The Other Side of Certain

of Certain

A Love for Certain Novel
Book I

Cover and interior design by Jacqueline Cook

ISBN: 978-1-7366203-8-0 (Paperback)
ISBN: 978-1-7366203-9-7 (e-book)

10 9 8 7 6 5 4 3 2 1

BISAC Subject Headings:
FIC027270 FICTION / Romance / Clean & Wholesome
FIC027360 FICTION / Romance / Historical American
FIC066000 FICTION / Small Town & Rural

Address all correspondence to:
Fireship Press, LLC
P.O. Box 68412
Tucson, AZ 85737

Or visit our website at:
www.fireshippress.com

*For my mom, who loved to read and
always made sure we had plenty of books.*

The Other Side of Certain

A Love for Certain Novel
Book I

Amy Willoughby-Burle

FIRESHIP
PRESS

Chapter 1

Mattie

When I stepped out of my father's 1936 Studebaker and onto the gravel in front of the Certain, Kentucky Works Progress Administration library headquarters, I felt as much like Alice falling down the rabbit hole as I'd had any time in all my life. My father's driver unceremoniously left me and my bags and boxes on the curb and drove away as if he might be trapped in this dismal Wonderland forever should he not make an immediate getaway. I was all but standing there in a cloud of dust as he drove off.

Waving the cloud of dirt and fumes away, I shielded my eyes against the mid-summer sun as it radiated off the old stone church building in front of me that housed the library. I could feel the heat sidling up beside me like an unwelcome but expected guest. Nevertheless, I was not to be daunted, and I straightened my shoulders and made ready to push open the large wooden doors of the make-shift library where I was to help two days a week while I got the small town of Certain, Kentucky's school program reinstated.

This was not the path I had planned for my life, but my life never had gone according to plan. I was not one to be shaken by things going awry, and this new "turn of events" the country found itself the victim of was certainly not going to be the first thing to stop me, no matter how devastating. When things had gotten tough, Eleanor Roosevelt had put on her best walking shoes and hit the pavement and that's what I was going to do, too.

When I entered the old church, the smell of books found my nose immediately, and I breathed in deeply. My eyes closed for a moment, and I imagined all the stories around me coming to life. I didn't yet know which books were there, but I could sense their characters in the corners of my imagination and hear them whispering to each other, one story to the next as if they were all connected somehow.

OK, so I've been accused of being a little fanciful and flighty. Is that really the worst thing?

The heavy door closed behind me and my eyes fluttered open. All around me was color and light. The shifting summer sun found each panel of the stained-glass windows along both walls of the small church and cast a swirl of color around the room. It reminded me of the kaleidoscope my mother had given to me when I was six. My hands would find it whenever escape was needed, especially during the years when she was no longer there. The sliding together and edging apart of color and shape mesmerized me. The seemingly endless combination of patterns pulled at my mind, creating a diversion from the world around me. The silent beauty entranced me, and I thought, then, that there was some way I could slip inside the pools of color and join their ebb and flow. I could almost feel the cool of the blues and greens like the waters of a lake and the warmth of the golds and yellows like the sun on my skin after a summer swim. At night, I could close my eyes and envision the swirl of light and magic and drift off to sleep with the idea that the world was a beautiful place. It had been, once.

"Mattie?"

The sound of someone saying my name startled me. I turned to see a woman who appeared to be around my age, late twenties or maybe just beyond, standing at a large wooden desk like the ones teachers used in the classrooms in which I had hoped to work when I graduated from college a couple of years ago. My eyes let go of the colors streaming through the windows and looked around the inside of the church. One side of the building had been emptied of pews, and in their place, a couple of tables and a desk filled the space where the seats had likely been. Pews remained on the other side of the church, and it seemed they were used as bookshelves. Strange, but practical. I had read about the ingenuity of the poorer regions; how they made use of everything in the most imaginative ways. I had also been warned that they didn't take kindly to strangers, and that I should work to fit in as best I could. That would prove to be hard for me as fitting in was not my greatest ability.

"Yes," I answered the woman, stepping in her direction. "Mattie Mobley. You are?"

"Ava," she said, coming from behind the desk to greet me.

She was tall to my short stature and much more elegant than I, even though her clothes were out of fashion and worn a little at the edges. Black satin hair and eyes the same cool blue as the sky outside might have given her a cold appearance, but she was pleasant to the soul.

"Where is everyone?" I asked.

"It's mostly just me," she said and shook my hand. "We've one other librarian here. Ruby. She'll be here later as it's repair and report today."

I couldn't take my eyes from the freshness of her skin and the shine of her hair. She looked like one of the angels from my mother's Bible.

"I serve as the headquarters librarian," Ava said, gesturing to the inside of the church turned library. "I'll show you to your accommodations. You'll be staying in the old parsonage. I suppose you'll end up holding classes there if you're able to get any of the children to come to town. It's brave of you to try. We appreciate it, no matter how it might seem."

I nodded, my mind stumbling over her words. I hadn't thought I'd have to convince the children to come to school. I was under the impression that they had requested me.

Ava reached to take one of my suitcases, but the last thing I wanted to do was to seem like a spoiled socialite. I politely refused her help and took the cases on my own. Ava led me out a side door at the front of the church and around to a small, whitewashed clapboard house. It was a humbly built structure, but it seemed very homey.

Ava stopped at the steps that led up to the covered porch. She took a breath and ascended them quickly. She pulled a set of keys from her dress pocket and opened the front door. I hefted the cases up the stairs and dropped them on the porch. I thought we might go in, but Ava didn't cross the threshold.

"You will find that there are two bedrooms, both upstairs, a kitchen, living, and bath downstairs," Ava said, still standing outside the door. "It's a pretty grand house for these parts. You should find everything you need in the kitchen. The cupboards are stocked. If you find personal effects, just leave them be."

"Am I staying with the preacher's family?" I asked. "Are they home?"

"No one lives here." She spoke quickly as if she couldn't wait to have this part over with. "The church has been closed for some time as well as the school. We're just the library now."

"Oh," was all I could think to say. Way to impress them with my wit and intelligence.

"I'll head back over to the library," she said, stepping back down off the porch. One of the steps creaked and I could see where the wood had warped, and the nail had pulled loose. She smiled at me somewhat apologetically. "Take your time to settle in. Come over when you're ready, and I'll show you around. I'll tell you what I can about the children and let you go through our donations to see if there are any materials you can use for school."

"Thank you, Ava," I said most sincerely. "I appreciate the accommodations and the opportunity to be here."

She turned and walked back down the path that led around to the church. From the porch, I could see what I assumed to be most of the town. The main street I'd come in on seemed to be one of just two roads that I could discern from where I stood. Perhaps there were others farther out. None of them were paved as best I could tell. I could see the imprints of automobile wheels left behind. That was a comfort. There were cars here somewhere. Or maybe those were the indentations made by my father's Studebaker. I felt rather like I'd shown up in a limousine for all it was worth, and I was quite glad my father's driver had dumped me out and driven away in his haughty haste.

Diagonally across the street was a short row of two-story brick buildings—three that were connected by shared walls and one that sat by itself. The corner one was the grocery based on the sign and the advertisements painted along the windows. There appeared to be a barber next to it, although I couldn't tell if it was open, and the last of the connected stores was a feed and seed and hardware establishment. The lone-standing building seemed deserted. The windows were covered in posters and flyers, government propaganda and the like as I had seen in Asheville, too. All the bright colors and emboldened statements didn't really fool anyone into thinking things would be better soon. As I stood looking at the building, I could make out the words *Certain Herald* in faded paint along the brick over the door. A newspaper? It seemed closed, though. I wondered how they got information about the rest of the world. Perhaps they didn't. Perhaps they didn't want it.

Beyond those buildings I could see others and even a few houses as the town seemed to give way to the less beaten path. One of the roads led around behind the church and I could make out what was likely a post office. So, there was contact with the outside world at least. My father had talked as if I was going to the ends of the Earth.

"Honestly, Mathilda," he'd said. "If you're looking for some charity work, there is plenty to be done here in Asheville. We have poor people too, you know."

"I'm aware of that, Pop," I had said. "I don't want to do charity work. I want to teach and there are no jobs here. I read that the schools in the more rural areas have all but closed. I could be useful there."

"But all the way in Kentucky?" he had asked. "Why not stay home. I can get you a position at the library here if you need something to occupy your time."

"There's a library there as well," I said, sensing an opportunity to win him over. He was a major benefactor of the Asheville library. "I read an article in the paper about Eleanor's library project and how it's helping to fight illiteracy. I've volunteered to help them through the summer."

"You do love books," he had said, his eyes focusing less on me and more on a distant memory. "Your mother did, too. She's why I got involved in the library here, you know."

"I know," I said, keeping my voice light and positive. "So many of the schools there have closed due to this crash. I can be useful in getting them back on their feet."

"Downturn," he said hopefully of the wrecked economy. "Just a brief hiccup."

"See, Pop," I said and hugged him. "You are ever the optimist, just like me. Wonder where I get that from?"

"Must you really go all the way to Kentucky?" he said, sadness in his eyes.

"If it's good enough for Eleanor, it's good enough for me."

"You're on a first name basis with the first lady, I see." He winked at me. "Your mother would be proud of your efforts to step out of the socialite circles and make a difference in the world."

"I guess I'm just like both of you," I said, a lump forming in my throat. I still missed her all these years later. I always would. I took in a deep breath and smiled at my father. I knew I had won him over. I didn't need his permission to go, but I wanted his approval.

"You don't have to work at all you know," he said. "I'm sure that beau of yours would be happy to marry you and set you up nicely."

"I don't have a beau," I said, pointedly, knowing he was referring to the son of a friend that he would like to see me marry, but with whom I had barely stomached one date. "I don't really have an interest in romance right now, Pop."

Marriage, love, the whole losing yourself to someone was not that interesting to me. It seemed a scary and unpredictable course of action.

"Fine. So, you say," he had said. "You'll come back soon, though. You're just to go over there and help them get started, right? Come back as soon as there's a position for you here."

"That's the plan."

Well, now I had certainly come to a place in need. This was nothing like the busy streets and noisy sidewalks of Asheville. There was no one in sight and save the loud neighing of a spotted mare in a pen between the parsonage and the church, there was almost no sound at all.

I picked up my suitcases and took them inside the house. It was a far cry from the Mobley estate, but I found that charming. No oriental rugs under Victorian style furniture. No chandeliers, crystal vases, and other expensive things I was not allowed to touch. No housekeeper other than me, for sure. This looked like a place where people might actually live. A home as opposed to a house. I surveyed the living room. The floral-patterned couch and cushioned sitting chairs positioned around a coffee table, looked worn, but still comfortable. Ava had suggested that I might have school here. It seemed quite small. I'd have to remove this furniture, but that could be done. Somewhere there must be desks. It could work. If I could convince anyone to come, apparently.

In the next room was the small kitchen, with a dining room table in the middle. The sink, stove, and icebox along the walls rounded things out.

I'd have to ask Ava how to light the stove as it was older than the one I had at home, and I was not really used to cooking on my own, but I was sure I'd figure it out well enough. I didn't have a choice, really.

At the top of the stairs were two doors, each leading into equally sized bedrooms. One had two twin sized beds with an end table and an oil lamp between them. A dresser and bookcase stood against the other wall. I was drawn to the books, of course. There weren't many, less than a dozen and all for children. A nice little collection though. I read from the spines. *The Jungle Book. The Secret Garden. Alice in Wonderland.* Someone read aloud to children here once, I suspected. It seemed a shame that they hadn't taken their books. Perhaps they had outgrown them.

The other bedroom had one larger bed and a bassinet. A baby. I had not expected that.

"I suppose this room will do," I said aloud and sat down on the bed. The feather stuffed mattress was adequate at best, but the metal frame was sturdy. I sat for a long moment getting my wits back about me. I found that I was trembling slightly with nerves, and I had the sensation that I had been out on a boat or some other event that left me floating and unsteady. Through the window I could see the back of the stone church. The horse pen I'd spotted from the front was bigger and better kept than I'd given it credit for. A small but adequate stable and feed trough under a sturdy overhang sat at the far corner leaving quite a bit of walking around room for the mare.

"Well, here you are, Mattie," I spoke out loud to myself. I tended to do that. "You wanted to be useful. Let's gather ourselves together and get started." I stood up with purpose. "Well, after we drag our suitcases up the stairs that is. And who are you talking to anyway? It's just you here, silly Mattie. Just you." I looked around and my shoulders slumped. "This might have been a terrible mistake."

I breathed in deeply again and stood up straight. Admitting defeat was not in my nature. *Just me,* I thought. That was quite nice. I had not had a place of my own or a life I had chosen for myself before. I could sense however, that I was terribly unprepared and about to get in way over my head for sure, but then again, so began all the best of adventures.

Chapter 2

Daniel

I tried not to go into town any more often than I needed to, especially in the summer when there was food to eat from the yard. But if I missed a week trading at Gibbons', Liam was fit to be tied. Liam and I weren't kin no more, not really, but he was used to telling me what to do like a big brother and it was hard to get him to mind his own business. When I did go to town, I tried to keep my eyes from finding the church across the street from the grocery, but it was hard not to look at it. Mostly, I went into the store from the back, so I only caught a glimpse of the old house and church as I pulled into town. It had been right at four years, but I still felt the shame of what I did.

"Whoa, Cody," I called to my steed as he tried to steer himself toward the front door. "Let's just take in our haul and go. I ain't aiming to get wound up in any new gossip today."

Gibbons was the first face I saw when I pulled the cart up to the back of the store. His smile reminded me that not everyone thought of me poorly. Mr. Gibbons had known me as a boy and known my father even, yet he still treated me with respect. He was one of the few people who actually knew what happened back then, that night in particular. Sometimes I wondered if I would have been better off just staying at home after my folks died. Maybe I should have just kept to myself. Then again, I'd have not had Emily or the kids if I hadn't been taken in by Pastor Collins and his family. At least I still had my children. So long as I stayed mostly out of sight, people seemed to forget I existed. It was better that way.

"Pull on up, son," Mr. Gibbons called, waving me in close to the door. "You got a right big haul today."

I pulled on Cody's reins and stopped alongside the back wall of the store. "This time of year is good for growing." I jumped from the seat and shook Mr. Gibbons' outstretched hand. I appreciated the gesture of respect and friendliness. "Got those chairs you ordered, too."

I had a little garden and woodworking business that kept me and the kids from starving. Some people in town knew it was my goods they bought from Gibbons. A couple were sympathetic like he was, but mostly people didn't say anything out of fear they'd be accused of associating with me. If there was anywhere else to get produce or have a thing fixed or made around here, they'd not have anything of mine. Most people, though, didn't have any idea my hands had been any part of it.

No matter. I didn't so much care anymore. I was used to life like me and the kids knew it. I had grown up realizing that life didn't do like you wanted it to. It did like it did, and you made the best of it or you didn't. Maybe I wasn't making the best of it yet, but I was trying. I'd longed for better once upon a time, and I'd gotten it. For a while. I didn't trust myself to long for it again. I figured it was safer not to have, than to have it taken away.

Safer on the heart, that is.

"Have you heard about the new teacher?" Gibbons asked as he took a crate of tomatoes from the wagon.

"Where's Liam?" I asked instead, looking over my shoulder lest he surprise me.

"Laurel says he's held up in the mine a little longer than usual."

Gibbons registered my relief and clapped me on the shoulder with his free hand. "Let's take these things in and get you on your way." He shifted the crate to both hands and nodded me forward.

He wasn't trying to get rid of me, just keeping things in line for the betterment of everyone.

"You'll tell him I was here?" I asked, shouldering the door open as I followed Mr. Gibbons inside. "He'll come asking, I'm sure of it."

"He will indeed," Mr. Gibbons said and took the crate I carried from me. "This is a fine-looking yield. I don't know how you manage to make things grow like you do."

"You work at something, you'll get it going," I said. "I'm making sure to work at the right things best I can."

Mr. Gibbons clapped me on the shoulder again and winked at me. "I know you are, son. Now, let's see those chairs."

We took the set of four ladder-back chairs into the store with Mr. Gibbons going on and on about the craftsmanship. I appreciated it, but I didn't say so. I was good at making things, that was true. I wasn't always good at making the best decisions though, and I didn't want to let myself get a big head over anything.

"Here's your usual," Mr. Gibbons said, pulling two crates of goods from behind the counter. "I threw in a little something extra for the children."

I shook my head and held up my hand. "You don't need to do that. I know you don't have things to spare any more than I do."

"It's a couple of little books, is all," he said. "I know how your kids like a good story."

"They come from the library?" I asked, looking over Gibbons' shoulder where I could see out through the front of the store and across the street. I let my eyes fall on the sign that had been affixed out front, but when I found myself looking at the stained-glass windows I turned away.

"Ms. Ava brought them over for you," he said and looked at me cautiously.

I grimaced but nodded. "Tell her thank you."

I picked up one of the crates and he took the other. We went out to the cart and loaded them in. He told me to watch the turns along the way, so I didn't jostle my wares along as I rode. He didn't need to tell me these things, but I liked that he did. He cared, was all.

"Are you going to send your little ones down to the new school come fall?" he asked.

I ran my hand over my beard and kicked the dirt at my feet. "I don't reckon so."

"You heard about the new teacher?" he asked again, and I nodded. "You should think about coming out of the hills, son. You don't need to be up there all alone."

"People…" I started in, but he held up his hand to stop me.

"People need to let bygones be bygones," he said. "And you need to forgive and forget. For those kids, if not yourself, Daniel. You hear me?"

I nodded, but I couldn't find any words to offer back to him.

He patted Cody and stood by while I got up into the seat and took the reins. Gibbons put his hand on Cody's bridle to stop me signaling her. "Son, you need to give life a chance when it comes at you now."

I nodded again and he stepped back. As I headed out and back toward the path to home, I glanced over at the church. I wanted to try to forget, but all I could see was old memories and pain.

Chapter 3

Mattie

Back in the church, I discovered that the pews did serve as bookshelves. Volumes of literature of all types were categorized along the rows, spine out or flat down for magazines and other things.

"That's clever," I said, pointing to a bookend made from a license plate folded at a ninety-degree angle. I could see them all through the rows.

"We make do," Ava said, coming to stand beside me. "People send all sorts of things as donations. Nothing goes to waste. When you don't have much, much care is given to everything."

Perhaps I imagined it, but I thought her eyes flickered across the rhinestone clasp that I had fastened into my hair. I touched my fingers to it, thinking how no matter what people had, they still wished for something else. I had always wanted to have spectacular hair, perhaps the bright red or shiny blonde of some of the ladies in my circle. Instead, I had hair the color of plain brown mud, so I glittered it up with clasps and headdresses as if it really changed anything.

As Ava continued to show me around, my gaze fell on one of the stained-glass windows that had obviously been broken out at some point and was in a state of moderately effective repair.

"What do you do if it rains?" I asked, motioning to the window.

The middle section of glass was gone, and small chunks of the other sections were missing as well. Jesus' toes were gone, as was an angel's halo. The busted-out middle section had been patched up with horizontal wooden planks, but there were still gaps where the light shone through.

"There was an early snow right after the window was broken," Ava said with a wry smile of sorts on her face. "My kids made a tiny snowman before my father made them clean it out. It was snowing through the hole even as we worked to patch it up."

"Like a snow globe."

She smiled at me, but the smile turned sad. "Yes, it was." She walked away from the window, and I hurried after her, trying not to miss anything she said. "We weren't able to get the glass fixed. Maybe one day. And it doesn't get very wet even when it rains. The roof overhang mostly keeps the weather out. That snow was," she paused, "a fluke. We cover it better in the winter, so that it's not as cold in here."

I looked back at the window, imagining the glittering white flakes as they flurried in just above Jesus and the little lamb and the angels all around Him.

"What happened?" I asked, imagining a child tossing a toy or some other innocuous accident.

She spoke without looking at me. "It was years ago. Old ghost long forgotten."

"What was in the center pane?" I asked, almost bumping into Ava where she had stopped in front of me. I also had the bad habit of asking too many questions.

"Mary," she said, her voice quiet as if perhaps she didn't want to arouse the ghosts she had spoken of. "Holding the baby Jesus."

I looked back one more time at the broken window. Ava cleared her throat, and I turned my attention back to her. I didn't know if she meant real ghosts or old secrets. I felt like this was a place where either of those things might be true.

"So, this is a large town?" I asked, sitting in the seat beside her desk. "Will there be many children coming to school?"

This made Ava laugh. She had a wonderful laugh. "No and not likely, but you might win them over with the sheer novelty of it all. It's been a few years since we held classes. There were never that many children in school here anyway, but things are very different now. People are just trying to survive. We exist, but it's not often the same as living."

I nodded, but I didn't really have much experience with the level of hardship that I had read about in these parts. I cleared my throat hoping to change the subject.

"So where are all the children?" I asked. "The town seems pretty deserted."

"All along the creek," she said. "Which reminds me—I made you some maps."

"The creek?"

"The Hell for Certain," she said, and I could tell she was waiting for a reaction. When my eyebrows lifted, she smiled and launched into a tale. "Folks claim that an adventurous pioneer was making his way through these parts and on one leg of his journey he had an accident and cut his shin. Hence the Cut Shin Creek up the way, and the next day he found himself trying to navigate our waters here after a flood and declared that he was in 'hell fer sartin' and the name stuck."

"Quite a perilous journey," I said. "Just like in a book."

She looked at me more seriously. "I imagine some folks here think he was right."

"If that's the case, why do they stay?"

"People have nowhere else to go," Ava said. "And this is home."

A cloud covered the sun outside and the colors coming in through the window faded. I stood up and looked back across the church at the plethora of books.

"I'm happy to be here," I said. "Although I'm a tad overwhelmed, I think."

She winked at me, and I felt a little hint of sisterhood. My heart fluttered at it, which surprised me in the best of ways. I didn't have real friends back in Asheville. I had the staff at my father's home and the ladies in the tea and small talk circles that I imagined didn't like me very much because I tended to say what I thought. I was laughed at for attending college and getting a teaching degree. Apparently, I should have been content to marry for money and spend my days lunching with the ladies. I suppose it's a fine life, and I never thought poorly of the other ladies for wanting it. It just wasn't for me.

"I noticed some nice titles in the parsonage," I said, letting thoughts of the past go back there. "Upstairs in one of the bedrooms. Should I bring those down? They could circulate, too."

Ava looked at me sharply and then shook her head. "No, those stay where they are."

Again, another story I didn't dare ask about. Not yet anyway.

"Let's look for books that you might use in your school," she said, changing the subject. "I know we got some nice readers the other day. You can have those."

"Thank you," I said, pretending that I was not at all surprised that there were no books and materials at the ready.

"The best part about taking a couple of library routes is that you'll get to know the children and parents," Ava said, handing me two books right away. "This is really a Godsend—you coming here."

"It is?" I asked. I'd found it a bit easier to get placement here than I thought. I had to pass a certification test which I did with ease, and my college degree far surpassed the mere months of educational training required.

"They've talked about sending our kids over to one of the city schools where there are books and buildings and all the things that accompany school," Ava said and handed me another book. "But it costs too much to get our kids out of the holler and over to the city, so we're left to our own devices."

"Costs too much?"

"To send motorbuses and such," she said and pointed me toward another row of books. "And passable roads," she laughed a little. "You'll see soon enough that we don't qualify."

I shifted my stack of books in my arms and followed her to the next row. "Perhaps we could work on that. Getting the kids to the better school, I mean. I don't want to hold anyone back by being here."

Ava waved off my concern. "You're not. The parents aren't going to send their kids over to the city anyway. It's just not how we do things here. We take care of ourselves."

I nodded. "In that case, let's get these books together and I'll start planning my lessons."

This was going to be a more daunting task than I figured. No building. No desks. No textbooks. My first problem though—no students. Well, I had the rest of the summer and an opportunity to change people's minds. And with books no less. I could do that.

"And besides," Ava said, inspecting a book, but then putting it back. "We need another carrier. Lizzie, our other librarian, had to leave to care for her mother. Her route has gone without books for a month. So, your being here is good in a couple of ways." Her voice seemed a little less positive of that than her words implied.

I smiled anyway. Even if she had reservations, she seemed pleased that I was here. I hoped others would be as well. Ava told me all about how Certain had come to be part of the library initiative and how they had been working to help decrease the illiteracy rate by providing reading materials and staying a while at the houses to read and teach when there was time. Listening to the passion in Ava's voice was like finding my place in the world. I belonged here.

She and I both had a fondness for the work of our country's first lady, and we lost ourselves in conversation about her as we finished searching the rows for schoolbooks.

"Thank goodness that Mrs. Roosevelt is such a champion for literature," Ava said, folding her arms over her chest in that way people do when they've completed a big task. "The Works Progress Administration has given people a modicum of hope again. This little initiative has brought some life back to our town and we needed it. We need more of it, to be honest, but this is a start."

I was determined to be part of that hope no matter what was happening in the world. Still, it concerned me.

"Times do seem to keep getting worse," I said, setting my haul of books on the circulation table and patting down my pristine outfit and shuffling in my new pumps. "I know it must not look like I know about bad times having been driven here like I was, but things are not always what they seem."

Ava nodded at me. "Indeed. I hope you will remember that once you are along your route."

I was about to ask more questions when the side door opened and a lady wearing farmer's coveralls came inside. She had a straw hat in her hand and her wiry brown hair was spun around in a knot at the back of her neck.

"Here's Ruby," Ava said and waved the gal toward us. "Ruby, this is Mattie Mobley from Asheville."

Ruby walked right up to me and stuck her hand out to shake. I obliged. Her grip was firm like a man's and right away I was impressed.

"Welcome," she said, sitting her hat on the desk and loosening her hair from its knot. "You must be the city girl here to take up the schooling and help with the routes. I'm glad for a break out there." She spoke with a thick accent that I struggled to understand but liked the sound of.

"We've been trying to take up the slack a portion at a time," Ava explained, although I understood. "Still, there are places we've not gotten to in a while."

"You'll be needing to mind the grizzly at the top of your route tomorrow though," Ruby said, sitting down hard in the chair and pulling off her man-style boots. "I might would have taken that leg, but I try to stay clear of Devil's Jump."

"Where?" I questioned.

Ava brushed the comment off. "A little branch along the creek that's more folklore than anything worth bothering over." Ava looked at Ruby thoughtfully. "Are you OK, you seem like you've been on a hard day's work, not headed in for repair and report."

"My report is that I didn't make the end of my route yesterday and had to finish today," Ruby said and sighed. "Molly threw a shoe right by a nest of yellow jackets and let's just say, neither one of us fared all that well. I called it a day and had to finish the rest of the route on the way here."

Ava made a pained face and then looked at me with raised eyebrows. "The least of the reported injuries. Do you think you're up for this?"

My mind was spinning across everything as I took it in. Really, all I'd come to do was teach. Not get stung by yellow jackets and fight off bears. Was there really a bear?

"I'm sorry," I said, my mind catching on a word and needing to clarify. "Did you say there is a bear along the route I will take up? Isn't that rather dangerous?" I looked quickly back and forth between Ava and Ruby.

Ruby winked at me. "A right grizzly indeed."

Ava looked at me with concern. "He's nothing to fret over."

"So, there is a bear?"

A creek called the Hell for Certain with a beast along the route. I'd been a sucker to take this job. I feared they'd given me the teaching job just to distract me from the worst of my duties.

"Ava has a soft spot for the wildlife around here," Ruby said as if joking, but then a more serious tone found its way into her voice. "You of all people, Ava, should be the last to care about the fate of one lone grizzly."

"You know better of him, Ruby," Ava said with a soft scold.

I quickly surmised that this was not a bear, but a person. One of a dubious nature.

"Tread lightly, Mattie," Ruby said to me, and it seemed like a genuine word of concern. "He's a grizzly bear indeed, and he won't take kindly to strangers coming up to his place."

"Maybe I ought not go. He sounds like a bit of a beast."

"He wasn't always that way," Ava said and patted my shoulder. "Now, why don't you watch as I check in some of the returns. I'll help you make some selections for your route and that way you'll be all set for tomorrow morning."

Suddenly, I felt extremely unprepared. "So soon? I don't even know the lay of the land."

"I have maps for you," Ava said. "And Opal knows the way. She'll be a big help."

"Who is Opal?"

"Your horse. The spotted mare in the yard. Have you seen her?"

"Yes," I said with a sigh. The one warning me loudly at my arrival to jump back in the Studebaker and head for the safety of the Blue Ridge Mountains from whence I'd come.

"You ride, don't you?" Ava asked, seeming suddenly concerned that perhaps I didn't.

"Best in show for three years running," I said proudly.

Back in the parsonage that evening, I curled up on the couch to study the hand drawn maps Ava had made for me. There was one for each of the two routes I'd take. I could see right away why they called these ladies pack horse librarians and why the school system had not planned to send their kids to the city or even other county schools. My father's Studebaker would be of no use out here, and a motorbus would have been laughable. There were a few houses I would visit across the lengths of my routes that had roads leading to them, but most called for me to ride along the creek bed and up and around what I hoped would be visible paths like the ones Ava had marked. "Road" was a relative term out here.

I knew all this before getting here. I knew the arrangement called for me to assist the librarians while I set up school for the fall. I had researched the library program as much as I could find and had asked questions, but none of that had really prepared me for doing the job. And I figured none of my planning and memorizing the map tonight would prepare me for tomorrow. But this was a good chance to meet the families and get to know the children. I knew that the first secret of being able to learn was wanting to learn. Desire led to effort and effort would lead to success. Books and stories were the perfect things to tempt little minds into wanting to learn. A great opportunity awaited tomorrow. Still, I was nervous.

I looked at the end of the route where Ruby had taken the map and circled the last stop, writing the word "grizzly" before giving it back to me. My first day would be a challenge. I traced my finger along the mark that indicated the creek. The name loomed ominous to me—Hell for Certain. I sure hoped it wasn't.

Chapter 4

Mattie

The next morning, it was yet dark out when I got up to start my day. I figured out how to work the stove and upon making myself a nice cup of tea, I stepped out onto the front porch of the parsonage. I had a small moment of readjustment when I didn't hear the sounds of a city already waking around me like I was used to back home. No people calling back and forth, no honking of horns from impatient drivers, no calling of the dailies from the newsboy on the corner.

I sat down in one of the two rocking chairs on the porch and sipped at my tea. I could smell the dew and the still lifting fog. I listened to the "sweet, sweet, sweet" chirp of a cardinal somewhere in the trees. Off in the distance, another one called its reply. The cup I held was warm in my hands and the tactile reality of it helped me stay grounded. The stillness around me was eerie, but interesting. I sat quietly and finished my tea before going inside to ready for the day.

Standing in the bedroom, looking at the clothes I had brought with me, I realized how little I knew about what I was getting into. I had had enough sense not to bring anything truly fancy, but I might as well have for the useful items I had at my disposal. I had expected to stand at a blackboard in front of a classroom of children. I figured they would be of various ages and likely all together like the one room schoolhouses I had read about. I had known I would be riding a horse to deliver books for the library, but honestly, I don't think I'd really understood the nature of either of the jobs I'd end up doing here.

At least if I had brought my society gowns, I could have made a joke of it, coming across the creek in my satin and lace. Not that I'd worn any of those things anywhere in years. The Mobleys had more cushion than most, so it was taking longer for the pantry to run dry so to speak, but the crash had knocked the wind out of us to say the least. My father had most of his money tied up in property rather than Wall Street, but some of it had been there. He thought he was being sly now, selling things off and buying new cars like the one I'd been driven here in. It was a dangerous game of keeping up appearances and trying not to lose everything at the same time. This place didn't seem caught up in that and it was a relief of sorts.

I had thought that packing simple day dresses and some smart skirts and blouses was the best thing to do. Still, I somehow looked completely out of place in comparison to Ava and Ruby yesterday. The worst offense was my footwear. I had meant to bring some sports shoes at least, but I had forgotten them. The only riding boots I had were purely for show horses, but had I packed them? No. Even a pair of saddle shoes would have been more acceptable. I rolled my eyes at myself now, having only the pumps I wore and one pair of black T-straps in case there was anything of a dressier nature that I was called to attend. Really? What had I thought I would be doing with my time here?

The best option I had was the pair of light brown Oxfords I'd worn here. They only had a Cuban heel—I'd at least not been silly enough to think I'd need a Spanish heel out in the hills of Kentucky. So, off I would go to ride a horse down the Hell for Certain creek while wearing Oxfords and a brand-new dress. Sensible was relative.

My first stop was a house just off the main road of town. An actual road—not the creek bed. Easy enough. The Studebaker could have gotten there. The house was much like the parsonage where I was staying. Simply built with clapboard walls, and small covered porch. The whitewash paint was chipped so much that in all honesty, it was less painted than more. The lady of the house met me at the door, keeping it mostly closed behind her.

"I'm Mattie Mobley," I said, sounding too formal as if I was running for office. "I'm opening the school in the fall. Up at the church. Do you have children here?" At that she stepped back inside a bit, looking behind her as if she were guarding the contents of her house and I was the witch from Hansel and Gretel. *Come out little ones, so I can bake you in a pie.*

She said nothing, just looked at me sternly. Her eyes traveled the length of me all the way to my shoes. She raised an eyebrow. I cleared my throat and tried again.

"I'm also the new carrier for your library route," I said, pointing to Opal, my horse. I held out the books Ava had helped me pick for this house. Children's books included. The lady took them, stepped back inside her house, and closed the door.

I wasn't offended by that at all. She had never seen me before and it was probably a great show of hospitality that she came out at all. I'd have to take things one step at a time.

"So far so good, Opal," I said to my steed once I had mounted and pulled the reins to lead her forward. Good was also relative. At least Opal had been accepting of me that morning. She sighed as if she had decided to give up warning me off and just accept that her fate was now tied with mine. It wasn't encouraging, but it was the best I figured I could hope for. Plus, I had bribed her with a sugar cube.

Ava was correct that Opal would be a help. As soon as we left the first house, Opal headed instinctively to the next and the next. This must have been the horse that Lizzy used.

I thought that I might be done early if I didn't stay at any one house longer than it took to pick up the last loans and give out new materials. That would probably be for the best as I was already a little afraid of riding back in the dark. I didn't really know how long these routes would take. It seemed most of the time was spent riding from one homestead to the next. Ava had said that some carriers rode as much as 200 miles in a week. That was further than it was from Asheville to here and on a horse no less. My week would be easier than that though, only two days out. I was grateful, but it did make me appreciate Ruby's work even more.

It was a lovely ride mostly. The day had lightened and warmed up with the sun. The sky, when we were out of the trees and able to see it, was a bright and clear blue. I breathed in deeply, enjoying the clean smell of the air. I had no idea how far away I was from anything. I felt I'd been out there all day. I didn't even know what hour it might be. I especially adored the rustling sound the leaves made as the wind wound through them. There were not nearly this many trees in the town parts of Asheville. I did already miss the open views of the Blue Ridge though. I felt a little closed in here, but I supposed I'd get used to it.

As I rode, following the maps, I was indeed in the very creek bed itself quite a bit of the time. A lovely stretch of clear water, it wound around as if it too was lost in the woods. Not more than shin deep in most places, the creek was beautiful, but hard to navigate as the ground was awfully rocky—as if someone had dumped the rocks there on purpose. Opal obviously did not care for walking in the creek, but she obliged. She much preferred the more open land or the paths to the individual homes.

The deeper into the hills we rode, the more I felt like I was indeed going back in time. The homes closer to town were already a far cry more meager than what I was used to in Asheville, to say the least. But some of the homes out along the hills looked so worn and aged that they might cave in at the slightest breeze. I felt awfully spoiled in the face of such want and need. At the same time, I felt peaceful, as if somehow, I had been searching for this place and had finally found it. I knew that sounded fanciful and poetic for the mere sake of it, but it was true. Perhaps it was the quiet. Perhaps it was the chance to make a difference. I imagined all the children who would come to school in the fall, fabricating their little faces in my mind. I pondered it all as I climbed one hill and descended another along this twisty and treacherous path upon which I found myself.

After a while, Opal and I entered under a canopy of trees and the heat lifted as the sun was blocked out save for some dappling here and there. I couldn't imagine the creek flooding and flowing hard enough to scare a grown man, but then again, it seemed this place was filled with stories, and that was something quite appealing to a booksy girl like me. Opal stopped once again, and I chided her forward with a tap of my foot to her side. She moved briefly, but then stopped again.

"Let's go, girl." I said and tapped with both feet at once.

She whinnied and walked forward. Trees grew very close to the edge of the creek, and I could see that in several places we'd have to go back into the water to navigate around them. I wondered if the creek I saw this day was high or low, fast, or slow.

"What say you about the creek, Opal? Is this water hiding a rougher tale?" We'd been alongside the creek often, but the land had mostly been more open and easier to navigate even with the rocks. Here, everything came in very close, and there was nothing to do but go through it.

Opal whinnied again but walked forward. We stepped into the edge of the creek just as some small animal scurried in the brush, and Opal stamped her feet and raised up on her hind legs.

"Whoa," I shouted, but I think I only startled her more.

She tried to back out of the creek, but something behind us spooked her, too, and she lurched forward. I lost my balance, and in my panic to right myself and hang on, I managed to kick the saddlebag hard enough to loosen it and send it falling into the creek. In a panic, I slipped over the saddle and slid down off Opal's back. She kept running forward, and I threw myself into the creek to try and retrieve the books. I snatched the bag out of the water and flung it to the shallow bank hoping I had reached the bag before the water penetrated. A few of the books had flown from the open side pocket and were floating down the creek.

I splashed through the water and grabbed for them, tucking each under my arm and reaching for the next with the other hand. Six in all. Six books that I had sent into the Hell for Certain on my very first day. Indeed.

I tromped out of the water and made my way back to the saddlebags. I sat the wet books on the bank and opened the bag with one eye closed, fearing the worst. Luckily most things fared pretty well. There were a few titles that I took from the bag and opened them along with the sopping wet ones and hung them like laundry over the tree branches. Not branches that extended over the water, that is. Lesson learned.

After that was done, I sat down on the ground, bumping a tree root harder than I meant to, and breathed out a few heavy breaths. I was not, no matter what, going to cry on my first day. I got my wits about me and stood back up. I was soaked nearly to my neck from all the splashing and thrashing about, and my inappropriate shoes were covered with mud. And my horse was nowhere in sight.

"Opal," I called out. "Get back here. Opal."

I listened for the sound of her hooves coming back toward me, but all I heard was the happy chirping of birds and the continued warbling of the creek. I had no choice but to leave the books to dry. I'd pick them up on the way home. I called for Opal again, but again there was no hint of her. I hefted the saddlebag over my own shoulders, balancing the two packs on either side.

"Pack horse librarian indeed." I lamented gruffly.

I tromped forward, slipping in the dark and dank mud almost immediately thanks to my Oxfords. I grabbed a tree branch to keep myself from falling. The thin tree limbs didn't hold me that well and I slipped and slid and grabbed and grumbled my way along.

According to the map that I must have lost, I now realized, the next house was just up the way. I remembered that my note was to look for a tree with a heart carved into the trunk and to proceed up the hill directly behind it.

"Tree with a heart," I said aloud when I spotted it. I struggled up the incline still talking to myself. "This would probably be much easier were I riding a horse. I should get a horse. Oh wait, I was riding a horse." I was getting down-right snooty with no one in particular, when I crested the hill to see the house I was looking for, and what else, my horse—waiting there in the yard as if nothing at all had happened.

"Well thank you very much, Opal," I said approaching her. I took the saddlebags from off my own shoulders and fitted them across her back. She snorted but sat still and let me fasten them tightly.

After the creek incident there were still several families on the route. Most of them were happy to see me and grateful that books were coming again. I was thrilled to see the children and even got a positive nod or two when I mentioned the school opening. Still, some folks regarded me with suspicion, not that happy to see a stranger. Were it not for the books and for Opal whom they all recognized, I might have found myself summarily run off a time or two. I got a raised eyebrow and a chuckle here and there at being wet. No one asked what had happened, but I'm sure they all surmised it. My misfortune seemed to endear me to them, even if only slightly. I did, at least, start to dry off the longer the day went on.

Still, I felt good about what I was doing. This was important work, and I felt important doing it. I could tell that the kids were hungry for story and that alone made this day, yes, even my swim in the creek, worthwhile. I couldn't wait to get to know them all better. I looked forward to knowing my route well enough, and being welcome enough, to sit and share some time with my patrons. It would be good to get to know them as the summer gave way to fall. I wouldn't be nearly the stranger, at least to the families on my route, when it came time for school to start. Every little bit of acceptance would help.

I was feeling pretty good as Opal and I left out for the last house. The other route I had, according to the maps, made more of a circle so that I was delivering on the way out and on the way back. This one stopped at the grizzly and then backtracked mostly along the winding creek. I wondered if after a trip to this house, all a carrier wanted to do was break quickly for home.

I discovered that my map was in my bag after all. I must have tucked it in as we neared the creek. I was happy to have it, as the last house was reachable by a series of turns and switchbacks that made me think there should have been an X marking the spot at the end. Instead, there was the circle around the word "grizzly." Come to think of it, I guess there was an X marking the spot. Not much of a prize, though.

"One more, Opal, and then we head home." My clothes had mostly dried in the heat of the day, but I had sweated enough to make everything damp again. Even with the moderate temperature, this was a hard day's work. I could feel a slight chill in the breeze that would have made me happy were it not accompanied by a roll of thunder in the way off from time to time. Hopefully it wouldn't amount to anything. I had books hung out to dry, and I hoped they'd stay that way.

Opal and I walked the rocky bed of the creek and when I neared the turn-off that would lead to the grizzly's house, I found myself entering under a canopy of growth that all but formed a little doorway. A secret entrance.

Opal and I entered in, and I was taken aback. I'd already seen that most of the homes along the route were older and smaller than what I knew of back in Asheville. Most were made of clapboard and many more looked like log cabins built in the 1800s, which they likely were. I don't know what I thought I'd find at the grizzly's house, but a nicely built log home was not what I had expected. It was clearly old and quite small but had been well kept. It was somewhat cluttered around with buckets and boxes and things that needed tidying up, but it was homey also. Flowers sprang wild in the yard and chickens pecked at the grass and grit. A brown mare was standing off to the side, munching calmly on some hay from a cart. I'd seen a horse and cart here and there in the places that a car couldn't reach. I wasn't sure how a cart would get from here to town given the tight curves of the creek.

I surveyed the homestead as I approached. Something about this house made me think that if I got any closer to it, it might disappear like a mirage or fade away like a dream sifting just out of reach as sleep gives way to waking.

"Are you sure this is the place, old girl? Doesn't look that bad to me."

I didn't see any movement, save for the chickens. The sun sifted through again, and suddenly so brightly that it caused me to shield my eyes. I blinked a couple of times and thought I saw children running toward me. I didn't see from whence they had come.

"It's the book woman come back, Da," the oldest of the girls shouted at a parent whom I didn't see. "Here we are," she shouted at me, waving her hands like I didn't see her and might turn around and leave.

I smiled and dismounted. Three little ones crowded around me jumping up and down with excitement. The chickens scattered in their wake.

"This is the best welcome I've gotten all day."

I studied the children's faces like I had at every other house. This would take a while, but I wanted to know them all. Two girls, one who seemed to be about thirteen or so and a younger one who might have been ten. There was also a little boy no more than four years old at best. The older girl scooped him up, so that he was able to see better, I supposed. Little bear cubs, no doubt. I should have known from the books Ava chose for this house that there would be children here.

"Hugh," the older girl said to him. "Look, I told you they'd send us a new book woman, and here she is." The girl jostled the little boy on her hip just like a mother would do.

"Hi Miss Book Lady," the little boy said with a sweet and soft voice. His light brown hair was tufted up like it hadn't been combed in a while.

"Hello. My name is Mattie. I'm filling in for a while."

"Miss Mattie," the younger of the girls repeated my name and nodded her head as if she approved.

I looked across the yard for any signs of a bear. None.

"I have three books left for you all," I said. "I admit, I would have had more of a choice for you, but Opal here got spooked by the creek, and I and some of the books got launched in."

Their little eyes opened wide, and Hugh began to giggle. His oldest sister scolded him.

"It's not polite to laugh at someone else's misfortune."

"I's sorry," Hugh said and looked sad.

"Oh, you can laugh," I said. "It was right funny. Not at the time, but now that I think about it. It was like a scene right out of a movie. Opal even left me there and I had to carry the saddlebag on my shoulders as if I was a pack mule."

They all smiled at that. Their faces were slightly dirty, and their hair needed a good washing, but the light in their eyes shone past all that.

"Opal is a feared of water," the smaller girl said. "Everybody knows that."

"You know Opal, too?" I asked, putting my hands on my hips, and tilting my head.

"Everybody does," she said.

"Is that so," I said. "Well, tell me your names."

"I'm Ella," the oldest one said and then pointed at her sister. "That's Marie."

"It ain't polite to point," Marie said, happily, as if she'd caught her sister doing something she shouldn't for a change. "Mama told us that."

Ella rolled her eyes at her sister. "This is Hugh. He's our baby brother."

"I figured as much," I said and gave his little cheek a squeeze. "He looks just like you both. Same mischievous dark eyes and delightful smile."

Yes, I was sucking up to the children. I could tell the little ones would be my best avenue for acceptance.

"Da says we all look just like our mother," Ella said proudly.

"Is she inside?" I asked. "I'd love to meet her. I'm new in town, I'm sure you know. Trying to learn who everyone is."

"Mama is in Heaven," Hugh said, and I had to work hard to not gasp at the sound of his little voice proclaiming such a sad thing with such an uplift in his tone.

"I am sorry to hear that, little ones." I looked at Ella's face and saw the same eyes I see in the mirror when I think about my own mother. "Mine is as well."

We stood for another moment, and then I cleared away the ghosts of loss by reaching into my bag and pulling out the books I had for them.

"Now, two of these are easy enough," I said, handing them all to Ella once she had set Hugh back on his feet. "This other, *Treasure Island*, is a bit harder, but perhaps your father can read it to you."

"Da don't read." Marie said. "Ella is a real good reader. She don't do the voices as best as Mama did, but she tries."

"Thank you for that strange compliment," Ella said with her brow furrowed.

Ella's wry sense of humor made me smile. I saw my own self in this girl right away. I knew that she and I would be good allies.

"I'm sure your sister will do fine," I said. "Where is your father? I should introduce myself. I ought not come onto his property and speak to his children without so much as a hello."

I was putting this picture together rather quickly, and my experiences so far this day had taught me that respect of privacy and boundaries was of the utmost importance.

Marie thumbed over her shoulder. "He's out there in the garden. Working. He said a storm's coming, and he wants to finish as soon as he can."

I nodded. I was sure that simple pleasures like reading seemed a waste of time to a hardworking man, especially now, when there was more to worry over than what happens in the next chapter of a story. This current chapter the world was on was hard enough to manage.

"I'll go and speak to him. You three enjoy these books and I'll be back in about two weeks. You can tell me whether or not Ella here managed to do a good job at the voices." I winked at her to show I was joking and to try and make an attempt at solidarity. She smiled at me, and I knew we were off to a good start. "I'll tell you all about my plans to start having school again as well."

Ella's eyes lit like the sun breaking through after a long dark night. "School? Really?"

I nodded and winked. "Indeed."

"That would be wonderful," she said as if she could hardly take it in.

Marie on the other hand rolled her eyes and grunted. "Lessons. I can do without them."

I chuckled. I liked these children very much already.

They ran up to the porch and opened one of the books right away. It thrilled my heart to see how eager they were. Ella sat in the rocking chair and the other two children sat at her feet.

"Now to find this bear," I said to myself, trying to make light of it, but worried nonetheless about a man people referred to as a grizzly.

I stepped forward cautiously. The sky was darkening more quickly than I was prepared for. I felt my heart begin to race.

"Mattie," I said out loud to myself, "you are being ridiculous. There is not an actual grizzly bear here. It is only a man and how scary could he possibly be. They are fooling with you."

I took a breath and went around the back of the cabin. There, in another section of this secret garden of sorts, I saw a man working about a third of the way into a decent sized plot of vegetables. The garden was beautiful—the way the beans climbed up the trellises bound together like little teepees, and how the tomatoes, cucumbers, peppers, melons even, grew in their own rows and squared plots bordered with smooth rocks. I couldn't seem to take it all in. It was like the gardens I had seen in magazines and nothing like the hardscrabble patches of dirt I'd seen other families trying to cultivate. This land was not fit for agriculture in the slightest, but here was this garden, nonetheless. This has taken effort and care and time. Much of it.

The man's back was to me, so I called out to him.

"Pardon, sir," I said, stepping over a border of small stones and walking into the garden. I stepped between the plants so as not to disturb anything. He didn't seem to hear me. "Sir, my name is Mattie Mobley. I'm one of the librarians from town." I stepped over a row of broccoli. "I'm taking over for Lizzy for a bit while I get a new school set up. I'd love to tell you all about it."

He didn't seem to mind me at all. Perhaps he couldn't hear. I reached out to tap him on the shoulder, and at that moment he turned around. Looming over me and just inches away, his face was nearly completely covered with a dark and tangled black beard. His hair protruded from his straw hat so that the wild locks covered most of his forehead. I could clearly see a pair of very stern and angry green eyes glaring at me. I tried to step backwards, but my heel sank into the dirt, and I found myself fumbling both forward and back at the same time on my stupid, mud caked Oxfords. The man seemed to lunge at me, and I put my hands up in front of my face to shield whatever attack was coming. He caught me by the arm and grabbed a hold of my shoulder.

"Sir, please," I said desperately, but even at the same time, I realized that he was not actually attacking me, but keeping me from falling.

I caught my breath and righted myself, not before turning my ankle again. He looked down at my feet and then again at my face. He was still holding onto my shoulder.

"I'm fine now. Thank you," I said, trying to sound confident and aloof, yet knowing I was talking to the very grizzly about whom I had been warned. Maybe he wasn't that bad. "As I was saying. I'm Mattie Mobley…"

"Leave the books and go," he grunted his interruption, proving me wrong. "Get out of my garden before you ruin my yield." He turned his back on me and went about his business.

My heart raced. I wasn't sure if I was angry at him for being so rude, or simply relieved that he'd turned away and given me an escape.

Either way, I left as instructed, and I did it as quickly as possible. Thankfully, Opal was as ready to get back to town as I was and made haste getting us there—creek water or not. She was none too happy when I stopped to pick up the drying books hanging from the branches. The sky was indeed darkening to an ominous gray, the storm now set to come in.

"We're almost home, girl. I'll make it quick."

I had been right to surmise that the reason there were no stops beyond the grizzly was the desire to make haste toward home. I put the books, mostly dry, but much worse for the wear, into my pack and we set out for town. The storm grew closer. The trees bent and the leaves rustled hard enough that some of them blew right off, swirling around us like a green tornado as we rode hard for home.

At the church, the storm had blown in fully and I felt like the winds of it blew me straight on inside the building. I beat the pouring rain by seconds.

"How was it?" Ava asked and then looked at me more thoroughly.

"You look like Opal dragged you through the creek."

"Pretty close." I said, trying to laugh it off. I didn't know how much sympathy she'd have for me once she saw the books I all but ruined.

The rain started to pelt on the roof of the church, and I looked up instinctively.

"It'll just be a little rain," Ava said, putting her hand on my shoulder. "It's all rumbling, but no real threat."

"Speaking of threats," I said. "I met the grizzly."

"How were the children?" she asked eagerly. "Did they seem well?"

"They were lovely," I said, happily recalling them. "Although I wish I had known that their mother had passed, so I wouldn't have asked to be introduced to her."

"My apologies," Ava said, a pained look on her face. "I forget that you're new and don't know our histories."

I could tell that this subject was a touchy one.

"I hope to learn them," I said, trying to sound as hopeful as possible.

Ava nodded and smiled at me, but it was that nod and smile that you give a person who has said something without understanding the magnitude of it. These histories were hurtful ones, and I knew I'd need to tread lightly.

I thought about the beautiful garden and the wild animal of a man and wondered what secrets everyone was keeping—even him. I wondered what was, just a rumbling, and what was an actual storm.

Chapter 5

Daniel

Ella and the kids ain't hardly put down those books they got from the book woman. I shouldn't have been so gruff with her, I suppose. Truth be told, she scared me right good. Nobody's been up here in months. Lizzie would sometimes drop a book, but she'd do it on the run. Me and the kids would joke that she must have given Opal wings because they'd fly by here, fling the books out, and soar away unnoticed. That won't true of course, but I'm pretty sure she didn't come to our house as often as she went to the others. That was fine, though. I wasn't that good with company. I doubted that we'd see that new lady again for a while, maybe ever by the looks of her.

"Da," Ella said, noticing that I'd stepped out on the porch with them. "You think that book woman will come back this way soon?"

"She might," I said, unbelieving.

Marie stood up and all but stomped her foot at me. "Well, you got to be more civil next time someone comes."

"Civil?"

"You know, pleasant and like a person," Marie said with a face that looked just like her mother giving me what for.

It made me smile to remember Emily, most of the time anyway. That hadn't always been the case, but these days the good memories outweighed the bad. I hadn't really noticed that change as it came on, but I could tell things sat differently as the years went by. I still had a bad day here and there, but these days it was less about Emily and more about the way things had turned out. Life was hard up here sometimes, and I got anxious.

"I know what the word civil means," I said to Marie, with my mouth set like I was about to give her a piece of my mind, but she knew I was joking.

"Maybe you ought to shave or comb your hair," Ella piped up.

"Ain't nobody care what I look like out here," I said and scratched at my beard. "Besides, Hugh wouldn't recognize me." I reached down and scooped him up, holding him tight to me.

Hugh was my measure of time. Four years since we left town. Since Emily died. Since I showed the town my true colors. Or at least they thought that's what they'd seen. I wasn't sure. Maybe it was.

Hugh tugged on my beard. "Cut it off, Da."

"Cut it off?" I said, indignant and set him back on his feet. I feared, though, that I might recognize myself too much if I did. I didn't know if I could put on the clothes of the man I used to be. I wasn't sure that I wanted to. "Tell me about the books you got," I said to change the subject.

Ella eyed me and I knew she had me figured out. She didn't answer me, she just went back to reading to her siblings and for a moment, I stood and watched them all. Most of the time we were fine out here, the four of us, but Ella was getting on in age, fourteen, and I worried there were things she needed to know that I couldn't tell her. Things she needed me to be that I wasn't.

Hugh tugged at my pant leg and held his hands for me to pick him back up. Maybe he was getting too big to be babied, but I picked him up anyway. I needed the feel of him in my arms.

"Come out to the garden with me and help me weed," I said to him, hoisting him up onto my shoulders like he liked for me to. "That book sounds boring anyway."

"It ain't too bad," he said from above me. "It's about a boat. Can we go fishing, Da?"

I liked the way his mind leapt from one thing to the next and never looked back. I envied him. I clasped my hands on his little thighs to keep him steady as we walked around the back of the house.

"How about we get some work done," I said, lifting him over my head and setting him down in front of me, "and then we'll get out poles."

Hugh clapped his hands and did this funny little dance he was wont to do when he was happy. I didn't know where he'd learned it; it seemed just a born-in expression of joy.

"You pick the dandelions but remember to put them in your basket. They're not for throwing away."

"Because you can fry them up with our eggs of a morning," Hugh said, finishing my sentence.

"That's right," I said and tousled his hair.

He ran to get his basket from the shed and began to pick the bright yellow flowers. I looked at his bare little feet and wondered how I'd go about getting him some shoes come fall and winter. Maybe I could make a trade with one of my customers who didn't mind it was me what built stuff, or perhaps Mr. Gibbons could order some and would take it out of my account. I supposed more likely, as soon as the weather turned, a pair would show up like so many other things had. Clothes for all the kids and random things I had need of but hadn't spoken out loud. I had a notion that Pastor Collins had something to do with it. He even sent me a hat when I left mine outside and it got unraveled by a crow. I'd worn it to town a time or two with a big hole in it, then one day a new one had shown up on the front porch. If I was of a mind to get my pride hurt, I'd say it felt like charity, but then I'd remember that Pastor always said the Lord provided, and so I tried my best to be thankful for everything.

Thinking on Hugh's feet reminded me of that book woman and the fancy shoes she had on. Ruined, but fancy. She was without a doubt the new teacher and carrier Mr. Gibbons told me about. All the way from Asheville, N.C. If her shoes were any indication, she wasn't going to last too long out here. I had an old pair of Emily's boots that she'd left here not long before she died. She'd been pregnant with Hugh and her feet were apt to swell. I remembered the day precisely. We'd come up to gather some herbs and things that grew wild around the house and to check on the place. Even though we lived in town, I still made sure to keep the cabin and grounds in good shape. It had been my home after all.

Pastor Collins had taken me in as a child once both my parents had died and for a long stretch, I'd lived there with him and his family. But as soon as I started having feelings for Emily, I told Pastor I needed to go on back home. I was old enough to care for myself then. He agreed so long as Liam and Zach came by to check on things and help me keep the house up. It had become part of our routine and the memories of the times we three spent up here were some of my favorites. Raised as an only child, I'd not had brothers before I went to live with Pastor Collins and the joy of their company was a novelty that never wore off for me. I missed that now, but things were what they were, and Liam and Zach had every right not to want me around anymore.

Every time Emily came with them to help clean or manage the grounds, especially after we were married, she always remarked at how she couldn't imagine being so far from town.

"What in the world would the kids do for entertainment out here?" she had said. "And all this far from the schoolhouse."

She liked that I had agreed to move into town when we got married. I think she always feared she'd end up living out here in the sticks as she called it. I joked with her that all of Kentucky was the "sticks," but she assured me that wasn't so. She had dreams of moving to a bigger city, getting her teaching certificate there and making something more of herself. I tried to convince her that "herself" was fine just where we were. I shouldn't have squandered her dream. I regret that. I don't know that I ever really managed to make her happy, but I tried. I was trying there at the last of it, but that's not the way anyone saw it.

The day she'd left her boots here was one of the first times I had felt little Hugh move inside her belly. Liam and Zach and I were cutting some timber and thinking on how to patch a rotten place in the porch, and she'd come running up to me with the girls in tow.

"Da," Ella had called out. "You can feel the baby moving in Mama's belly."

"Touch it," Marie squealed with an excitement she hadn't yet had for the new baby coming in to take her place as she said.

Emily had smiled at me and reached for my hand. She placed it on her stomach and sure enough I could feel the baby moving. I had had some doubts about the world and how things might turn out as times had already gotten bad, but that day I had hope. I made the decision then that I'd get Emily and the kids out of Certain and onto a better life, just like she wanted. No matter what I had to do.

What's that saying, the road to Hell is paved with good intentions. Indeed it is.

Emily and the girls had gone down the creek to splash some cool water on their faces and play around in the shade. She'd taken off her boots and then later when she'd gone to put them back on, her feet had swelled, and they wouldn't fit. I'd put them inside the cabin and there they were forgotten. That might have been one of my last happy days, other than when Hugh was born. But Emily died not long after he was born, and sometimes I forget the joy of his birth.

I really was just trying to make a better life for us.

And the boots were just boots now. I watched Hugh pile his little basket with dandelions, roots, and all in some cases, which was even better. I could use those, too. Hugh looked up and waved at me, holding up his basket for me to see his hard work. I realized I was wrong. There had been happy days since that night. Many of them. This was another one.

If I could keep myself straight and do what was right, there might be more happy days yet to come.

If.

Chapter 6

Mattie

I finished out my first two weeks by completing the other route I had taken over for Lizzie and amassing a lovely collection of schoolbooks that Ava had let me pilfer from the library. I had made some lists of the ages and grades of the children I had met as well as those that Ruby told me about from her route. I knew that only a small percentage of the children would come to school this fall, but a small start might not be the worst thing. Wanting to thank Ruby and Ava for all their help so far, I thought to have them over for tea. Also, I had spent quite enough time in my own company and really needed some companionship.

I walked across the street to the Certain Grocery to see if I might purchase some French biscuits or a chocolate cream cake. I entered the store and with one glance I had seen the whole establishment. The store consisted of one room with floor to ceiling shelves along two walls and a counter with glass cases along the third. The door where I'd come in was directly in the center of the front wall and barrels of grains and such sat at either side of the entrance. In the center of the store was an ornately carved table with a few baskets of colorful produce. At first glance, it all looked quite lovely with its deeply stained wood and clean feel.

Upon a longer look however, I could see that the shelves were not that well stocked. The store was tidy and well organized, but that seemed to be mostly an effort to disguise the sparseness. The grain bins were not full, and some shelves were empty altogether. It had been the colorful produce that drew my eye into thinking that all was well. This was yet another place that made me feel like Alice stumbling upon a new location in Wonderland; some place that seemed out of sorts even for the out of sorts.

"Hello, miss," the proprietor greeted me. He was a friendly looking man in his sixties most likely with white hair, but a strong build. The White Rabbit. "I was wondering when you would come in," he said.

"I had to, sooner or later." I smiled and reached my hand out for him to shake, which he did. "I'm Mattie Mobley, the new teacher and part-time book carrier."

He nodded as if he knew this already. "Gib," he said by way of his own name. "Sal Gibbons. Owner and sole employee of the Certain Grocery. You can call me Gib or Mr. Gibbons whatever suits you. Mostly just ring the bell and I'll turn up." He turned and dinged the bell on the counter to demonstrate. "Glad you decided to shop here."

"There doesn't appear to be any other place to get food in Certain except from one's garden."

"And most of those don't produce much around here," he said. "The devil's burden makes it hard to grow."

"The devil's burden?" I questioned.

"There's a story that goes like this," Mr. Gibbons said and leaned in close to me like he was telling a secret. "Just along a stretch of the Hell for Certain that we now call Devil's Jump, the Devil himself was hopping around from bank to bank, scooping up rocks and loading them into his apron—all giddy and pleased with himself because he was planning to further burden the land with his load."

I wrinkled my brow, but it came to me what he meant. "To make the soil too rocky to grow things?" I asked.

"Indeed," Mr. Gibbons said, nodding like he was pleased that I was picking it all up so fast. "But his apron string busted, and all the rocks landed in the creek."

"That's a good thing, then, right?" I asked. "He wasn't able to burden the land."

Mr. Gibbons smiled at me and winked. "The devil can do what he wants, busted apron strings or no. To this day, when there's a strange smattering of stones people say that the devil must have busted his apron strings along that path."

"But that's just an old tale, folklore," I said. "Right?"

Mr. Gibbons chuckled at my apparent uncertainty. "That it is, but it don't stop people from believing it. Catch my drift?"

I nodded. I wasn't sure that I did, but I felt like it was worth sussing out.

"Speaking of old tales," I said and picked up a basket and hung it on my arm. "What's the story behind the church being turned into a library?" I raised an eyebrow at him. I had a feeling that Mr. Gibbons and I might become easy friends and hoped he felt the same.

"Now that's a long story indeed," he said, and glanced around as if someone might hear him. "Been about four years since things went to the bad over there." He nodded his head in the direction of the building.

"Four years?" I put an item here and there in my basket. "That seems a long time for no one to use it. Has there not been a pastor in the church for that long as well?"

No wonder some of the pews were missing and the whole thing was now a library. I supposed if it was just sitting empty, the town might as well have made use of it.

"Perhaps Mrs. Ava would be a better person to ask," he said, stepping out from behind the register so he could follow close by me as we talked.

"Mrs.?" I had caught on his distinction of him calling me Miss and her Mrs. "Is Ava married?" I had noticed that she didn't wear a wedding ring.

"She is, but her husband is gone," he said and cleared his throat, looking around for an obvious escape.

"Gone?"

"Times are terribly rough," Mr. Gibbons said and shook his head. "Men leave to find work. Most of the time, they come back. Sometimes they don't."

"Does she have children?" I asked, putting a nice ripe tomato in my basket.

"Five, as a matter of fact."

"Five." I spoke as if he'd said twenty. "I had no idea."

I stood there letting that all sink in. I must have looked as though I'd suddenly become lost.

"So, what can I help you find, Miss?" He gestured to the store as if there were prizes of all sorts to be had.

"Well, Mr. Gibbons, I'm wanting some tea and perhaps some small sweets as I'd like to invite some ladies over for the afternoon. Whatever you might have from the bakery. A cake even, perhaps caramel layer or chocolate?"

Mr. Gibbons broke into a little fit of laughter. I understood my error, of course. I would have been offended, but his laugh was somehow endearing. I knew he wasn't laughing at me, but rather at the state of things.

"You have no bakery, I take it," I said and smiled sheepishly.

"We barely have the necessities these days."

"Why are the shelves so bare?" I couldn't help but ask.

"People have no money, plain and simple," he said matter-of-factly. "Which means I have no money to order more supplies. It's all I can do to pay the note and keep the lanterns lit. We'll see how long it all holds out." He said it with a hint of amusement, and I wondered how he could manage to smile in the face of his own financial demise.

"What will happen then?"

"Don't know, Miss," he said. "The Lord will take care of us."

I nodded. "I suppose afternoon tea isn't something that anyone cares much about here." I felt my cheeks burning slightly. "It was foolish to think of such things. I should do something more useful. More practical. Less frivolous."

"Never underestimate the importance of something frivolous," he said, kindly, putting his hand on my shoulder. "A little thing like a sweet morsel and a cup of tea makes a person feel like the world is right again. Like things are back to normal."

"You humor me," I said gratefully. "Do you really think something so simple could make people feel normal?"

"When you have nothing, the littlest something makes you feel like the world has righted itself. Even for just a small moment. There is hope in moments like that. Hope is important. Without it, we have nothing."

A thought occurred to me then. "If you have flour, sugar, eggs, and some butter or shortening, I think I'll take them."

His eyes lit up. "Ah, making your own bakery goods?"

"I'm not sure how good they'll be," I said, and he chuckled.

"Add a pinch of salt." He held his finger up for me to wait as he searched the shelves. "Aha," he said and came back triumphantly. "And a little vanilla and baking powder," he said and set them on the counter.

I watched out the window as he fetched the other items. Did people really not have the money to eat? The Mobley household had felt the sting of this downturn as my father insisted on calling it, but we had so much more cushion that life had not gotten to a place of hardship, merely a noticeable inconvenience of the finer things. My mind lit back upon the state of the houses and lives I'd glimpsed through the cracks in the open doors afforded me along my book routes. I'd seen dusty and disheveled children, spied elderly men and women curled on chairs or lying listless in rickety beds. Those who had talked to me a little more openly had told me of needing materials on how to repair things, grow things, and heal with home remedies. I had seen the hope in those requests, but that hope was a defense against the despair.

I knew cookies were not a cure, but perhaps they might be a buoy.

Having found everything I wanted, Mr. Gibbons rang up my purchase and I paid him easily. I had taken the last of the shortening on his shelves and that gave me pause.

"Thank you, Mr. Gibbons," I said.

"Thank you, dear," he said and opened the door for me as I left.

"Take care and come back soon."

I nodded and held the bag of goods close to my chest as I walked back down the road to the parsonage. It was strange not to see the church in use on a Sunday. I had grown up going to church with my mother, but when she passed, we didn't go anymore. I wanted to, but my father said Sunday was a day to prepare for Monday, which meant sleeping late and listening to the radio apparently. Sometimes we'd go for a Sunday drive or out to lunch if he felt like leaving the house. Often, we'd drive past a church as service was letting out. I always liked to see the ladies in their pretty dresses and hats and the children running around in the parking lots or playing along the grass. I missed my mother terribly in those moments, especially if I'd see a woman take hold of a child's hand. Still, even in the sadness, it made me happy to see them.

I looked at the empty church yard now as I approached it and wondered what on Earth had made them all stop going to church. Especially in small places like this where I imagined church was not just a religious moment on Sunday, but a way of life. Life had stopped here.

Inside the parsonage, I set all the ingredients on the table and realized I really had no idea how to make a cookie. I knew what went in the bowl because I was the one who retrieved the ingredients. "My little baker's assistant" my mother called me. I'd seen it done, and I'd even helped, but the last time I'd made cookies with my mother I was just twelve years old.

A sudden grief filled me at the thought mixing the ingredients and heating the oven. If only I had taken her up on the offer to bake together that last day when she died. How different might things be? How easily one small choice can change the world forever. I covered my mouth with my hands as emotion threatened to erupt from the depths of my throat, but soon lowered them and took a deep breath. I was not going to cry. I had managed not to cry when I'd fallen from Opal and then later when the dreadful bear had yelled at me, and I was not going to now. I had set out to make cookies, and that's what I was going to do.

"How are you going to bake a cookie?" I asked myself out loud. "You don't even have a recipe."

Even as the words left my mouth, I realized I had tons of recipes at my disposal. There were books and magazines that surely had recipes, as well as the scrapbooks that Ava and Ruby were compiling from the age-old secrets of the women of Certain. Of all the things at the library, I think I was most fascinated with the scrapbooks. Ava had told me that they had begun to make them when other books would start to fall apart too badly to be repaired. They'd combine like information on various topics and create a new sort of reference book. They had begun to collect recipes and quilt patterns from the local folks as well and were making completely new materials. There must surely be a baking scrapbook.

I hurried to the door in hopes that it was open. I figured my chances were slim as Ava most likely kept it locked and I was right. Then I remembered I had seen some keys in the kitchen drawer in the parsonage and rushed back to get them. Lo and behold, one of them worked. *Voilà!*

Being in the church with the lanterns not lit on a Sunday when service should be underway was strange. Sad. Quiet. It was as if the figures painted onto the windows knew what day it was, and they were sad too. I found myself tiptoeing toward the back even though there was no need to tread lightly. The late morning sun found its way in through the windows bringing back the kaleidoscope of color to the gloom. I looked without thinking at the broken window.

"What stories are you holding," I said, looking up into the eyes of Jesus made of colored glass. "What sad thing happened here to keep them away?" He didn't answer, but he looked sad too.

Sure enough, there were a few baking and cooking scrapbooks, and I took the one with the easier recipes. I found one very similar to the sugar cookies my mother used to make, or at least as close as my memory of all things sorted, sifted, and stirred allowed. I had simply enjoyed being in the kitchen with her. I was too young to really pay too much attention to the ins and outs. That could be said of just about everything a young girl could learn from a mother. I wish I had had more time. I wish I had paid better attention.

Back in the parsonage kitchen, I did my best to make her proud. I burnt a batch here and there, but I had a plan for those as well. Most of the cookies came out edible and that was success enough. I made a trip back over to the grocery for some parchment paper and string to package the cookies, taking Mr. Gibbons a few, of course. I paid him too much and if he noticed, he didn't say anything about it.

"These are not the worst cookies I've ever eaten," he said with a wink.

"I'll take that as a compliment," I said proudly.

"Life is all in how we choose to see it," he said and smiled.

"I chose to see it covered in flour," I said, noticing I was doused in it and leaving little poofs everywhere I turned. "Back to the factory."

"No ladies over for tea?" he asked.

"Bigger plans," I said. "And more baking. Much more baking."

"Soldier on," he said and saluted me.

I saluted in return, flour poofing everywhere.

The next day was repair and report day at the library, and I put all my little parchment packages of cookies in boxes I had found and took them over to the library.

"Did we get new donations?" Ava said rushing to help me when she saw me coming in trying to balance two boxes in my arms. She took one from me and was surprised. "This is so light. What is this, it's not books."

Ruby, even though she had to come from the other side of town, was already there working on the spine of a book. She set the repair down gingerly and came to see what I had.

"It's cookies," I said as Ava and I sat the boxes down on a table.

Ruby opened a box and took out a little parchment package. "Someone sent us cookies?"

"I made them," I said, standing up tall and straight. So long as they hadn't tasted them, I could still hold onto a little pride.

"What are they for?" Ava asked.

"Gifts for our patrons," I said. "I have some for us too. I'll be right back."

Their faces had been skeptical, but I hoped my return with tea and the best few of the batch would sway them. I hurried back to the house, gathered my mobile tea party as it were and went back to the church.

"What's all this?" Ruby asked, helping to unpack the tea service from the little set I had brought with me.

"It's silly, I know," I said as I arranged things. "I have no idea why I thought I would need this."

Ava turned the delicate cup over in her hand. "It's lovely. How did you get it here without breaking it?"

"I packed my clothes around it," I said and then sighed. "I filled up my suitcase so that I didn't have room for decent shoes." I held my feet out to show off my ruined, but at least scraped clean of mud, Oxfords.

Ruby laughed. "We should do something about that. I'll see what I have at home."

"Thank you," I said. "Tea anyone?"

The ladies pulled up chairs to the table and I set out tea service. So far so good. We sipped and chatted, and it felt a little as if I had been part of this place forever. I wanted these ladies to accept me. If they did, others would follow. And to be honest, I hoped for friends. Real ones. I hoped this was a good start.

"I hear the grocer only uses the lights on odd days," Ruby said when I mentioned having bought the cookie ingredients there. Her thick brown hair hung loose and wavy.

"What do you mean?" I asked, reaching for another cookie. "What makes a day odd?"

"The date," Ruby said and chuckled. "You know the first, the third, the fifth and so on."

"Oh," I said, embarrassed.

"It keeps the costs down," Ruby said, explaining. "We do the same thing with our lamp oil. At least we're still able to eat every day. For now."

"People don't eat every day?" I asked with the taste of sugar still in my mouth.

"With this downturn, as they call it," Ruby said, rolling her eyes, "going on for years now, people are lucky if they still have what we all used to think of as necessities. You really start to understand the difference between what's a want and what's a need real fast these days. Especially people like us. We thought we were already bad off. We didn't have any idea."

The poverty the people lived in was undeniable. I'd seen as much in North Carolina as well. Not all that far outside the city limits there was a whole other world. I knew it, but I'd never lived in it. I still didn't really if I was honest with myself. I felt as though I'd had my head in a hole all this time. I had read about people leaving their homes and wandering the country in search of work and housing. I had heard about people not being able to get proper medical care and about the cost of the simplest thing being out of reach, but it was all words to me, like a story in a book. This was real.

"I know cookies won't fix anything," I said, "but I made them, hoping you ladies would take some and pass them out to your patrons and family. I don't know, it sounds silly now that the words are out there. I just thought it would be nice."

Ava looked at me and smiled. "It is nice. The children, especially, will love it."

"Clever bribe," Ruby said and winked. "That's the way to get them to come to school indeed. Food."

I tilted my head at the thought. Yes. I was thinking too small with cookies. Food was the way to get them to come. I had a kitchen. I could offer lunches and snacks. I could get my father to send me the money. I could get him to send me the food if it was something that Gibbons didn't have. If nothing else, surely parents would send their children to school for a good meal. I also had plenty of space in the church yard for a garden. I might have to dig out a few rocks, but I could grow what I could and buy the rest from Mr. Gibbons.

I pointed my finger approvingly at Ruby. "You're absolutely right. And I know just what I'll do. I only wish I had gotten here sooner, but I suppose the ground will grow things still. Better late than never," I said, talking as much to myself as I was to the ladies.

Ava shook her head. "I'm not certain what's brewing in your mind there, but this is pretty hard ground to grow on."

I nodded. "I can see that, but there's plenty of room in the church yard for a Victory Garden for the school and loads of natural fertilizer thanks to Opal, and," I said, holding a finger up to make the most important point, "I know someone who can help. All I have to do is tame the beast."

Ruby's eyebrow shot up. "What sort of beast are you talking about?"

"Turns out that your grizzly bear is a bit of a good gardener," I said and sipped at my tea.

Ava nearly spit hers out.

Ruby shook her head. "There is no way that you'll ever get Daniel Barrett to help you with anything. Least of all coming to town to start a garden and least of that a garden here at the church."

Ah, so the bear had a name.

"Daniel Barrett," I said, letting the sound of it roll around in my mouth. "I knew there was a person underneath that scruff."

Ruby made a warning sound under her breath. "There's a person there indeed. One whose story is not pleasant. I don't think he'd be welcome here even if you could convince him to come."

"Why not?" I asked what seemed like, by the look on their faces, the most shocking question ever uttered.

The ladies looked at each other and I knew they were deciding what to tell me and what to leave out.

"There's a reason this isn't a church anymore," Ruby said hesitantly.

"Ruby," Ava challenged, and I could tell that, were it up to her, she'd not tell me anything at all.

"Pastor Collins made some decisions that turned out for the worst," Ruby said, eying Ava as she spoke. When I just sat and waited for more explanation she continued. "Sometimes people make mistakes that they can't come back from."

"Pastor Collins?" I asked. This name was new to me. "I thought we were talking about Daniel."

Ava cleared her throat. "Like she said, it's a very long story that really is of no use to tell." She raised her eyebrows at Ruby.

"The two of you know that I can see you making faces at each other, right?" I asked, mimicking their expressions back at them.

Ruby shrugged at me. "I guess it really isn't right to talk about him behind his back."

Ava scoffed. "That hasn't stopped people."

I watched them back and forth, but nothing more came of the tale. I could tell that it was in my best interest to change the subject.

"Well, anyway," I said. "I hope you will take some cookies to hand out on your routes. I think they'll hold for a while. Might get a little crunchy, but they're still sweet."

Ava's eyes told me she was grateful for the shift in conversation. I did love a good story, and this was shaping up to be one of interest. Ava seemed to have a soft spot for the town's grizzly bear. I wasn't sure what it was, but a booksy girl like me knew how to wait for things to unfold.

Chapter 7

Mattie

Opal and I walked through the cool creek water toward the Grizzly Den as I had come to think of it. Opal seemed not to mind too much if the water wasn't moving. The rest of the route had been mostly productive. Since I wasn't a complete stranger this time, most of the people spoke to me and most took a package of cookies and listened to my short, prepared speech about the opening of school that came with a promise of lunch and an afternoon snack. Ruby had been right; the mention of food had piqued people's interest. This made me sad, but hopeful that I could help. Some people also seemed to regard the offer with suspicion as if producing food from thin air was some magic I proposed to have. That was fine. I had all intentions of making good on my promises. And today, I planned to talk again to the one man who seemed to know how to grow a garden despite the soil being made of dust and stone.

The last push to reach the Barrett house saw us struggling to pass over a scattering of rocks, some the size of a small child. Opal hated this part most of all. I blew out a hard breath of determination and gave Opal a little tapping of my foot to get her moving.

When I passed through the overhang of the secret entrance and came into sight of the house, the three children I'd met that first day came pouring out of the cabin like white water over rocks. The littlest one, Hugh, almost fell, but his older sister, Ella—I was pretty good at remembering the names—caught him by the arm before he went over the steps head over heels. She didn't even pause, she just tucked him to her and kept coming, not setting him down until the ground was solid beneath him.

They all ran over to me as I was dismounting—each of them carrying a book, even the little one.

"We read these at least four times over," Ella said, looking up at me with her brown eyes and slightly buck-toothed smile. "Not the long one, I only read that one twice. Hugh and Marie didn't hardly listen to it the second time, but I read it out loud anyway because the words were so pretty, and I just love to read it slow so I can pretend I'm there, you know what I mean?"

I did. As a child, I became quite good at losing myself in a story. It was far easier to pretend a life than to actually live one. I appreciated her excited speech. I imagined she had waited a long time to tell me all that.

"I'm glad y'all enjoyed them," I said, taking the books from them and looking around for wild animals. I slipped the books they were returning into the saddlebag. I nestled them spine in, that's how I kept better track of what I was picking up versus what was going out. I made a selection for each of them, and they took the books from me like people starving.

"Will you stay and read one of them to us?" Marie asked. "Ella did an OK job of it, but I'd like to hear it the way Mama would have read it."

"What does that mean?" Ella said, one hand going to her hip.

I noticed that she was wearing a dress that had been mended rather poorly. The ruffle around the bottom had evidently come loose and someone with below average sewing skills had tried to reattach it. I wondered if I was looking at the sewing prowess of the local grizzly bear. I imagined his meaty paws threading the needle, one eye squinting closed, and his hairy face tuned up in frustration. I had to struggle to keep a smile off my own face. Though, one solid memory of him grunting at me to get off his property wiped the smile away quickly enough.

"Ella," Marie said, looking at her with bewilderment. "You know how Mama would do the voices and make it all dramatic. I bet Miss Mattie can do that, too."

"You said I did the voices OK enough," Ella protested. "I've been reading to you for a long time now."

"OK enough," Marie said, emphasizing the word. "That doesn't mean you did it right. A real grown-up is here. I want Miss Mattie to do it."

A real grown-up is here. The words clung to me with desperate fingers.

"Will you stay and read, Miss Mattie?" Marie urged.

Finally, someone wanted me to linger with them.

"I suppose I can," I said, thrilled that she had asked. Then I whispered to Ella, "I'm sure you did a fine job."

The children clapped their hands together in excitement.

"Wait," I said, reaching back into my bag to retrieve the tin I used to carry my sweet bribes. "I made you all cookies." I handed them each a little package.

They took the gift without hesitation. Marie opened it right away and shoved one in her mouth. Ella held her package to her nose and then closed the parcel protectively in her hand.

"I got one, too," Hugh said, holding it out. "For me."

I wondered if he even understood that it was something for him to eat or if he was just happy to have something—anything.

"OK, children," I said, a thrill rising at the thought of saying this to a whole classroom. "Let's read."

This was a fine chance to endear myself to the children. I would, of course, be reading to them at school. Story time was a must. Marie took hold of my hand and pulled me forward. Her fingers gripped tight, stronger than their smallness would suggest. Need was a powerful thing. The children led me up the steps to the porch which stretched from one side of the house to the next. Still the whole thing wasn't twenty feet across if that. The wide planks seemed to be sealed together with mud or some other substance that held the whole thing in place. I touched the side of the house as the kids were settling themselves on the floor by the rocking chair. The wood was rough in places, but smooth in others. I noticed how solid this house seemed to be in comparison to many of the others I'd delivered to. The steps were sturdy and the porch about as even as I'd seen. Someone here knew how to keep the place up.

A rather royal looking rooster followed us up the steps. His long black tail feathers were so shiny they were blue here and there when a bar of light caught them.

"Shoo, cockado," Hugh said and waved his hands at the bird who flapped his wings in protest, but left, nonetheless.

"Remind me," I said to Ella, "I have something for your chickens, too."

Ella handed me the book she had and asked that I read that one. *The Velveteen Rabbit*. It was one of my favorites. My father had bought a copy for me and had it sent all the way from England when the book was first published. I was too old for it, I had told him, but later I'd read it and loved it so much that I slept with it under my pillow. It was still in my room back home. I wished I had brought it with me. It just seemed wrong to take it away from the place it called home.

I took the book from Ella, my eyes lingering over the children's worn clothes and tangled hair. They were worn down to the natty little nothings, but they were loved. They were worse for the wear, but they were real. My throat caught tight, and I had to struggle out a few little jagged breaths before I could right myself.

They all sat down cross-legged on the porch. Hugh crawled up into Ella's lap, and I read. It was the single most magical moment of all my life I thought—reading this story that I had loved so deeply to these children who lived like little captives, not of scarlet fever or any real illness, but of exile whether they seemed to know it or not. I wasn't even sure why they all holed up here, but I could see that they did. This was part of the long story that Ruby and Ava had tried very hard not to tell me. The children made me want to know the rest of the story even more.

After I had finished reading and the children had begun to talk to each other about the story, forgetting me for a moment, I looked around the porch to get a sense of their world. A tub and washboard sat just outside the open front door, a feed sack, a harness of some sort, a wooden crate. A hand saw, a basket with hay and one egg, a milk bottle. It seemed that much of their living was done outside. There was one window to the right of the door, but no matching one on the other side.

"Why is there just one window?" I asked.

Ella piped up answering. "Da says it was built like this to keep the draft down in winter. Our beds are on the side without the window."

I nodded, "What about summer, like now?"

"Why's we keep the door open," she said. "Would be trifling hot. We have the back door open too, makes a cross breeze, Da says."

"Da put a window in that door so we could get some light," Ella said. "The window don't open, but it's sure pretty with the colored glass."

"I think it's creepy," Marie said. "Has baby toes on it and some lady's eyeball."

Toes. Perhaps Jesus's toes like the ones missing from the window in the church. Mary's watchful eye perhaps. Was this a piece of the puzzle? Literally. Was Daniel to do with the bad decision their Pastor Collins had made and the broken window?

Why keep the pieces then and build them into his house? The story grew more and more intriguing to me.

"Where's your father?" I asked, not at all sure that he'd be OK with me making myself at home on his porch and reading to his children. "That was him the other day in the garden, yes?" I asked the children.

Opal snorted in the yard and the sudden sound made me jump.

"He's around," Ella said, waving away the question.

"Is he at work?"

"He don't have a job no more," Marie said.

I just nodded.

"You did the voices real good," Marie said, nodding her head at me, causing her bangs to fall over her eyes. She pushed at them and then licked her dirty hand to slick her hair out of her face.

My heart ached for these little kids here with no mother and being raised by a bear. Mowglis, each of them. I was overcome.

I moved to get up from the rocker, but Hugh crawled up in my lap and kissed my cheek. "I like your face," he said, in that slow way little kids do when they know the words but making the sentence still requires thought. "You ain't hairy like Da."

"Don't say ain't," Ella corrected him. Ella stood up and took Hugh from my lap. She put the boy on her small hip just like a mother would do. She was no more than thirteen or fourteen, but that was as good as grown when times were hard like they were now.

She thanked me for reading to them and went on to bend my ear about how her mother used to read to her and Marie and how yes, she was very good at the voices. Marie and Hugh seemed easily bored and both took off into the house before long.

"Hugh was just a baby when she passed on, so he doesn't remember," Ella said sadly.

"That's a sorrow, I'm sure," I said to her sad little face. "But I bet you are rearing him correctly. Teaching him that lovely grammar I hear."

Sure, her speech still had a cadence I had to listen carefully to, and little broken bits of regional voice slipped in, but I could hear that there had been a time when someone schooled her on the finer points of speech. She practically beamed with pride.

"I trust that you'll come to school when it opens in the fall," I said and smiled at her. "You must have been a good student. I can tell."

Her face sank a bit. "We don't really go into town."

"I could talk to your father about it," I said hopefully. She made a face as if that was not a good idea. Still, she didn't tell me not to. "You seem to really enjoy reading and it would be a shame to miss out on school. What do you like most about learning?"

I knew to ask questions in a way that encouraged answers, not just shakes and nods of heads.

"I don't know if it's about learning, but I like to write stories that I make up myself," she said proudly. "We couldn't bring all our stuff when we moved here, and I missed my books. So, I figured I would just write some stories of my own. I think I'm pretty good at it," she said and then lowered her voice, looking over her shoulder and then back at me. "I think that I would like to publish a book of my own one day. If girls like me are able to do that."

I looked at her very intently. "Well, girls like you are able to do anything they want to. You remember that. There are quite a large number of writers who are women. I'd love to read a story that you wrote."

"Would you really?" she asked, pressing her wrinkled dress down and straightening her shoulders. "I'll write one special for you for when you come back. I'm almost out of paper though, so it might not be very long. I might let you read some of the ones I have already written. I'll have to read back over them and make sure they sound good."

I nodded at her professionalism. "You do that, and I will look forward to reading them." I thought for a moment, something occurring to me. If I could bring cookies, I could bring other things as well. "I'll see if I can get you some more paper and I bet you could use some pencils, too."

Her face lit up as if I had offered to bring her the latest toy in the window of FAO Schwarz all the way in New York City.

"That would be," she said, but then her voice caught in her throat, and she didn't say any more.

I touched the side of her face, and she closed her eyes. A lump formed so quickly in my throat that I knew I had only moments before the tears came.

"I better be getting along," I said, clearing the lump from my throat as best I could and peeking around one more time for any sign of wildlife.

Daniel

I had to stop her before she left. I had the boots in my hand but hadn't worked the courage to go out onto the porch and talk to her. Which was ridiculous. It was my porch, and she was just the book woman bringing stories, not the leader of an angry mob toting pitchforks and torches. Which had never really happened, it just felt that way sometimes. I stepped out the front door and cleared my throat.

"Ma'am," I said, softly as I'd already startled her the last time she was here. "Might I have a word?"

She held her hands out to her sides as if I was holding her up. "Sir, it is part of my job to read to the children, but I can understand that I should have obtained your permission first."

I shook my head and stepped closer to her. I held the pair of lace-up boots out to her, but she backed away.

"I should go," she said, taking a step backward, looking behind her quickly and then back at me. "My apologies."

I thrust the boots at her, and she let out a small scream. I didn't mean to be forceful. I just wanted her to have the boots, but it was clear I had scared her. She'd obviously been told a thing or two about me.

"Ma'am, I'm just aiming to give you these here boots. It's just shoes. Nothing to be afraid of." I held them up, more gently this time, and gave a nod to the shoes currently on her feet before looking her back in the eyes. She had nice eyes. Peaceful. Brown, like the richest soil. "I noticed last visit that you didn't have proper shoes."

"I'll have you know; these shoes are of the latest fashion and were quite expensive," she said and put her hands on her hips. She was insulted, but not in an arrogant way. It was endearing actually.

I tried to keep the amusement out of my voice. "I don't think you'd get much of a price for them anymore. Not around here least ways."

She stood there for a moment and looked at me quizzically. As if she was surprised to hear me speak in complete sentences.

"Thank you, Mr. Um, Mister, but I couldn't take them."

She looked at the girls who were standing to the side watching us talk. Hugh came back out of the house and pulled on my pant leg.

"Name's Barrett. Daniel Barrett." I patted Hugh with my free hand.

"Mattie Mobley," she said, and stuck out her hand for me to shake.

I put the boots in them instead. They were nice boots that shouldn't go to waste.

"I know who you are," I said and pushed my hands in the pockets of my overalls so that she wouldn't be able to give the boots back. "The kids done told me all about you. Ain't talked about hardly nothing else for the last two weeks."

She paused again and tilted her head as if trying to figure me out. It was unnerving in a way, but I appreciated it. No one had really stopped to think about what they thought of me in a long time. Minds were made up and there seemed no changing them.

"Library initiative," she said, finally and held the boots to her chest. "We bring literature to the homes. Books."

"I know what a library is for, and I know what a book is, ma'am," I said and folded my arms across my chest.

"I'm sorry, Mr. Barrett. I didn't mean to imply anything. I was just trying to justify my presence on your land."

I hadn't meant to be rude. I didn't get much chance to talk to people other than Mr. Gibbons and my brothers, if it was still appropriate to call them that. I wasn't sure when the last time was that I'd had a conversation with a lady.

"No need to apologize," I said and let my arms fall to a less threatening position. "I heard you speaking to Ella just now. She has fanciful ideas, and I tend to be more practical these days." I touched the top of Ella's head. "It was kind of you to entertain them."

"They aren't fanciful, Mr. Barrett. It's perfectly reasonable that she might be a writer one day. She seems well educated for," she stopped mid-sentence as if recalculating what she thought while she was speaking it.

I sighed, she'd certainly heard a tale or two about us here. I was glad she seemed to be the sort of person to make up her own mind but saddened by the thought that she'd been "warned" about me. I suppose I still hoped that people might forget even if they didn't forgive.

"You can call me Daniel," I said to clear her confusion about how to address me. "Mr. Barrett is too much a burden around here. Glad you dared come."

I tried to sound a little annoyed—mostly to cover up the truth of the matter—I was hurt.

"Well, Daniel, good day." She nodded and set the boots on the porch railing. She descended the stairs quickly without looking back.

I followed. She made it all the way back to Opal and had grabbed her reins when I reached out to her and took hold of her wrist. She stiffened and my heart sank. But she turned around to look at me, which was better than yanking free and riding away as fast as she could.

"My wife died shortly after our son was born," I said, holding the boots out to her. "These were hers and they are just going to the bad sitting around unused. Please take them."

"I'm sure Ella would grow into them. You should keep them for her," she said and glanced to the kids on the porch. "I've seen the state of people's shoes or at least what passed for shoes. It's too much to take from you."

"You were kind to Ella, and I owe you," I said, searching for the reasoning that would persuade her to accept them.

"You don't have to pay for kindness," she said. "It's my job to deliver the books, and if I have time to stay and read or chat, then that's part of the package. I was just trying to pique her interest, make a connection. I would have done the same for any family along my route."

I chuckled then and said, "We ain't just any family around here. I reckon you've been told as much, seeing as how you're hot to get out of here."

"I am not," she said indignantly.

I could tell right away that this lady valued her independence and wanted to be seen as strong willed and able to take care of herself. Maybe she was.

"I'm not surprised you got this route," I said, fishing for information. "I didn't figure Ava would take it. I see you've been fool enough to accept the job."

This offended her senses I could tell. I was pushing her, and I wasn't sure why. I liked having her here, but that wasn't apparent in the way I was acting.

"I am no fool, Mr. Barrett," she said, and I winced at my own name. "For one thing, I am able to make up my own mind on matters presented to me. For another, I am a teacher come here to Certain to start school in the fall. I'm helping out at the library as a thank you for the position."

"Teacher?" I said and cleared my throat. "I suppose it's been a while since we had one."

She straightened herself to her full height as if to square off with me, which was a waste of effort as no amount of standing up straight or raising on her toes would really make much difference as I was much taller than she was. Besides, I could tell she was a formidable woman, no matter being short. It looked like she was about to give me a piece of her, surely, well-educated mind, but before she had a chance to speak, I lowered my head and held the boots out one last time.

"Please take the boots, ma'am," I said. I really did want her to have them. "This is rougher terrain than the paved streets of your Asheville, and I don't mean just the road. Proper footwear will be the least of the adjustments you'll need to make. Let me help, at least in some small way."

She reached out and took the boots from me. "Thank you, Mr. Daniel." She shook her head. "Daniel."

"Go on before it gets dark down there along the creek bed," I said. "It ain't safe in the woods after dark and you don't want to get tongues wagging that you're keeping time at the Barrett's, no matter if it's part of your job or not."

She nodded toward the boots. "Thank you."

She slid the boots into her bag and pulled out a little paper sack of something. I took the bag she offered, opened it, and pulled out a very burnt cookie.

I smelled it and chuckled. "You don't have to pay for kindness," I offered her words back to her and winked. "Especially with burnt cookies."

"They're for the chickens," she said, obviously pretending to be offended. Perhaps she could tell that I was joking with her. "I'll have you know that I made some perfectly, well mostly, good ones as well that I shared with your children earlier."

I dropped the burnt cookie back into the bag and closed it in my hand. "Thank you," I said. "I'm sure they appreciated that. I'm not much of a baker."

"Me neither," she said and shrugged. "Thank you again, Daniel."

She lifted herself into the saddle and patted Opal, who hesitantly turned around to leave. I nodded to them as she gave the reins a soft clap to get Opal moving. I stood there even after they were gone, contemplating on this woman who had heard the tales, but had come, nonetheless. Who had met the grizzly, yes I knew the nickname, and had stayed to talk to him anyway.

I had liked the way my actual name sounded clean and clear when she said it. The way it rang like anyone else's name might. Like I might be just another person on her route.

"Mattie," I said her name out loud to see how it sounded. I didn't expect to, but I smiled. I rubbed my hand across my face, feeling the scratch and tangle of my beard, but also feeling the upturn of my mouth and the plumping of my cheeks. "Mattie," I said it again to see if the reaction was the same.

It was.

Chapter 8

Mattie

I woke up the next morning thinking about the fading light along the creek and the sound of the warbling water and the way I had noticed that Daniel's eyes were the same color as the leaves on the trees and that his hair was the same shade as the dark brown bark of the trunks when they're wet from the rain.

"Girl," I told myself right out loud, "you need to get your head on straight."

There was work to do today. Ruby and Ava had graciously offered to help me move the furniture out of my living room so that I could set things up for school. However, dark skies and low rumbling thunder overhead had us hurrying things out of the parsonage and into the church.

Setting the coffee table down in the back by the circulation desk we surveyed the mess we'd made. The loveseat, chairs, and end tables were set cattywampus and in the way of everything. We'd have to move it all again, but at least it was dry.

"I think we could make a nice little sitting area back here," Ruby said, plopping down in one of the chairs. "Maybe people might even come visit like you would an actual library."

Ava nodded her head and said to me, "I suppose you could take one of the worktables as a desk for yourself."

"Yes, take mine" Ruby agreed and put her feet up on the coffee table. "I won't be needing it since I'll be stretched out over here from now on."

I smiled at her and pushed the other armchair over by the coffee table to join her. "Indeed. I think this will make getting our work done here much easier." I put my feet up on the table as well."

"Where did you get those boots?" Ruby asked, looking at my feet. "Much better than your other shoes."

"Daniel Barrett," I said, and Ruby gasped. "That was a little melodramatic," I chuckled. "He gave them to me. He said he had seen that I needed some shoes and that he wanted me to have these. I felt a little strange taking them. He said they had been his wife's." I made an apologetic face and moved my feet off the table where the boots were less visible.

Ava knelt down to look at my shoes. "Let me see," she said and touched the laces and then turned like she was going to walk away, but she didn't.

"You talked to Daniel?" Ruby asked as if I was out of my mind. "Like an actual conversation. Didn't I explain to you who he is?"

"Truth be told," I countered, "not really."

"You shouldn't take things from him," Ruby said and looked worried. "He might have cursed them or something."

Thunder rumbled again and the first drops of rain fell hard and thick on the roof.

"That's ridiculous," I said. "He practically begged me to take them." I held up one foot, turning it to show off the brown leather lace-ups as there was no reason to hide them. "I tried to decline the offer, but he wouldn't stop insisting."

"He spoke to you about Emily?" Ava asked, turning back toward us. "And gave away her shoes?"

Emily. That must have been his wife's name. I was going to have to take notes on who was who and what was what as it seemed plain that no one aimed to tell me the whole story.

"That was nice of him to give you the boots," Ava said and pressed her lips together. She took another step closer. "Why did he do that?"

"He said he was thanking me for being nice to Ella."

Ava's eyes reddened and she turned away quickly. She went back over to her desk, sat down, and returned to her work as if she had not been talking to me at all.

"I did something wrong, didn't I?" I whispered to Ruby, feeling awful. "Does she think the boots are cursed, too? Should I not wear them in here?"

"Daniel Barrett is a subject best left alone," Ruby said quietly, glancing at Ava. "I know you have to take him books and be courteous, but it's best to just pop in and out and let it go. I'd advise against spending much time there. Especially if you're hoping to win people over and come to your school. Being acquaintances with Daniel Barrett won't win you friends."

At that, Ava got up and walked out the front doors of the church letting a stiff wind in around her. It blew some of the papers off her desk. Ruby got up and called after her, but Ava didn't turn back. Ruby pulled the doors closed and wrapped her arms around herself.

"She'll be OK," Ruby said and sat down on the table in front of me.

I shook my head and sighed. "I just don't understand," I said. "He doesn't seem that bad. I mean, sure, he's scruffy and a little bearish in his towering over you sort of way, but he seemed pleasant enough and his children were happy and seemed well cared for. I just don't understand," I repeated.

Rain pelted steady on the roof above us. Without the sun to light the colored windows the room seemed as dark and ominous as our conversation.

"It was years ago," Ruby said, referring to what must have been one heck of a thing as if that tiny pronoun explained things to me. "You're not from here. Of course, you don't see it. It's just," she paused.

And I finished her sentence. "A long story."

She shrugged. "You're trying to fit in here, start a school, serve as a carrier. Trust me, leave Daniel Barrett out of it."

It; I decided that my first lesson this fall would be about the use of pronouns.

"Ava seemed particularly upset by the whole exchange," I said and looked at the boots. "Daniel mentioned her. They know each other, I guess."

Ruby started to say something, but the door opened, and Ava came back in. The chill of rain followed her in, and it almost made me shiver. She came back over to me and folded her hands in front of her like she was praying. I stood up, unsure of what I was supposed to say or do.

"Forgive me," she said. "Please keep the boots. It will be an insult to return them, and you did need better shoes. It was a very kind gesture on Daniel's part. I had forgotten his kind nature. I think most people have."

I opened my mouth to ask about a million questions at once, but over Ava's shoulder Ruby shook her head.

Ava went back to work, and Ruby stood beside me. "The Daniel thing is tricky around here. Just tread lightly."

"I'll try," I said. "I feel like I misstep at every turn. I want people to trust me. They have to at least not hate me if I hope to have any students."

"Folks are wary of outlanders, is all," she said and tugged me toward the front of the church, presumably to give Ava some space.

"Outlanders?" I asked, pulling against her urge forward.

"People coming in telling us what to think and how to live."

"I would never presume to do that," I said, although I could see how I must look to them—city girl come in to teach them a thing or two. Turns out that it was me who probably had the most to learn.

"I know," she said, touching my arm. "Give it time and stay away from Daniel."

"Should I just toss the books at him from the creek-side," I said and made a face to let her know I was joking.

"I think you've damaged enough books already," she said and punched me playfully on the shoulder.

I opened my mouth wide and feigned insult. She laughed openly and I became very aware of an occurrence that was entirely new to me. I had made a friend and we were making sport of each other. This was what the beginning of a friendship felt like. I could feel tears welling in my eyes and I cleared my throat to shoo them away.

"Want to move the student desks?" Ruby asked.

"There are desks?" I had figured I'd have to send for some or perhaps have the students sit on the floor.

"Only five, but they're in good shape," Ruby said. "They're stored behind the baptismal. To keep them safe."

"From what?"

Somehow, I knew the answer was Daniel, although that made no sense at all.

"Let's just get them and take them over before the weather gets any worse," Ruby said. "Maybe we can have tea again. If it's not too windy let's sit on the porch," she was saying as she led me toward the desks. "I love a summer storm."

I thought about Daniel's front porch and if he and the kids were sitting out there watching the clouds churn the sky and listening to the rain fall. I imagined him in the rocking chair and Hugh tucked in his lap. Maybe Ella was reading them a book and Marie was giving her a hard time about not getting the voices right.

No, I didn't see how I was going to be able to leave Daniel out of it, whatever *it* was, at all.

Chapter 9

Mattie

I'd been in Certain for a month. I felt as though I had been here much longer, and that I'd just arrived at the same time. Preparing for my book route, I stopped in the classroom, as I now officially called it, and took in a purposeful breath. Just being in the room excited me. I found that I often came in just to straighten something that was fine to start with or to reorder the stack of books on my table. I liked to start my day in the classroom.

I had worked hard to remember all the names of my library route patrons and to connect the dots of family and friends as relationships were revealed to me, but I still had a way to go to feel like I knew everyone. I was welcomed by most folks and the houses at which my reception had been chilly at best, had at least improved slightly. Trying to see the silver lining, I imagined the cool thaw of people's reception to blow over me like a nice breeze on a steamy Kentucky afternoon. I hoped that meant I was seen less as an outlander and more like a friend—or at least someone with the potential to be. I had a few children and parents who showed interest in school, especially when I mentioned that I'd be providing lunch and a snack. I had a kitchen after all and if I could talk Daniel into helping with a garden in the church yard, I'd be all set. I knew Ruby wouldn't approve of that last part of my plan, but so be it.

Pulling up near one of the larger homesteads on my route, I found a whole brood of kids waiting on me and Opal down by the water along the creek. As we made our way up the bank, they walked alongside us as if leading me to the castle gates. I'd seen some of them before, but they'd stayed on their porches or in their yards. This was a new level of welcome.

I had noticed on my first visit that this homestead consisted of four houses—built in a sort of semicircle with a big, shared yard. One house looked much older than the other three, and I surmised it was the original home around which the others were built as the children grew up and got married. I was the only child of only children, and I liked this grouping together of family. Aunts and uncles, plenty of cousins, and an older couple I took for the matriarch and patriarch—the granny and gramps. None of them had spoken to me much the last time I was here. They seemed very familiar with who I was and what I was doing there, but that hadn't garnered me much conversation.

The children, at least, seemed keen to talk to me today and it was a relief that they'd come to wait on me, happy to have me back again.

"Whatcha got for us this time, book lady?" The elder boy, perhaps fourteen, asked, as he held back a tree limb that crossed my path.

"I done read all those others."

"You got any mystery stories?"

"I'm hoping for a book with pictures this time."

I couldn't tell who was speaking what, they were all talking over each other in their excitement. I looked down from my perch on Opal's back into the eager faces of the children.

"I want something what will teach me how to make a birdhouse," the older boy said. "Uncle Liam says I have to read up on it and then he'll help me use the tools. I told him since he knows already, he oughten to just teach me himself, but he's of the mind I should learn on it on my own."

"Well," I said looking down toward the boy's uplifted face as I pulled up on Opal's reins where she tried to lurch forward. She'd done that the last time we came, "that sounds like a good plan to me and yes, I actually do have something that teaches you to build a birdhouse."

"I bet my Aunt Ava picked that out for me," he said and suddenly the whole group of them took off running in front of me.

Aunt Ava? Another puzzle piece no one had informed me of. How would I ever figure this place out without the picture on the top of the box? I remembered, quite suddenly, my mother and myself doing a puzzle at our kitchen table. When I was little, there were no pictures to go by. In fact, people would have thought you a cheat if you knew what the picture ended up being before you started. I supposed my time in Certain would be much like that.

I followed the children as they ushered me in. They called ahead, announcing my arrival. I saw the two women I'd seen the last week come out of the houses I remembered them from. I pulled up into the enclosure of their small personal village and dismounted. The children clamored around—their hands out for new books. I gave the boy the book I had mentioned. Ava had indeed picked that book. I had thought she was just very good at this job when she picked it—so precise, but I saw, then, that she had the special insight of being part of this family—one of these houses must be hers and some of these children as well. It made me smile, but I did wonder why she hadn't told me her family was on one of my routes. I looked to the empty porch at the farthest part of the little camp of houses and surmised that must be hers. I thought again about her husband being gone and I imagined I could actually see her loneliness sitting on the chair on the front porch waiting for her to get home from work. I wondered if that was why she seemed to always be at the library.

One of the women came forward—her arms loaded with books to return. "I'm Sarah," she said, and pointed to the children. "Some of those are mine. I won't burden you with which ones." She smiled at me, knowing, I suppose that remembering the names would take a while.

"I'll learn them," I said. "I'm Mattie."

"I know," she said and pointed toward the porch where another woman about her age stood looking toward us. "That's Laurel, Liam's wife. I'm married to Zachary." She told me these things as if I knew who Zachary and Liam were. "I will warn you that they are both home this afternoon and eager to talk to you."

"To me," I said, pointing at myself. "Avid readers, are they?"

She laughed. "Not a lick. Not that they can't, mind you. We had a good upbringing, but no, they'd rather use a book as target practice. No offense to the book, they would use just about anything as target practice."

"What do they want to talk to me about?" I asked, tightening the straps of the saddlebag where it was coming loose. I felt nervous and needed something to do with my hands.

"Daniel Barrett," a deep voice said behind me, and I actually jumped.

I put my hand to my heart and turned around. A man wearing a miner's style cap stuck out his hand to me. "I'm Liam Collins." He looked just like Ava—they both had those blue eyes that seemed too blue to look at, framed by dark hair that offset their pale skin in another worldly sort of way. His face was clean shaven, and he was harshly attractive.

Collins. The name stuck out in my mind. Pastor Collins. I remembered that Ruby had mentioned some bad decisions that a Pastor Collins had made. Mr. Gibbons had mentioned him too. Surely this wasn't him. He didn't seem the pastoral type. I glanced at the older gentleman on the porch instead. More likely that was the pastor.

"Mattie," I said and shook Liam's hand. His nails were caked in soot, and I supposed because of his job, they always looked that way whether his hands had been washed or not. It was dark and dirty work in the mines. Many wives had told me stories already. "I don't know that I can tell you much about Mr. Barrett that you probably don't already know."

"Let it rest, Liam," another man, who I supposed was Zachary, spoke as he approached. He was bigger than Liam, but somehow seemed less formidable. "What good does it do to ask after him, brother?"

Zachary put his hand on Liam's shoulder, but Liam jerked away.

"I'm going inside to start supper," Sarah said and handed me the books she had cradled in her arms. "It was lovely to meet you, Mattie. Pardon my brother-in-law, he's got an ax to grind or a few."

"With good reason," Liam said, but he didn't seem angry with her for calling him out on it. "I just want to know if you've seen him. He still over there? Hiding out on the other side of Hell, or did it finally suck him in?"

Zachary stepped up and put his hand on Liam again. "That's a bit of a stretch, brother. Let him hide if that's what he's a mind to do. Makes things easier, don't it?"

"For who?" Liam asked and his eyes looked pained. "He missed his last trade appointment."

"I don't know why you call them that," Zachary said. "The man's free to come and go as he pleases. You make it sound so serious."

"There's an order to things and it's in his best interest that he keeps it."

I looked from one to the next as they talked. I had thought that perhaps Daniel was just reclusive, but this sounded more like he was imprisoned and that the exile was not his own.

"Are you surprised he didn't come this week," Zachary said with a sort of laugh. "Y'all near about came to fisticuffs last time. I'm not surprised he kept his distance."

"I just want to know if he's shining again. Especially with them youngins there," Liam said, his eyes wide and worried, looking back at me. "Ain't no good gonna come from going back to that kind of work."

Zachary nodded in concession. I could see that there was a fair amount of bad blood between Liam and Daniel. It was etched across Liam's face just as visible and vivid as if it were a tattoo.

"Shining?" I asked, catching on the word.

"Running moonshine," Zachary clarified. "Making and selling. It's a right cutthroat business in these hills, ma'am. Best you be careful."

"I didn't see any evidence of such a thing," I said, feeling defensive of Daniel, which surprised me.

Liam snorted. "Of course not. The man's got more sense than to leave it out in the open. Probably out in the woods somewhere."

"Daniel ain't going to risk his kids, Liam," Zachary said.

"I don't know," Liam said, his blue eyes wide. "I fear he would. Look what happened to Emily because of it."

"Long years ago, brother," Zachary said with a sigh.

"Time don't make her any less our sister or any less dead."

Zachary's eyes squeezed shut at the words. I stood still as a deer struck fearful. I didn't move anything except my eyes back and forth as the men talked. If Ava was their sister and so was Emily, then Emily was Ava's sister or sister-in-law depending on how her missing husband fit in with the rest of them and although I couldn't understand why she didn't tell me that, it did explain her behavior.

Eventually they quieted down, and Liam blew out a hard breath.

"I just want to know if them kids are OK," Liam said, looking sternly at me. "Is he there? Do they look alright?" His voice was harsh and insistent. He wiped at the sweat forming on his brow. He wanted an answer and wasn't going away without it.

I opened my mouth and stammered one out. "Of course, he was there." I didn't know why I had said of course. I clearly didn't know the man as well as they did. "The kids looked fine. Happy."

"Did he speak to you?" Liam's words were blunt and choppy.

I glanced at my infamous boots and tried not to shuffle my feet lest they draw attention.

Zachary pressed his lips together and pulled his brother back by the arm. "That'll do. You heard her. They're all alright. We'd hear if they wasn't. Mattie would tell us, right?"

Here I thought that Zachary was my protector in this awkward encounter, but instead he'd drawn a line and asked me to choose a side. I could see that etched on his face as well.

"I said they were fine." Now my words were blunt and choppy.

Liam stalked off, and I released a breath.

"I'm sorry, ma'am," Zachary said. "That was shameful of us to put you on the spot like that. I know you're hearing all sorts of things about Daniel and suffice it to say, he's best off where he is."

"Daniel was your brother-in-law?" I asked, but I knew the answer. "I'm real sorry to hear about your sister's passing. I don't know the history, really. It seems a well-guarded secret, but I take it people hold Daniel accountable for Emily passing and perhaps some other things as well."

"Daniel and us," Zachary said and waved to the whole homestead. "We've known each other forever. Daniel practically grew up here. He was like a brother to me and Liam. I don't have hardly a story that don't involve him in some way." Zachary looked past me as if he could see one of those stories playing out in the air behind me. He almost smiled, but anger lit his eyes fast on the heels of it and he shoved his hands in his pockets. "It ain't that way no more. No, Daniel's best up there by Devil's Jump. Right where he can remember what he done and where we can keep things in order."

A wind stirred up in the trees and blew across the grit covered ground like a warning. I expected to hear some whistling music like in a gunslinger scene from one of the cowboy movies that my father liked so much.

"I've got to make another stop or two," I said, but before I could return to the safety of Opal's saddle, Zachary stopped me.

"Will you stay for a moment? I'd like to introduce you to my parents. It's hard for my mother to get around much these days. Can you come up to the porch?"

"Sure," I said. "Where can I tie Opal?"

"She'll stay right there," Zachary said and patted her neck. "Good girl."

I followed Zachary up to the house where the older couple sat watching us approach.

"Ma, Pa, this is Mattie," he said, stopping us at the bottom of the steps and nodding toward me. "She's taken Lizzy's place on the routes. Bringing books."

I smiled for lack of anything to say. The grandfather stood and came down off the porch to greet me. I could tell that it took some of the wind out of him, but when he spoke to me his voice was strong and his eyes were full of life. He reached for my hand and then put his other one over the top of it, squeezing slightly.

"Pardon Ma," he said and nodded his head to her where she sat. "She's not really of this world anymore. I'm still hoping for a return."

"Is she ill?" I asked.

"Brokenhearted."

Zachary looked at the ground then shuffled his feet.

"They still housing the books in the church?" Zachary's father asked.

"Yes, sir," I said. "I mean, Pastor."

He nodded and made an expression that was somewhere between dismay and acceptance. "At least it's getting some use." He looked at me, obviously sizing me up. "Ava speaks highly of you."

"I'm so pleased to hear that," I said. "She's been very kind."

"She says you're really here as a teacher," he said and looked way off like Zachary had done. "Certain could use one again. Thank you for bringing books back to our little establishment. Ava was bringing home a stack or two here and there, but the children really like to see the book woman coming up the creek and Ava has been reluctant to take some of the other homes on the route. You can imagine why."

"It's my pleasure to bring the books," I said for lack of how to address the other situation.

"I know the rest of your route is a rough one," he said, and I thought he was going to speak ill about Daniel again, but he didn't. "The Hell for Certain is a rough patch of water. You be careful out there."

At that, he patted my shoulder, told Zachary to round up the children for afternoon prayer and nodded his goodbye to me.

I found myself standing in the yard alone until a girl I had not seen yet, came running up to me. She seemed to be fifteen or so, a young woman by sight, but still a child in movement. She held out a piece of paper to me.

"I want to thank you for bringing the books," she said as I took the paper.

The drawing was fantastically realistic, yet magical in some way. It was of the creek, right where I had turned to head up to the houses here. Every branch of each tree, every clump of briar and bush, even the certain bend in the land where the water had worn it away was all there in pencil sketch.

"This is unbelievably good," I said, not able to hide both my surprise and appreciation. "Where did you get it? Did you draw this?" I asked, understanding even as I asked it.

She nodded shyly and looked away. "It would be better with color, but alls I have is that pencil."

"I thank you for it," I said. "It's the creek right here, leaf for leaf. You're really quite talented."

"Ain't nothing, just a doodle," she said, and pushed her blonde hair behind her ears.

"You have a gift, and you should be proud to use it," I said. "You could really do something with a talent like this."

"I'm just a girl," she said, and waved the comment off.

I stood up straight and reached out to lift her chin so that she pulled up straight as well. "I am a girl too and look at this important job that I'm doing. Our own first lady, Eleanor Roosevelt, is also a girl and look at the strides she makes for the betterment of the world around her. Never say the word 'just' before the very important term 'a girl.' Promise?"

"I promise," she said and smiled at me proudly, straightening up even more.

"Will you tell me your name?"

"Adaline Bell," she said. "Mrs. Ava is my mama."

She must look just like her father with her light hair and dark eyes. The opposite of Ava herself. Bell, not Collins, so Ava was Emily's sister indeed.

"I'm Mattie Mobley," I replied. "I can keep this?" I asked and pulled it close to my heart.

She smiled and the light from within her shone beyond the ragged state of her clothes and the lopsided nature of the pins in her hair that I had noticed before. Not "just a girl" indeed. An artist and I had a sudden thought to make it more so.

"I will treasure it," I said and meant it.

Ella had wanted paper and Adaline had want of colored pencils. I had the means to procure them both. Suddenly, I knew what I would do for these girls. I was going to make a scrapbook of Adaline's art and Ella's stories. Cousins. I was going to bring this family back together with words and pictures. I didn't so much care what Daniel had done. I was sorry for the loss of his wife and to see his children growing up without a mother, and I could see that he'd made some decisions that had given him a bad reputation, but I'd also seen a kindness in him, and I knew how old hurts festered if you let them. I knew the impact that story could have, and I was going to use story to fight story as it were.

Chapter 10

Mattie

I was a bit later than usual getting to Daniel's house this third time I'd come. As I approached the house, I could see a stranger sitting in the rocking chair on the front porch. He was dressed in simple, but nice clothes—light blue shirt and gray slacks, suspenders over his broad shoulders. His back was to me slightly where he had angled the chair toward the garden at the side of the house. He wore a hat that he had tipped down over his eyes, likely to keep the lower afternoon sun out of them as he read. It looked to be a Bible that he had open on his lap.

Liam's words came back to me, and I wondered suddenly if something had happened to Daniel or the children. What if Liam and Zachary had been right to worry over them so. They certainly made it seem like the children's welfare was in danger. Maybe this was someone from town or the government or the moon. I wasn't sure, but suddenly my heart beat a little faster at the thought that something had happened.

Missed his last trade appointment

Near about came to fisticuffs
Best right here where we can keep things in order.

I suddenly felt as though perhaps I had not given Liam's words their proper due. Apparently, Daniel had been, or was still, a moonshiner and it had been something to do with the death of his wife.

I hoped to see the kids come running out to greet me, but it was the man on the porch who made the first move. I was already dismounting when he noticed me. He must have been lost in his reading and not heard me approach. He glanced up quickly and then even more quickly closed the Bible and slid it under the chair like a child caught with something he'd been told not to touch.

I pulled a few books from my bag and walked up to the porch where the man now stood waiting on me. No children, no chickens, silence. I felt a flurry of fear.

I rushed up the stairs and stuck my hand out to shake his. I had been told this wasn't ladylike, but I had been raised by my father and his example had been strong.

"I'm Mattie Mobley, the book carrier," I said, clasping my hand around his reluctant acceptance of the greeting. "Has something happened with Mr. Barrett or the children?"

The man chuckled at first and then broke into a fit of laughter. I had no idea at all what to make of such hilarity.

"I'm quite serious. Are they alright? This is not a humorous matter."

"You don't recognize me, do you?" The man asked and stepped a bit closer.

I stepped to the side of him to get a better look. The cabin door was open, and I peered in to see if I could see anyone being held hostage or the like inside the house. I shook my head at my own imaginings. What can I say—I'm booksy. The house seemed empty, which I wasn't sure was a good thing or bad. The wide front porch was cleaner than the last time I stopped by. Without the buckets and piles of this and that, I could see that it was quite spacious.

"I'm sorry," I said, looking at this quite terribly tall and now that I looked with more clear eyes, attractive stranger. "Have we met?"

Surely, I would remember a face like this—firm jaw, full lips, smooth skin.

"We have indeed," he said and opened his arms as if to give me a better look.

I stepped closer as something quite amazing dawned on me. Those eyes. Green like the moss along the creek. The deep and slow voice.

"Daniel?" I asked with more incredulity than I meant for him to hear.

"The same," he said.

"I beg to differ," I said and reached up as if I was going to touch his face but stopped myself. "Quite different indeed."

"Better?" He asked as if not sure.

This new turn of events did nothing to help clarify my thoughts about him.

"You're more handsome than Gary Cooper," I said, still finding myself a might startled that something so attractive was hiding behind all that beard and hair.

"Is that your old beau in the big city of Asheville?" He put his hands in the pockets of his pants and leaned against the porch railing.

"Heavens no," I said, still very blatantly staring at him. "Gary Cooper is every woman's dream, but he's not from Asheville. He's out in Hollywood."

"Hollywood?" Daniel said and wrinkled his brow. "I don't think I've heard of it."

"You haven't heard of Hollywood?" The thought utterly flabbergasted me. I shook my head and then thought better of my surprise. "I suspect you all don't get to see too many movies out this way. Well, Hollywood is where they make films and Gary Cooper, oh my." I could feel my face flushing and I hoped that Daniel wouldn't realize that he was the one rising the pink in my cheeks much more than the thought of Gary Cooper. "It's out in California. All the way across the country."

He looked at me and smiled with one corner of his mouth. "I know what Hollywood is, ma'am. I know where California is, too." He winked at me. "And although you are correct, I have not been to see a movie, I have seen the posters and advertisements, and I don't think I look anything like Gary Cooper."

He had been pulling my leg. Sporting with me. A playful grizzly?

"If you'll recall, I said you were more handsome than Gary Cooper," I said, deciding to own my embarrassing comment. "Not that you looked like him."

Far more handsome, I thought, trying not to go all moony again.

He smiled at me, and I was grateful that he hadn't taken offense at my accidental insult. He seemed a rather gracious grizzly if you asked me. Devilish good looks perhaps, but a pleasant spirit.

"Maybe I ought to go out to Hollywood and see if I can make a go of it. You think? Might be a fair amount easier out there for the likes of someone like me than it is around here. Less of a Lion's Den if you can imagine it."

I knew he was joking about going to Hollywood, but in a different time under different circumstances, I'd say he might have a shot. I let the Lion's Den comment roll away, but I knew what he meant. He was not oblivious to his station in town.

This Daniel was different than the one who had grunted at me to get out of his garden and nothing at all like the one Liam and Zachary openly loathed. Rather he was like the Daniel that Ava seemed to imply he was. More like the one who had given me the shoes, for sure.

Daniel looked at me curiously. "Have you been to Hollywood?"

"Nowhere close," I said. "But I have been to the movies. Often even. You could be Fred Astaire and I could be Ginger Rogers," I said, excited, actually, to tell him about the last movie I had seen. "From *Top Hat*. I saw that just last fall. It was divine."

I admit I forgot myself then and grabbed Daniel by the hands. I pulled him closer to me and pushed a pair of our joined hands out in front of us.

"I love this part. It goes like this…" And then I sang. Not all that well, but I tried. "Heaven, I'm in Heaven."

Daniel held his ground, a shocked look across his face. "What are you doing?" he asked.

"Come on," I said, pulling him down the porch steps and into the yard. "Dance with me." And I sang again. "Heaven, I'm in Heaven, and my heart beats so that I can hardly speak…"

He moved a little then—reluctantly. I pressed us forward, swaying us back and forth. "And I seem to find the happiness I seek…"

Suddenly, Daniel pulled me a little tighter and twirled me around, spinning me away from him, but not letting go of my hand.

I was the one in shock then, but I kept the song going "… when we're out together dancing cheek to cheek." As if on cue, he pulled me back to him.

Squeals and laughter erupted from the porch, and we looked over to see the children, who started to clap. Daniel turned me loose and bowed. He nodded for me to do the same.

"Do again," Hugh said, clapping his little hands.

"Another time, little one," Daniel said. His voice was so soft and loving toward his son. "You three are late coming back from your walk. I gather you tried to sneak in the back door and hoped I wouldn't notice." He folded his hand over his chest, obviously pretending to be angry. "Go on around back and get washed up. The pump is primed. You can get your books when your little hands and faces are clean."

The children ran down the stairs on their way past us.

Ella looked at Daniel with a smirk on her face. "I told you she'd like you better if you shaved and let me cut your hair."

Daniel blushed and I bit my lip at seeing the color in his cheeks.

"I believe you were right," he said to her, "but stop smarting off and go wash up."

I could tell that he wasn't angry with her. It was nice to see him so kind with his children. My father was a good father, but not one to show emotion very often. On occasion, though, he did, and this exchange between Daniel and his children reminded me of the best of times between my father and me. The children ran off and Daniel and I were left standing out in the yard with Opal.

Daniel

With the children gone to clean up, I was alone with Mattie and very aware of it. Well, save for Opal.

"I didn't dislike you before," Mattie said.

"Pardon?"

She waved her hand around in the general area of my missing beard. "You scared me a bit, but I'm a pretty stubborn woman when it comes to being frightened off."

"You're here for a third time," I said. "I suppose you're right about that."

"Where did you learn to dance?" she asked, putting her hands on her hips like she was trying to suss out some very important information. "You don't seem like the ballroom dancing type."

"I assure you that I am not," I said, touching my chin out of habit and being surprised to feel my own face. I found that I felt a little vulnerable, exposed.

"I disagree," she said, and put her hands to her face as if she was trying to hide the pink in her cheeks.

"Dancing is easy," I said, trying to make light of the whole exchange so as not to have to give too much credence to the flutter in my chest. "You just lean into each other. Nothing special."

At this I stepped away and put my hands in my pockets. I had almost reached out to her in the moment as if to take her for another spin across the yard. I shook my head at myself.

"I am so sorry, Mr. Barrett," she said in a rush, mistaking my gesture no doubt. "I just got carried away. I didn't mean anything improper. I just…"

She was not the one who needed to apologize.

"It's been a long while since I danced with someone," I said. "I didn't expect to enjoy it, which I did. Very much."

"It was silly and trite," she said, shaking her head and patting her hair. "Look at me gushing like a schoolgirl at your looks and singing Hollywood tunes. I must seem ridiculous." She put her hands to her cheeks again. "Going on about movies and showing up here the first day in my fancy shoes."

"You don't seem ridiculous, Mattie," I said, liking the feel of her name on my lips just as much as I had before. "You made my children happy. That goes a long way with me."

Birds chirped somewhere unseen in the trees. A small breeze wound its way through the yard and into the curl of Mattie's hair.

The children came wheeling around the house then calling for their books. Our time alone was through. She curtsied to me, and I bowed. She smiled and looked at me as if she was surprised I knew anything about such displays of formality.

"Da," Marie said, even though Ella was pinching her and trying to pull her away. "Could we have a dance like we used to? One where you and our uncles play the strings, and we dance with all the cousins." She started humming a tune and doing a little jig. "Like when Mama was alive. Maybe Miss Mattie could come."

Even Ella looked at me hopefully. "Not right now, love," I said, patting her head.

"When are we going to see them all again?" Marie asked, dejected. "I miss them. And I mean see them for real, not on accident at the grocery like that one time before."

I looked nervously to Mattie, not really sure exactly what she knew. "We'll talk about that another time."

Ella spoke up then. "You always say that."

Her voice was so broken, and it made me ache.

"I have a few minutes before I need to go," Mattie said cheerfully, and I knew she was coming to my rescue. "Who would like to learn to dance just like they do in Hollywood? I can teach you some tap if you'd like to learn a little. It won't make the noise of course, but the moves are the same."

"Can we, Da?" They all seemed to ask in unison.

"You may," I said and looked at Mattie with gratitude. "I'll go inside and start the stove. We'll need to set about making dinner soon, so not too long."

"Can Miss Mobley stay?" Ella asked and I stopped short.

"I'm sure she's got a better dinner planned than our oatmeal and tomato slices." I said looking at her apologetically. "Perhaps if we had something better to offer."

"What you have is fine," she replied emphatically, finding my eyes with hers and holding my gaze with purpose.

I stood, struck still like a deer. She was certainly sending me a message and it was one that I had not heard in years.

"What about when we have leftovers from the garden after market-day?" Marie asked, oblivious to any deeper meanings. "Miss Mattie, it's a feast once we know what we have that's ours."

I opened my mouth to say something, but nothing came out. I let the children take the conversation as they were excitedly jumping all around her.

"You can come for ugly baby stew," Ella said and clapped her hands together.

Mattie's eyebrows shot up, but she smiled when she said, "Well that sounds positively dreadful."

"It's not a real baby," Hugh said, his eyes wide as he'd made that frightening assumption before. It made me laugh a bit. Mattie laughed too.

"It's all the ugly harvest," Ella said explaining what I'm sure Mattie already understood. "They taste just as good as the pretty produce."

"I'd be happy to join you any time," Mattie said, looking first at the children and then again at me.

She turned back to the children. "Now, I will demonstrate some simple steps and then we'll practice them. Does that sound good?"

The kids all nodded, and Mattie readied herself in the yard. She counted off from five to eight and then began again at one. Then right there in my yard, she started to tap dance, or something like it. I had never seen such a thing happen in my yard. No one hardly even came here, much less stayed to dance.

"This ain't much different than the clogging we do," Marie said and broke into a jig of her own.

Mattie watched with a look of delight on her face and said, "You're right. They are very similar, and you are a good dancer, just like your father." She glanced at me, and I felt myself blush.

"I think I'll go on in and fix some supper," I said, needing to get away before I showed my hand too much.

Mattie nodded at me, and the edges of her mouth turned up very slightly and very briefly before she turned back to the kids. I went up onto the porch and glanced back at them all.

"We should get Da to play the fiddle," I heard Marie say.

"You know he doesn't play anymore," Ella's voice warned. "Let it be. Let's learn to dance."

I went on into the house and pretended I hadn't heard. I peeked out the door a time or two to watch them. The children were taking the lesson quite seriously, even Hugh, although he wasn't really learning it all that well, which was cute. I had been afraid that Mattie wouldn't come back to us, or that if she did, she'd have some agenda that I couldn't trust. I watched her now with hope. That was a dangerous thing to do, but I couldn't help myself.

I gave them some time together while I fixed our meager supper. Shortly, I went back out onto the porch and cleared my throat to announce myself.

"We have an audience, children," Mattie said and curtsied to me. "Please come and have a seat."

She motioned for me to sit on the front steps and the children lined up in front of me.

She stood off to the side and counted again. "And a one, and a two, and a three." She sang a little more of the tune from the movie and the children danced.

Mattie

I watched Daniel watch them and the smile on his face rivaled any beauty one might find on the faces of any star in Hollywood. No sunny day, no moonlit night, not even the trees alight with fireflies could compare. I was astounded at the level to which watching him watch his children moved me. When the kids were through, he clapped as if it was the best production he had ever seen.

"That was quite nice," he said to them. "Now, run inside and get ready to eat."

They all dashed up the steps and into the cabin.

"May I join you for a moment before I head back?" I asked and nodded at the stairs. "Unless I'll cause you to eat cold supper."

"It will be worth it." He patted the spot beside him, and I sat. "Thank you for coming to my rescue," he said, looking out toward the creek. "Family is a difficult subject. We left our other home quite suddenly and the children don't see their relatives that often." He looked at me and bit his lip. "I suppose you know the relatives I speak of."

I nodded and then changed the subject to allow him to let it go. "How did you know I was from Asheville?"

"I know you're not from here," he said and looked at my feet. "Your shoes gave that away. I'm happy to see that Emily's boots are working out for you."

I looked at the brown boots on my feet. Plain, but sturdy. Much more appropriate. "They are. Thank you." He shook his head as if to say it was of no concern, but I knew what a thing it was to have given them away. "Still, that doesn't tell you where I'm from?"

"I'm not a hermit up here," he said and smiled slyly. "I'd like to be, but I've got mouths to feed and that takes me into town and to other houses where people will still have me. People might not talk to me, but I hear them talking to each other."

Daniel spoke of his apparent exile with such neutrality that I wasn't sure what to make of it.

"Word gets around, I guess," I said. "I suppose it's nice to have someone else be the fresh topic of gossip."

I knew I was laying it all out on the table—telling him that I knew how people talked about him.

"Indeed," he said appreciatively. "Though you are spoken about far better than I am."

That small exchange between us seemed to open the gates of respect and honesty. I could see that much in his face. Perhaps my tendency to put my foot in my mouth by saying what I was thinking was actually a benefit here. I decided to return to the original conversation.

"Have you been to Asheville?"

He chuckled. "No, my travels never took me that far, but I have seen pictures in the paper, and it looks like quite the booming place. I imagine the house you left there offers quite a bit more luxury than this little cabin. Running water to say the least."

"Electricity even," I said.

He laughed and I was very grateful that he understood my playful joking. Daniel seemed to understand me from the outset. We were both outsiders here for one reason, or the next. Perhaps we both needed someone to talk to who would speak to us without reservation.

"The children were used to more comforts than this at our last home, but we make do."

"This is a lovely house," I said, nodding back toward it. "Kept up well. I'm sure it can feel crowded though."

"I like having the kids underfoot, actually," Daniel said. "I spent too much time away before. It is one of my greatest regrets. I don't want to let them out of my sight any longer than need be."

Running shine, like Liam said? Leaving his wife home with the children? Perhaps gone when she died? I tried to sort him out like the plot of a book.

"How did you find this place?" I asked so that I wouldn't pose any of those more delicate questions.

"I grew up here." Daniel answered.

"In this cabin?"

"Yes," he said. "Many years ago. But that's a story for another day. It's getting late and the creek will darken quickly under the canopy. You should get going. I'm not actually the wildest animal in these woods."

He stood up and offered his hand to me. I didn't need it to stand, but it was a very gentlemanly gesture, and I accepted. His hand was warm and strong around mine, and I liked the feel of it very much. He saw me to my horse, but before I mounted, Ella came running out of the house with a stack of papers.

"This is a story that I wrote," she said nervously. "This is my last paper, but I want you to read it. Will you take care of it?"

I held the story to my heart, thinking of the drawing that I had from her cousin. "I most certainly will. Thank you. This is a great honor."

She smiled broadly, and I tucked the story into my pack. Daniel had turned loose of my hand as soon as Ella came into view, and he offered it back to me to help me mount Opal. Again, I didn't need the help, but I found that I longed for the touch of his hand again, so I accepted.

"Thank you for caring for my children like you do," Daniel said. "I know it's part of the job, but I appreciate it. They didn't get to bring their books with them when we left, and it means so much for them to have things to read now. That was a special time that my wife used to spend with them, and they miss it. Thank you for reading to them."

"You could make it a new tradition," I said. "You could read with them now."

He nodded. "She was good at the voices."

"I've heard."

"I don't read that well, truth be told," he said and looked down at the ground.

"That's easily remedied," I said, gripping the reins where Opal tried to pull away, ready to leave. "I'd be happy to teach you. I am a teacher after all. I'm sure the kids would love for you to be able to read to them. It is a rather special gift."

"I suppose I could humble myself to a reading lesson," he said, putting his hands in his pockets. "What pride I once had is long gone."

We stood there rather awkwardly for a moment, until Opal whinnied her annoyance.

"Well," Daniel said. "I hope you will forgive me whatever stories you're being told about me. I'm sure you're getting an earful. I admire your courage to stay and converse with me. Know that some of it is true, but that some of it isn't."

"I'm able to sort out fact from fiction."

He looked up at me and the light hit his eyes so that they shone like emeralds.

"The children look forward to your visits, Mattie." Daniel looked at the house and then back at me. He slipped his hands from his pockets and ran his fingers through his hair. "I admit I was as much looking forward to your arrival today as they were."

"It's been my pleasure," I said, stalling to leave, having to grip the reins tight to keep Opal put.

"Mine, too," he said and then cleared his throat and stepped back. "You really should go. It's getting late. I don't want people telling stories about you as well. Beware the company you keep."

I had never cared less about riding home in the dark as I did then. Wild animals or no, stories or no, I wanted to linger. It would still be a while before the sun had set, but he was right, the thick canopy across the creek would make it very shady in places even on the brightest day.

I loosened my grip and reluctantly gave Opal a pat. She stomped her feet and turned around in a circle. Daniel tried not to laugh, but only partly succeeded.

"She does this on purpose, I swear it," I said. "She was just chomping at the bit to leave and now she's going to stall on purpose."

"Maybe you should sing to her," he said and winked. "It worked to get me moving."

Opal lurched forward like she was going to push him out of the way.

"You ornery thing," I said.

"Are you talking to me?" Daniel asked, biting his lip to keep from laughing again.

"Perhaps," I joked as Opal circled me around again.

"Well, if you ever get out of here, I will be glad to see you return." He put his hands in his pockets again and stepped back as if he was doubting my ability to make it out of his yard. I could see it was all a joke. I enjoyed his teasing.

"I've got some work to do tomorrow, but the following day I'm available," I said, feeling brave and maybe foolish, but going for it. "I could come back and give you a reading lesson."

His eyes were locked on mine as if searching my sincerity. He nodded but didn't say anything.

"Great," I said, considering it a yes. "I'll see you in two days. I'll have you reading well in no time. I'll even teach you to do the voices."

He smiled and nodded again.

Opal took a step, but I pulled up on the reins and stopped her. "Daniel," I said, and he looked up at me, "I really do know the difference between fact and fiction."

He nodded again and turned back toward his house.

Chapter 11

Mattie

The next day, I couldn't get Daniel Barrett off my mind. I tried to spend the day planning for classes, checking in books, making new selections, but all I'd really done was craft elaborate daydreams that had nothing to do with any of those things. I shook my head and stood up from the kitchen table where I was unsuccessfully making notes about what to serve for lunch and snack at school. I decided I needed to see what was available before I went too much further in my planning. And I really needed to clear my head of dark hair, green eyes, and soft smiles.

The bell dinged over the door of the grocer's as I entered. Mr. Gibbons looked up, giving a smile and a nod of his head.

"Hello there, Miss Mattie. What brings you in on this hot day?"

"The want of a cold soda from the fountain," I said, knowing full well there wasn't one there, but imagining one was almost as good.

"Now that does sound delicious," Mr. Gibbons said, closing his eyes as if dreaming of the taste. "How about some freshly brewed sassafras tea over a chunk of ice?"

My eyes opened wide. "That sounds even better."

He gave a nod and went behind the counter. I heard his footsteps ascending toward his living quarters. I thought how I'd be much the same soon, the proprietor working and living on the same property. I liked the idea of it very much. How nice to just come down the stairs in the morning, ready to greet my students.

While I waited, I looked around the store and pondered if there was something that I needed. I was drawn as always to the colorful produce on the table in the middle of the store. I picked up a clutch of tomatoes on the vine and held them to my nose. I loved the smell of the stalk and the fruit together.

"I wouldn't buy those if I were you," a female voice said behind me, and I startled. I had noticed someone else in the store when I entered, but her back was to me. "I'm Claire," she said and stuck her hand out to shake.

I put the tomatoes back on the table and shook her hand. "I'm Mattie. I'm the new teacher come fall. I'm helping out at the library for a while."

She looked me up and down somewhat disapprovingly I thought. "I know who you are."

"Everyone seems to," I said, smiling at her despite the off-putting feeling she gave me. "I'm not even sure why I bother to introduce myself." I laughed, going for a joke, but she didn't seem to possess much humor.

"I hope you're not here to upset the apple cart," she said and glanced at the produce. "We have our ways."

I felt like I was getting the shakedown like in one of those gangster movies or something. "Who are you, again?"

"A concerned citizen," she said, stepping closer to me which caused me to step back. The smile on her face told me she was pleased by that. "You're new here. I just don't want to see you make friends with the wrong people." She said it as if she meant it, but not quite.

I raised an eyebrow at her. "I'm a good judge of character," I said and smiled at her knowingly. "I think I'll be alright."

I eased past her and picked up my clutch of tomatoes again. I selected a little bag of green beans as well.

"Do you know who grows those?" she asked.

I'd only seen one decent garden in these parts, so, yes, I had a good idea. I decided to see if I could get a rise out of her as she was clearly trying to prove a point to me.

"Speaking of our friend up the creek, I wonder if Mr. Gibbons keeps any moonshine behind the counter?" I said and tried to look genuinely hopeful.

Her mouth dropped open and then closed quickly. She squinted her eyes at me, and I could tell that she knew I knew a thing or two about the town talk.

"Have you seen a still or the makings for it," she asked me sternly. "If you have, you need to report it. This is not something to joke about."

"For Pete's sake, no," I said, recalling Liam and Zachary fretting over the same thing. "Is this about Mr. Barrett? From what I know of the man, he's not at all like everyone says." I pushed past her again and put my produce up by the register. "Sure, he looked a little worse for the wear when I first saw him, but he's shaved and cut his hair, and honestly he could pass for a movie star."

Claire scoffed. "Nobody said he wasn't pretty to look at. The Devil's always dressed in a nice suit."

I couldn't help it, but I laughed. "The Devil? That's ridiculous. The man's not anywhere close to that."

"And you'd know, having dropped books off to his children a time or two?"

"How exactly is it that you know so much about me?"

"This is a very small town, Mattie," she said and looked me over again. "Loyalties run deep."

I opened my mouth to ask about hers, but Mr. Gibbons came back down to the counter carrying two glasses of tea. The sound of the ice clinking in the glass was like a heavenly chorus.

"Hello, Miss Claire," Mr. Gibbons nodded at her. "Is there something I can help you find?" He handed a glass out to me, and I stepped closer to take it and to be nearer to him, as I could tell that allegiances were being noticed.

"I was actually looking for some baking powder," she said, although she'd been on the other side of the store from the baking goods.

Mr. Gibbons nodded in the right direction. "Right over there, where it always is." He winked at me.

Claire plucked a can of baking powder from the shelves and brought it to the register.

Mr. Gibbons held his hand out to her and smiled. "I'll put it on your account. You can pay me later."

She nodded at him curtly and cut her eyes at me. Once she had left, I turned back to Mr. Gibbons in confusion.

"Why did you let her leave without paying?"

"For one, I wanted her to go ahead and skedaddle out of here," he said. "For two, her husband has been out of work for a while, and I know they're struggling a little extra right now."

I nodded at his compassion. "That's nice of you. Will you put that powder on my account then? I'd love to help out."

He smiled broadly. "Oh, you'll really get her goat by doing that," he said and chuckled. "But it's kind of you. She's a bit of a pistol on the best of days, but people in pain, whatever that pain is, often come across as the worst version of themselves. We all do. Try not to let her get the best of you."

I took a sip of the tea. "This is deliciously fresh," I said. I touched the produce I had selected. "Did Daniel really grow these and all of that." I nodded back toward the table.

"He did," Mr. Gibbons said. "Some people don't buy it because they know. Some people don't know but wouldn't buy it if they did. And a few don't mind either way."

"I'm surprised Claire hasn't ridden through the town announcing it loudly for all to hear."

"Well," he said and sighed, "Claire has an interest in the matter that keeps things a little more raw for her than others."

"Regarding Daniel?"

"She and Emily were the best of friends," he said, looking out the window and then back at me. "She blames Daniel for Emily's death, just like everyone else does, but it's a little more personal for her."

"I see," I said, wondering what had happened that caused him to be held responsible. Wondering if it was true. "I don't know the details, but I don't see why the whole town hates him. People die. Not to sound callous, but he seems like some exiled traitor."

Mr. Gibbons nodded. "I suppose that's a good word for how people see him."

"But not you? You don't see him that way?" I figured since Daniel's goods were in the store.

Mr. Gibbons put his hand on mine where I had it resting on the counter. "Nor you? I'm glad." It was an answer without saying as much. "Daniel could use a friend. Someone who doesn't know his every mistake just yet. Someone who doesn't hold his family history against him. The stories are long and many."

He didn't say anything more and I figured he wasn't going to be the one to tell me the tales. Although, his not telling me didn't feel like a secret kept. It felt like a chance given.

"In that case," I said and returned to the produce baskets, "I'll take this broccoli and some of these carrots. They're absolutely beautiful." I thought about Hugh's ugly baby stew and smiled.

Mr. Gibbons nodded approvingly at me and rang me up for the produce and Claire's baking powder. Chances given, indeed. He bagged my purchases and I left feeling even more refreshed than I had hoped for.

Walking back across to the parsonage, I saw a truck pull up in front of the church. I headed toward it instead of to the house. The driver got out, went around to the back, and brought out a large box.

"Is there a Mattie Mobley here?" he asked.

"That's me," I said, shifting the bag of groceries to one arm.

"This is for you," he said and dropped the heavy package at my feet.

"Are you from the post office?" I asked.

"Look, lady," he said, already headed back to his vehicle, "I just want to get out of here. I drove all the way from Asheville, and I have to drive all the way back."

Asheville? I looked at the box and then back toward the man, but he was already in his truck.

"Nice day to you, too," I called as he drove away.

I set my groceries on the church steps and looked at the box. I saw my father's handwriting on the package. He had addressed it himself, which made me smile.

"I know what this is," I said aloud to myself.

I hurried my groceries to the house and came back for the box. I peeked into the library expecting to see Ava, but Ruby was there.

"Where's Ava?" I asked. "I didn't expect you here today."

"Just getting a jump on things, and coming by to check on Ava," Ruby said.

I nodded. "I've got a delivery out here; can you help me get it in?"

Ruby put down the scrapbook she was working on and came to meet me at the door. "More books?"

I shook my head and smiled excitedly.

"More cookies?" She asked, somewhat hopefully, which made me smile.

"No, something from my father."

Ruby came out on the steps with me, and her eyes widened at the size of the box. "Let me put a rock against the door. I think that will take both of us to move."

Ruby and I hefted the box inside and sat it on the circulation desk. "Is Ava OK?" I asked, touching my fingers to the label and my father's handwriting. "You said you were checking on her."

"It's just a hard day," Ruby said, kicking the rock away from the door and coming back to the desk. "The anniversary of a loss."

I took some scissors from the desk and sliced through the tape as best I could. I tore open the box and took out some newspaper.

"Emily?" I asked, tilting my head at her. "Her sister."

Ruby made a surprised face and then grimaced. "We should have told you that."

I shrugged. "I guess it doesn't really matter, in the grand scheme of things whether or not I knew." I wondered though how Daniel and the children were doing today. "I mean, it is what it is. I hope Ava is alright as well."

Ruby smiled at me and sighed. "Can I have that?" she asked,

reaching out for the newspaper I'd taken from the box. "I made some paper dolls out of old book jackets. I bet I could make them some newspaper clothes." I handed it to her, and she looked it over quickly. "Oh, it's from Asheville. I wonder what news you've been missing. Do you want it back?"

I shook my head. I didn't really care what was going on back home. "I'll see it on your doll's dresses. You can tell me if you read anything of interest."

I reached in the box and pulled out package after package of paper and pencils. There were colored pastels and drawing supplies of all sorts—notebooks and a pencil sharpener. It was fantastic. Ruby revered the items as I set them out on the desk as if I was pulling gold and gems from a treasure chest.

"Oh my," she said. "These are glorious. Where is it all from?"

"I asked my father to send some paper and pencils. He sent so much more than what I expected." Three or four times more. I was overwhelmed. I had wondered if he'd send anything at all. I knew he wanted me to come back to Asheville and not settle in Certain. I had thought that might be my plan as well, but now I wasn't so sure.

Ruby continued to sort through the supplies as I talked.

"Daniel's oldest daughter is a writer and actually," I said and stopped, looking to see if mentioning him was OK or not. Ruby didn't seem to mind, and I was grateful. I wanted to be able to talk about him. "I promised her more paper and some pencils."

"I didn't know that about Ella," Ruby said and raised her eyebrows as if she should have. "I haven't seen the kids since they left and moved up the creek. I hear that they used to come with Daniel when he'd come to trade, but I don't think they do anymore. From what I hear, he just buys and sells and goes back home. Liam keeps a tight rein on him. So, what about all the art supplies," she asked before I could comment on anything she had just said.

"These are for Adaline," I said and then I looked at Ruby firmly. "Aside from Emily being her sister, I had no idea that Ava's kids and her brothers, I take it, are all on my route. Why didn't she tell me that? I guess she didn't want me to know that she's related to Daniel." I answered my own question, I supposed.

"It's a touchy subject," Ruby said, picking up a pack of pencils and touching it reverently. "I'm sure she just didn't want you to think badly of her by association. She's actually more empathetic to Daniel than most people."

"Considering that it's Daniel's fault Emily died?" I asked, hoping that Ruby might tell me more, assuming that I already know enough to be let in on the rest.

"We could all learn a lesson from the amount of grace she shows," Ruby said instead.

I nodded, thinking about what it would be like to lose a sister. Not having one, I imagined I'd never really know. I had lost a mother though. I knew the pain of losing family before it was time.

"The children will be thrilled," Ruby said. "They've not had things like this in years. Most of them never have."

"It's indulgent, I know," I said, feeling guilty for asking my father to send such luxuries as if it was the most common of things to do. "I just want to encourage them. I plan to use them at school as well. I suppose it's frivolous."

"It's marvelous, is what it is," Ruby said, looking over a package of colored pastels. "Perhaps a small thing to you, but a huge thing to the children." She paused and sighed. "It's just what they need."

My spirits soared at the thought of making a difference. I looked around the church. "Where did they used to do school?" I asked. "Here?"

"Yes. Here in the church on weekdays." Ruby motioned around. "But now there's no school or church, so we get a library."

I bit my lip but asked anyway. "Why is there no church? I understand that many schools have closed, but it seems like people could still come to church."

Ruby looked over her shoulder as if someone might be listening, but we were alone.

"Pastor Collins, Ava's father, made some decisions that didn't go over well," Ruby said quietly, nervously like someone might hear. "A lot of them. Daniel was like a son to him and when he went wild and tore everything up, Pastor Collins still took his side, but it was the last straw for everyone else."

"Wild?" I asked, thinking about grizzly bears and scary things in the woods. "Do you mean Daniel?"

She nodded and looked around again. My eyes lighted on the broken window.

"Daniel's not from very good stock," she said and shook her head. "Long line of bad men. Pastor gave him a chance to change, and things didn't go well."

My hands had found their way to my hips. "That doesn't explain why people don't come to church. Because the pastor gave someone a chance? Isn't that what pastor types are supposed to do?"

"People felt betrayed," she said and shrugged. "And times were tough, and people just lost faith in everything."

"And Daniel takes the blame for it all?" I asked, but it wasn't really a question. I knew the answer.

"Lines were drawn, and people forgot how to see things from the other person's perspective," Ruby said. "I'm not defending any of it. I'm just telling you."

Finally.

"What about the people who don't hate Daniel?" I asked, getting a little irritated. "Why doesn't anyone defend him?"

"More trouble than it's worth, I guess."

"Probably not for Daniel."

Ruby looked at the floor and I thought maybe I'd embarrassed her, which I felt bad about, but when she looked back up at me, there was this look in her eyes as if I was the naive one and she was wondering how to set me straight without hurting my feelings.

"Daniel didn't make it easy on anyone to take his side," Ruby said. "He led people to believe he was one sort of man, but then it seemed like he was just the opposite and people felt betrayed. Daniel has a way with words and he's pretty easy on the eyes, or at least he used to be. People felt tricked and he didn't do or say anything to defend himself or set anything straight."

I thought of Mr. Gibbons saying that Daniel was a traitor in some people's eyes. I didn't know what to think. I did know that I didn't know as much as I thought I knew.

Was Daniel a trickster who had cleaned up to lure me into some deception. I remembered something he said. *When someone gives you a warning, you best heed it.* I felt out of sorts and unsteady.

Light shone in through the window behind me and splashed color across the desk and onto the wall behind it. I reached out in front of me and tried to close my hands around the light, but my fingers slipped through the dancing colors—blue, red, orange, and yellow. Just like the colors of my childhood kaleidoscope, I could see them, but I couldn't grab hold.

Chapter 12

Mattie

Daniel's house was quiet when I rode up and dismounted on the day of our reading lesson. I could see his own horse in the way off, grazing. Cody, the kids had told me the name of the horse. They said it had been their grandpa's. She wasn't tied and I didn't see a fence. Free to go, but evidently, she was happy where she was. I walked up to the porch, but no one came out. When I knocked on the open door, the house was silent.

"Daniel," I called into the house. "Are you here?"

I stepped in cautiously. I could see right away that there were two rooms—one in front of the other, separated partially by a double-sided fireplace and a doorway from one room to the next. The front room was sectioned off into a living space and a bedroom. Just as the kids had said, the side of the house with the window was the living room and the bedroom side had no window. The bedroom had a full-sized bed on one wall and a set of bunked beds on the other. There wasn't more space between the beds than a man could stand in. I thought of the large rooms at the Mobley estate, and the difference astounded me.

I figured Daniel probably slept on the full bed. Its covers were laying askew still, as if someone had just risen from sleep. I knew I shouldn't, but I went over to the bed and touched the patchwork quilt that lay bundled up across the foot of the bed. The quilt was soft and worn against my fingers. Daniel's quilt. I wanted to sit on the bed, but I didn't dare. I ran my hand across the faded blue pillowcase where Daniel, no doubt, rested his head. I glanced back at the door lest I be surprised by someone catching me. My eyes flitted to the bunk beds along the wall. The wood had been built affixed to the wall so they wouldn't topple or shake, and I could tell by the lumpiness that each bed boasted the same sort of worn-out feather mattress that Daniel's bed had. The girls must sleep there, I surmised. What of Hugh? I turned back to Daniel's bed and pulled back the threadbare sheets to reveal an equally threadbare stuffed animal. I picked the little bear up and turned it over in my hands. A Velveteen Bear. This nubby stuffed animal had seen more children's love than just Hugh, I could tell. Probably a hand-me-down from his sisters. I pulled the bear to my face and kissed the spot his missing button nose would be. I could almost smell little Hugh in the very fibers of the stuffed toy. I placed it back where I'd found it and drew the sheet back up like it had been. The image of Daniel cuddling here with his son struck me with such a fierce passion for this family that I could hardly contain myself. I wanted to take Daniel's pillow into my arms and hug it to me for lack of anything else to do, but instead I stepped away from the intimacy of their sleeping room and after glancing once more at the door, looked to the living area.

A small couch and two lovely, handcrafted chairs sat facing the fireplace which was slightly right of center. A Bible lay open on the chair closest to the fireplace. A small end table sat between the chairs and a lantern sat upon the table. I thought of Daniel sitting there with the Bible open in front of him—feeling the sense of the words even if they were difficult to read. What sort of devil would do that? None that I knew of. Perhaps Ella read to them all at night.

Through an archway to the left of the double-sided fireplace, I could see a small table and what looked like shelves with cans and jars of various sort. The kitchen. The whole thing was a clever design, making the fireplace useful for heat and cooking at the same time. The kitchen had probably been added sometime after the house was built. The fireplace had probably been the back wall, but the house had been opened up and added on to. I wondered if Daniel had done this or if his parents had. I thought about a young Daniel running through the room past me and out onto the front porch. I felt self-conscious being in the house without anyone there, but comfortable as well. I wanted to stay there. I stepped deeper into the house, wanting to go into the kitchen, but I'd already have a hard time explaining myself if someone caught me where I stood. I peeked toward the back though. I could see the back door and the colored glass in the window. It was a rudimentary welding together of various pieces that I knew had come from the window in the church. Daniel had obviously brought the broken pieces home with him after he "went wild."

Reluctantly, I stepped back toward the door. I saw a note tacked to the wall just inside the doorframe.

Walk. Creek. Back dinner.

I touched the writing, recognizing Ella's script, but knowing her ability far outstretched this. I realized that it was written so that Daniel could read it. These were probably words he saw often, and Ella had likely told him what they said. She had learned to read somewhere. Her mother? School before times got tough and things shut down? Maybe she'd even sat in one of those little school desks I'd gotten from the church and now sat empty but expectant in the parsonage.

I didn't want to leave the house, but I wanted to find Daniel, so I stepped back out onto the porch and went out into the yard. I rounded the back of the cabin looking for him. The late afternoon sun shone on the wide planks of the house turning them the warm color of rich caramel. The sky was a perfect and clear blue, and the light made the whole place look like it was part of a painting and not a real thing that a person could reach out and touch.

Daniel stood in the yard with his back to me and an axe raised over his head. He wore overalls with only what appeared to be an undershirt beneath. I tried not to notice the way his muscles flexed, but I failed.

I thought it a pleasant thing that I had stumbled upon, but when he swung the axe down on the log in front of him, he yelled out so loudly that I jumped. The noise he made wasn't that of a man expending energy with his whole body and voice. The sound was a guttural cry of anguish and anger. I thought of Ruby telling me that the day before had been the anniversary of Emily's death. Daniel put another log on the block and raised the axe again. Again, he swung and cried out. I took in a breath and stepped toward him but stopped again when this time he tossed the axe to the ground and put his hands on his head. He sank down on his knees, and I was struck cold and still.

"What do you have to say for yourself?" he asked out loud and I thought he somehow knew I was there and was talking to me. "How am I supposed to take care of these kids, Lord, when I don't have nothing but what grows up out of the ground? It ain't enough. You know all I need happen is for someone like Claire to get fed up and tell folks where it come from, and I'm done for. Ain't nobody going to buy the Devil's produce." Daniel sat back on his heels and made a sound something like laughing, but that kind you do when you're about to cry.

I took a step backward trying very carefully not to make any noise.

His voice became more of a whisper, but I could hear it carried on the breeze. I knew he was talking to God and the way he spoke, so familiar like, moved me.

"You already took Emily, Lord and I deserved it, I know, but I can't lose my kids. Please." His back was still to me, but I could see him put his hands over his face and fold forward so far his head almost touched the dirt in front of him. After a moment he looked up at the sky. "Please, I know you have no use of me, but just help us make it through. I won't leave again. I won't do that. I learned my lesson the last time. I won't make those same mistakes again." He bent forward as if he was trying to press himself into the very ground. After a moment, a moment in which I should have taken my leave, he straightened up and spoke again. "Forgive me of my many and terrible sins. Your will be done, Lord. Amen."

I wasn't much of the praying type after all these years of not being in church, but I knew "amen" meant it was over, and he was about to stand up and see me there so close behind him there was no way I could retreat fast enough. Still, I tried, stepping back a tiny step and then turning around.

"Mattie," his voice rang behind me softly.

Daniel

I had forgotten she was coming today. I had forgotten everything since yesterday. Mattie stopped at the sound of her name and turned around. She had a smile affixed to her face that I imagined was an effort to cover up what she'd surely seen and heard.

"Daniel," she said cheerfully, "I was just coming by for that reading lesson."

"Yes, I forgot," I said, my voice felt worn out and tired. "I've not had a very good couple of days or nights. I am so sorry. I forgot our appointment."

"It's no worry," she said and fiddled with the collar of her blouse for want of anything else to do with her nervous hands it seemed.

I hadn't meant to make her uneasy. I didn't know anyone was there. I hoped the children hadn't seen.

"Are the kids inside?" I asked, looking around for them. "Have they returned?"

"They're not here," she said, and shrugged. She didn't make haste to leave though, which I hoped was a good sign. She motioned toward the creek. "Probably off playing in the water."

"I haven't been the easiest to be around since yesterday and sometimes they go for a walk to give me some space," I said, running my hands over my face. I looked down at myself—completely unpresentable to a lady. "My apologies, Mattie, I regret terribly that I drove them away on a day you were coming. I told them after you left the other evening that you'd be back right away, and they've been beside themselves waiting for you. I think the hope of you coming and the joy of the last time you were here helped us more than you know. Especially on these days."

"I could come back still," she said, sounding hopeful. "I was looking forward to this visit, too, but I can see that today might not be a good day."

"That was not my finest moment," I said, looking her straight in the eyes. I didn't intend to hide anything from her. I'd learned my lessons on truth and honesty. "Not my worst either, I hate to admit."

She reached out and touched my arm and the small gesture of intimacy made me feel a little weak in the knees.

"Daniel, please don't apologize," she said. "I'm the one who needs to be sorry for imposing on your privacy. Ruby told me about the anniversary of Emily's passing. I'm sure it's always a hard time."

I looked at her hand on my arm and nodded. I put my hand over hers. "I appreciate you, Mattie. Your kindness is uplifting. You needn't worry. It's been a while and we're mostly alright." I don't know what came over me, but I rubbed my thumb across the back of her hand. Her skin was so soft. I shook my head suddenly at myself and stepped back from her.

"Will you walk with me to the creek?" I asked, not wanting her to leave. "That's where the children have gone, I'm sure. Perhaps they will be making their way back up."

"Of course," she said.

We walked in silence a long way up the bank to Devil's Jump. I stopped and picked up a rock, tossing it into the water.

"It's beautiful, isn't it?" I asked. "The scattering of rocks is just like the very stars in the sky, don't you think?"

She smiled at me and nodded. The water itself glistened in the dappled light. As a child I had thought it looked like pure magic the way the sparkles from the sun danced across the water.

"There," I said and drew my finger across the air in front of us like tracing a constellation. "That's Singing Bird. See how the rocks make the wings, one up and one down and the beak points up to the sky like she's singing."

Mattie stepped closer and touched my arm again. "I see it," she said, pointing and tracing her finger in the air as well.

I took her hand and led us a few steps farther along the bank. We stepped over the tree roots, her fingers grasping mine as the path got unsteady. My heart raced at her touch. I was being reckless, and I knew it, but I couldn't help it.

"Hugh named this one," I said, stopping us and pointing at another cluster with my free hand. "Big fish with splashy tail. See the outline of the fish?" I asked and she nodded. "When the creek is just a little higher, those rocks at its tail cause the water to splash if it flows just so."

I felt her fingers wiggle around mine, finding a comfortable hold.

She said, looking up at me, "Opal and I have been along this path, but I didn't notice the rocks this way. I just thought of them as an obstacle. They're like constellations," she said, just as I had thought. "It's just like the stars."

"Heaven and Hell you might say," I said, coming back to my senses just a bit. "It's just a matter of time before he comes for me."

"Who?" she asked, looking concerned.

"The devil," I said. "He's just biding his time. I see him dancing out here, skipping across the rocks he's strewn, waiting for me."

"You mean the story about the apron strings?" she asked, her brow furrowed.

"It's not a story," I said, and tugged at her hand to move us up away from the water. "It's true." I nodded at a place along the bank I liked, and we both sat down. She let go of my hand to do so and I wasn't sure I should take hold of it back.

"I don't so much believe in a living, breathing devil," she said with certainty.

"I do," I said. "And if he's coming for anyone in Certain, it's me."

"That's just silly," she said. She stretched her legs out in front of her. She was wearing the boots I'd given her. I was happy that they fit.

"I thought people had told you about me."

"Bits and pieces," she said and as best I could tell she didn't know the worst of it.

I wanted to think that she knew and that none of it mattered. But if she really didn't know about me—I couldn't let her go on like this—keeping time with me and letting me hold onto her hand.

"There's a reason the Barretts have lived on this side of the Hell for Certain, way up in the unreachable places," I said.

"What reason is that?" She asked almost like she was challenging me.

"I was eight when my mother died," I said, starting as far back as I figured she cared to hear for now. I closed my eyes and turned my face up toward the pieces of light that tried to make their way through the trees. "People thought my father killed her."

"Why?" Mattie asked.

"Because he might have," I said and shook my head. The water in the creek warbled as if it agreed. "He wasn't a good man. He was a good-looking man," I said, "but his heart was ugly. When she died, he wouldn't let anyone come for her. She didn't have any family out this way. She was from over the mountain ridge like you." I stopped to look at Mattie. She had turned to face me and was listening intently. "She laid on the bed for three days before he buried her."

Mattie gasped. "Oh, Daniel, I'm so sorry."

I shook my head at the memory of it. "He was drunk. He might not have realized how much time was passing," I said.

I did, though. I remembered everything.

"That's no excuse," Mattie said and grabbed hold of my hand.

I looked at the fingers entwined so tightly around mine. "He finally dug a hole for her, but he passed out before he took her to it. I couldn't stand it anymore, so I took her myself."

"But how," she said. "You were so little."

I opened my mouth to tell her how I'd used the sheet on the bed to slide her to the floor and then drag her down the steps and through the yard, but I couldn't find the words that went with such a thing as the way she fell to the floor and the way we tumbled off the steps. I couldn't settle on the words that would paint the way my heart thundered and the way I cried so hard I could barely see where we were going, so my mouth closed without anything coming out. I tried to speak again and tell her what sound it made when my mother's body landed at the bottom of the too shallow grave my father had dug and how it had been too hard to use the shovel to cover her up so I'd ended up pushing the dirt over her with my hands, but those words wouldn't come either.

Mattie tugged on my arm, pulling me closer to her. "Daniel," she said with such sorrow as if perhaps she could read my mind.

I cleared my throat and managed to croak out the last of it. "I fell asleep on her grave that night, I was so exhausted."

"I'm so sorry," she said. "I know what it's like to lose a parent too soon, but none of that is your fault. The devil, even if he's real, isn't after you. You know that right?"

Maybe.

"I'm just another in a long line of bad Barrett men. It's expected."

She shook her head hard. "No, you are not."

I sighed. "I appreciate that, but you don't know me that well. You clearly haven't been told the worst of what I've done. It's OK. I appreciate your willingness to give me the benefit of the doubt, more than you know, but everyone is right about me."

She took in a breath and blew it out hard. I thought she was going to let it rest, but she only changed the subject slightly.

"What about your father? Where is he now?"

"Long dead and probably deserving," I said. "A few years later he turned up home with a gunshot wound to the gut. I was eleven. He died in the same bed my mother did." I dug my fingers into the loamy soil and pulled a rock free. I tossed it into the creek. "He was drunk again and barely able to speak. I didn't even help him, Mattie. I just let him die." I pulled my hand loose from hers and covered my face and closed my eyes.

Neither of us said anything for a minute and I thought that when I opened my eyes again, she'd be gone, but she was still there.

"I'm sure a lot happened in those years that caused you to let him go without doing anything. And what could a child have done, anyway."

I looked at her sharply, somewhat amazed. I nodded. That was an understatement, great and wide. As I said, my father was not a good man. Her simple statement was offered as a pass, a forgiveness, and an understanding that I wasn't sure anyone had offered me before. Those years had not been acknowledged, at best merely accepted as an unfortunate time in a young boy's life.

"Where did you go after that?" she asked.

"I stayed here," I said.

"You grew up here all by yourself?" she asked, astonished.

"I tried to keep it a secret that he'd died," I said. "I didn't have anywhere to go and I wasn't sure what happened to kids with no parents. I thought maybe people would see a chance to get rid of me, too. I knew what people thought of the Barretts."

She put her hand to her heart. "Certainly no one would have hurt a child."

I shrugged. "Well, I only made it about six or seven months here by myself."

"What happened?"

"Pastor Collins came for me," I said. "Didn't give me no choice— as if I would have said no. Told me to pack my things and that I was coming to live with them. That's what I did. Grew up right there with them. Liam and Zachary took me in like their very own brother." I smiled at the thought of it. "I had a family. They never once said or acted like they'd heard anything about the Barretts, even though I was sure they had. The Barretts had been despised for generations and rightly so." I sighed, remembering that day that Pastor had come to get me. "I was theirs from that moment on. I went with them into town on a Saturday and then back to church Sunday morning. Over the years, people started to forget who I was. Heck, I started to forget."

"Daniel, if you think you have to explain yourself, you don't," Mattie said. "I don't care that your father and your father's father were liars and leches and who knows what else. That doesn't mean you are."

I shook my head. "It's nice that you think so. But I am. Turns out, I am just like them." I stopped and looked at her intently. She needed to remember who she was dealing with. "I did what they say I did. Mattie, you need to know that."

"But I don't know what that is," she said, somewhat impatiently. "Did you do something to Emily?"

I nodded. "I fell in love with her, and I thought I could be a good person. I tried to do right by my family, but I was doing it the wrong way. Things ended badly and people remembered who I was after all. And here I am back where I belong. Long story short."

"You don't have to hide up here. You don't have to live like this."

"It's a fair punishment," I said. "It reminds me to do better."

"Punishment?" She asked, drawing her legs underneath her and turning toward me. "What about forgiveness?"

"Too late," I said. "The devil's rocks are what they are no matter what pretty picture I try to turn them into. The path is laid."

"Why don't you move them, then," she said. "Pick up the devil's path from there to you and scatter it back in a different direction."

"I tried that a time or two," I said and looked out at the water and the rocks. "I married a good respectable girl, had me some kids, even got to play the fiddle every Sunday in church. Them rocks seem to fall back into place just like they were, no matter what I do. The devil makes a new path one rock at a time and there ain't nothing I can do but try to claim it out from under him."

"I don't see the devil out here, Daniel," she said, taking my hand back in hers. "All I see is you."

I hadn't realized that my eyes had welled up a little, until a tear fell loose and rolled down my cheek. Embarrassed, I made to brush it away, but Mattie beat me to it. She pressed her thumb to my cheek and caught the tear, then she put her thumb to her lip and kissed the tear off. I was struck still like a deer again. It was as if she had eaten my sadness. I didn't know what that meant or how to process it, but it was one of the kindest things anyone had ever done.

"If you don't mind, Mattie," I said, unable to think beyond this moment, "I think I should go back to the house and see if I can pull myself together before the children return."

"Of course," she stammered, her cheeks pinking up. "I didn't mean to outstay my welcome."

"You haven't," I said and touched my own burning cheek for a second. "I want you to stay, but I am bad company today. If your offer to return still stands, I know the children would love to see you. I would as well. You probably had a lesson prepared and I've gone and sent us in another direction."

She smiled as if my words were a great relief. She had a very pleasant smile. A real one. Did people smile around me? I wasn't even sure. Mr. Gibbons, certainly. The children. How strange a thing to suddenly realize. The loss of smiles.

"I'll bring a pie," she said, and I think I might have missed the first of the sentence. "I just bought some wonderful blackberries from the grocery," she said and winked at me.

Mine.

"Will it be better than the cookies," I said, letting a joke take the place of my sadness for a moment.

She opened her mouth in shock as if she was truly offended, but then she punched me in the arm. "I can't promise it will."

I pretended to think it over then gave a feigned sigh. "Well, the cookies didn't kill us, so I suppose we could give your pie a whirl."

"Daniel Barrett," she said and smiled widely. "You are simply the worst." But it sounded like I might be the opposite the way she said it, and it was the best thing, oddly enough, anyone had said to me in a long time.

"Let's get back to the house," I said. "The kids will turn up sooner or later. Watch those tree roots, it's tricky around here." I held my hand out to her and she took it.

I listened to the wind through the leaves and the water over the rocks every day. I felt the sun on my skin and smelled the sweetness of the mossy creek bank even in my sleep. It was nothing new. Except today, it was. It was all new. Everything was different.

Chapter 13

Mattie

I made the pie I had blabbered on about. It was as ugly as sin as my grandmother always said when she messed up the looks of an otherwise decent dish. The old wood burning stove in the parsonage was a beast to cook on, but I was getting the hang of it. Sort of.

I hadn't thought through the travel requirements of pie though, and now I had ridden the whole of the route balancing a pie with one hand and holding Opal's reins with the other. Maybe I had not been very skilled at navigating this terrain when I first got here, but I had become an expert. No pies in the creeks for me.

Daniel came down the porch stairs and made fast steps toward me when he saw me enter the clearing at his house. I was relieved to see him, having been worried that he might feel awkward and standoffish given the way he'd opened up to me and especially the way I'd all but told him I had feelings for him. Well, not outright, but I had touched him several times for no real reason other than I wanted to and then I'd made him cry and kissed his tear off my own finger. Talk about being forward.

I pulled Opal to a stop, just as the kids came racing around from the back of the house—Hugh pulling up the rear but keeping time pretty well on his little legs. Daniel reached up and took the pie which he handed to Ella. He offered me his hand to help me dismount from Opal. When I jumped from Opal, I landed a little closer to Daniel than I meant to and I placed my hand against the firmness of his chest to steady myself from falling. I blushed deeply and stepped back from him. His eyes caught mine and we both looked away.

"Will you come in?" he asked after a moment. "I'm sure the kids would like to show you around."

"I'd love to," I said, pretending as though I hadn't already sneaked in there and seen most of it already.

"It's not much," he said, not knowing.

"I'm sure it's perfect." Which I already knew it was.

Marie took my hand and pulled me up the steps and into the house. The wood underfoot creaked a bit as Daniel stepped in behind me.

"This is it," he said, his voice apologetic behind me. "Not much of a tour to be had."

I turned back to him. "It's lovely, Daniel," I said, willing him to hear my sincerity.

He made an appreciative sort of face, but I wasn't sure that he believed that I meant it.

Ella and Marie scurried around setting places at the table and Hugh sat on the floor by the couch playing with a set of blank wooden blocks of all sizes and shapes. He had built a bit of a tower. Marie came back through into the bedroom area and quickly tucked the covers of the bottom bunk into place before returning to the kitchen to help Ella. I noticed that Daniel's and Hugh's bed was nicely made, and that the little teddy bear slept on one of the pillows.

"Watch this, Miss Mattie," Hugh said and stood up. He promptly kicked the blocks over and squealed with delight. "I do it again." He sat down and started building.

"Those are nice," I said, pointing to the blocks and then asking Daniel, "where did you buy them?"

"I ain't bought next to nothing in years," he said, stepping forward and picking up one of the blocks. "I made them. Took near about forever to get them sanded down enough it was safe to let him play with them."

Daniel handed the block to me, and I ran my fingers over it. The block was smooth as velvet to the touch.

"How do you manage?" I asked, thinking about the rumors of moonshine distillery and distribution. "To get the things you need, I mean." I thought about the trade appointments that Liam had mentioned.

Daniel stood in the opening between the living room and the kitchen. Behind him, the girls sliced the pie and in front, Hugh continued to play.

"I do a fair amount of bartering," Daniel said, putting his hands in the pockets of his pants. I noticed that he did that when he was nervous. He needn't be. He continued. "You've seen the garden and the chickens. That affords me most of what we need. In the summertime at least. And it gives us something to eat as well."

He looked extremely handsome in his clean blue shirt and suspenders. His hair was combed and his face cleanly shaven. I liked him just as well the scruffier way he'd looked the day before. Although the nicer manner that seemed to come with a shave had been an improvement.

"You do other things on the side?"

He looked at me and nodded, but he didn't say what. I was going to have to ask if I wanted to know. I wasn't sure that I did. Maybe it wasn't the worst thing to make a little shine and sell it.

"Your garden is quite impressive," I said, too much of a coward to ask the other question. "I've seen some other ones, but they seem sort of spiteful if that makes any sense."

He smiled and nodded. "I know what you mean. This is tough ground. It wasn't an easy task to cultivate this land into something that would grow anything at all, much less into what it has come to be. Many prayers and a right much hard work went into it. But I've got mouths to feed, and a person has to do what has to be done."

He pointed to the couch. He sat on one end, and I sat on the other. The piece of furniture was small, like a love seat, and we weren't very far apart from one another. We watched Hugh play and I was desperately aware of the warmth of Daniel's body so close to me. He stretched his arm across the back of the couch, and I tried to scoot a little closer without him noticing. I didn't really get very far because Ella called us to the table.

"Pie's cut and plated. Can we eat?"

Daniel took his arm from the back of the couch and ran his hand through his hair. The dark locks fell back into place as if he'd not ever touched them at all—save one little piece in the front. His eyes, somewhat sullen, but reluctantly hopeful, fixed on mine.

"We'll be right in," Daniel said and the girls nodded. Ella scooped up Hugh and they all went back to the table. Daniel sat forward but didn't get up. Looking not at me, but into the room at his children, he said, "I know you must want to know what I did. How it is that I'm shunned as it were." He still didn't look at me. He stared straight ahead. "I'll answer anything you want to know. All you have to do is ask. I warn you, it ain't a pretty story or a short one."

He looked at me then, as if waiting for the interrogation to begin.

"If I have questions, I'll let you know," I said and got up, without giving the matter another moment, and went to join the kids at the table. I looked back at Daniel still sitting on the couch. "You coming?"

He furrowed his brow at me, raised his eyebrows, and stood. He didn't join us though, rather stepped only as far as the fireplace. He put his hand to his mouth and then into his pocket.

"We ain't had pie in forever," Marie said, not seeming to notice the awkward moments of tension.

"Dig in, then," I said.

There were only four chairs at the table. One had a booster block of sorts on which sat Hugh, already eating his pie and getting it all over his face. The girls sat and then Ella stood back up.

"We ain't had company," she said and looked over to where Daniel was standing. "Da, where should Miss Mattie sit?"

"She can have my chair," he said and stepped on into the kitchen.

"I'll stand. It's fine."

The girls looked at each other and whispered something behind their hands.

"Ella and I will share," Marie said and dragged her plate to Ella's spot. The girls squeezed in the one seat together. "You sit by Miss Mattie, Da."

Daniel nodded and sat down. Ella jumped back up to fetch another plate. She sliced Daniel a piece of pie and pushed it toward him.

"I only cut four," she said. "I'm too used to it only being us here, Da."

"I love the way they call you Da," I said, as we all dug into my ugly pie. "Is that a holdover from when one of them was a baby."

Daniel smiled. He poured a glass of water from the pitcher and took a sip. "My mother's people were Scottish. That's how she referred to my father when she talked about him to me. She wanted him to act like a father and she wanted me to think of him as one. It's sort of a term of endearment. I never called him that. Whenever my mother would say it, I imagined some other man, some other father. I try to be that man that I imagined. I must have told Emily about it," he said and shook his head. "I guess she either didn't understand the story or thought she'd take the bad out of it by turning it on its ear. She was like that."

"They say it with such love," I said. "You must be doing a good job of being the father you imagined."

I smiled at him, and he smiled back, a small smile, but enough that it counted.

Daniel

We finished our pie, which was quite delicious even though it looked a little worse for the wear. Although even that was endearing. Everything Mattie did was endearing. I knew I needed to tread lightly. I didn't really have the luxury of intimate feelings. I instructed the children to go out back and wash the plates. Mattie and I went to sit on the front porch steps. The air was warm, but not uncomfortable. Sunlight sparked off the places along the creek that you could see between the trees. We hadn't sat there long before Mattie spoke.

"Daniel, I shouldn't have asked questions about your past."

"You only say that because you've been told I have one that is questionable," I said and winked at her. "It's alright. I do."

"I don't mind what people say," she offered.

I wished I could say the same, but it bothered me still. The sounds of the children laughing somewhere in the yard floated over to our ears.

"Sometimes I wonder if you're real or if we are all imagining you," I said, not daring to look at her in case I was right and when I turned to see her, I'd discover myself alone and talking to the wind.

She startled me by taking hold of my hand. "I'm real," she said.

I looked at our hands and then out into the yard. "I apologize for yesterday. The chopping block," I said and glanced quickly at her. "I'm embarrassed that you saw that."

"Please don't be," she said,

"I was just desperate," I said. "Did you hear me, nearly ordering the Lord around like he owes me something?"

"I shouldn't have been listening," she said, "but you seemed worried that you were going to lose the children. Is everything alright?"

"I always worry about that," I said. "I guess I figure that it's my due. You know."

"Not really," she said.

"They're all I have," I said. "And all I want." Mostly. I cleared my throat to knock back a knot I felt forming. "I guess I just figure that one day God will take them, too."

"Why would he do that?"

"He's got reason," I said.

"OK, that's it," she said and took her hand away. I thought that perhaps I'd convinced her, and she was leaving, because she stood up and went down the steps, but then she stopped, turned back to me, and put her hands on her hips. I tried not to chuckle, but her look was a cross between a petulant child and an angry schoolmarm. It didn't matter what look she wore, I thought she was beautiful. There, I'd admitted it. I was smitten. And about to be in trouble it looked like.

"I'm standing right here, Daniel," she said, stating the obvious, but

I knew what she was getting at. "Do you think I rode all the way out here balancing a pie in one hand and holding the reins of a horse in the other because of my Christian charity?"

"No?" I was afraid to answer.

"That's correct," she said, and I felt relieved. "Not that I have none, mind you. I came out here because I wanted to see you. To be with you. I don't even know how to make pie."

"You did a fine job."

"This is not about pie."

"It's not?" I asked, honest confusion and a little fear creeping into my belly.

"No," she said, her voice raised. "I want you. I want to get to know you and to be part of your life. There," she said and stomped her foot. "I said it."

"I ain't got nothing to offer you," I said and gestured back at the house. "You can see that without a second look." I didn't say it to turn her way. I wanted her, too, but I wanted it to be real. Not something from a storybook or some flight of fancy whose novelty would surely wear off.

"I didn't ask you for anything," she said.

"Are you leaving?" I asked.

"Do you want me to?" she replied, her eyebrows raised.

I shook my head. "I want you to come back and sit with me."

She did.

"The last years have seemed long," I said. "It's hard to imagine anything will be any different."

"I happen to have a great imagination," she said and scooted closer to me.

"I hope you're not lost in it now," I said. "This is what you get. I'm not anything more than what you see and likely, I'm less. Don't imagine me some hero from your books. I'm not. This might not be a happily ever after story. Look around."

"You know what my favorite place in Asheville is," she asked, and I shrugged. "The fountain in the middle of the square. There are always tons of people around, but when I go there, it's like I'm by myself.

Peaceful and quiet. I can drown out the sounds of the people and the noises of the street. All I hear is the water. Close your eyes, Daniel."

I knew where she was going with it, but I closed them. I understood that she wanted to show me that everything she really wanted was here also. I opened my eyes. "It's easy to close your eyes and dream, but when you open them, this ain't Asheville." Not even close. Emily had wanted out and Mattie would too.

"Indeed, it's not," Mattie said, her dark eyes seeming to find her home in her memory. "I liked the city. The colors of the stone and brick, the spires, and arches. And the glimpses of the mountains in the near distance visible at the end of the road. At certain times of day, it's quite breathtaking. The light plays on the buildings and the mountains at the same time, but in different ways. The bricks and stone take on a very real quality, but the mountains especially, look like a painting in all their hues of smoky blue. It looks like the whole city is part of a play and the mountains are hazy shades of painted-on blue in the background like a stage drop that could be lifted and something else put down in its place."

"It's not like that here," I said. "There's no picking up the scenery and making for a better day. This will lose its appeal. You'll miss your old world and go back home. Trust me."

"Do you know what I like about things here?" she asked as if she hadn't heard me at all. "I like the way things look clear here. The hills and mountains are so close that I can see the green of each individual leaf, slightly different than the leaf next to it. I can hear the sound of the water here, too." She looked off toward the creek. "Here at your place, that is. I miss the sound of it in town. I thought what I'd miss would be the sounds of the city street, the people calling to each other, horns honking. I thought I'd miss the noise. But really, I just miss the water. You know what I think of when I hear that creak babbling?"

I shook my head.

"You," she said. "And the kids."

"Because of all the babbling I do?" I asked and raised an eyebrow.

She punched me in the arm again. "I am trying to be poetic and meaningful here, Daniel."

"And I am trying to deflect the conversation because I'm worried that you won't stay, and I'll be sad when you go."

"I cannot figure you out," she said and tilted her head at me.

"I don't know why not," I said. "I just told you the plain and honest truth."

"That's what I mean."

I shook my head and reached out for her hand. She twined her fingers around mine.

"It's hard for me to trust people," I said. "I'm used to this life that we have here by ourselves. I know this. You know what I mean?"

She nodded but didn't comment.

I ran my thumb over the smooth skin of her hand holding mine. I peeked at her to see what her reaction was. She was looking at our hands. A small smile played across my lips, I couldn't help it. We sat there for the longest time listening to the sound of Ella's voice in the house as she read a story to the other children and warbling of the water of the Hell for Certain creek as it ran its path in front of us from one side of what I knew to the other.

Chapter 14

Mattie

I tossed the letter from Asheville on the kitchen table and poured myself another cup of hot tea. I needed to steady myself before heading out onto my route. It was Daniel day as I called it, yes, I know silly and girlish, but I was drawn to him so deeply that all the other days seemed only part of the process of getting back to him. Today we were reading, no matter what other distraction he created.

I had homed in on his honest statement that it was hard for him to trust people. I was going to be someone he could trust. I could have kicked myself for starting to believe that people were right about him. I had seen enough to know that there were, indeed, two sides to this story. I didn't really know what the story was, but I knew he wasn't the antagonist that people made him out to be.

I took my mug of tea to the table and sat down to read the letter again. I would have to answer it. I just wasn't sure what that answer would be. I was too afraid to tell my father outright that I didn't want to come home. There had been a time when what was in that letter would have been excellent news. That time had passed.

> *Dear Mattie,*
>
> *You will be thrilled to learn that a teaching position is coming open here in Asheville this fall. There is some competition for the spot, so it's prudent that we send your resume and recommendations right away. I will include your service to the community of Certain, Ky. as part of your volunteer efforts to further education in needy areas. I believe that your time spent there setting up a school for them will sway the board in your favor. What a smart move on your part. I hope all is well out there in the wilds. I will see you soon.*
>
> *Most sincerely,*
> *Your loving father*

I let the letter fall from my fingers and took a sip of Earl Grey. I breathed in the scent of it, reminding myself that I only had a few more bags left from the canister I'd brought with me. I held the cup close to my nose.

"You could just go home," I said out loud, the steam of the tea rising around my face. "It would be easier. Maybe for the best, before you get attached."

I laughed out loud. It was too late for that, and I didn't want to go home. Sure, I was worried about what would happen if the school here was a flop and they didn't need me. And how would I make a living really? I was getting a small sum for working as a carrier, and I have been provided a place to live. But I was mostly getting by on my father's money. In the best of times a town like this probably couldn't afford a teacher, and these were not the best of times.

Perhaps I needed to be practical. I pulled out a piece of paper and wrote a quick letter to my father before I had time to think better of it.

> *Dear Pop,*
>
> *It was so good to see your handwriting and to hear your voice in your words. Things here in the wild are going very well indeed. I'm surprised to hear of the job opening*

in Asheville and I suppose it wouldn't be the worst thing to go ahead and send my information to them. Meanwhile, I am hard at work setting up school here. There has been some interest from the local children and their parents which is very exciting.

I miss you,
Your loving daughter

I sealed and addressed the envelope quickly. I thought the suggestion to go ahead and send my resume, although I didn't really want the job, might appease him for the moment. But really, I hoped that he would read into my words and see that I was happy here. I left the letter from my father on the table and put my empty cup in the sink. I needed to get my route started if I wanted to leave time for lessons with Daniel and to see the kids at the end. I wanted to see what new story idea Ella had, and I couldn't wait to present her with the paper and pencils. I decided to drop the letter to my father in the post on the way out of town. It would buy me some time at least. And there was nothing to say that I would even get the position in Asheville. No need to worry about it now.

The lingering summer heat was building to a slow boil on the route, but Opal and I plowed forward. Thoughts of my last visit to Daniel's house floated around me along the journey. Those thoughts lit a fire within me that caused me to stop a time or two by the creek to douse my hot cheeks with cool water, lest I show up with my face pink and sweat on my brow. Opal, getting more used to the water, even dipped her head to take a drink. I was anxious to run her to Daniel's door, but nervous to get there at the same time. A week had passed since I'd sat out on the porch with him. I had hardly slept without dreaming of him—mostly pleasant, but an occasional vision of a bear and the dark murkiness of waters running too rampant to catch. I worried that I had imagined his feelings for me. As I had told him, I did have a good imagination. Perhaps when I arrived, I would find that I'd made the whole thing up in my mind.

As I approached, I could hear fiddle music coming from the house and at first, I thought it to be a radio program until I remembered that there was no radio here. Someone was playing. The music stopped as soon as Opal let out a whinny and Daniel appeared quickly on the porch with the instrument in hand.

He hurried to greet me, which caused my hands to shake with sudden relief that the days had not turned his mind from me.

"You're late," he said and tucked the violin and its bow under his arm. He reached for my hand. "I was worried that you were hurt or that you might not come at all. It's been a whole week."

"No dangers encountered," I said, taking his offered hand to help me from the horse. He let his fingers linger on mine a moment more than necessary before turning my hand loose. "Just long-winded stories and indecision about which books to choose."

He seemed relieved. "The kids are in the garden," he said and nodded us that way.

I secured Opal, gathered the books for the kids and followed Daniel around the side of the house. Once there, I closed my eyes so that my mind could see. Behind my lids I saw the tall buildings of Asheville, the shops and busy establishments, the automobiles along the streets. When I opened my eyes the summer sun glinted off the tiller blades by the shed across from the garden, and everything in my other world of Asheville seemed to lift from my shoulders and sift off like a disappearing cloud. I thought for a moment to try and reach out and take hold of it—it was a wonderful city and in it I had a good life which was not one I had thought to escape when I'd left. But as the scene before me retook its shape—the children now running along the edge of the garden playing, Daniel smiling over at me when my eyes lit across his, the cloudless blue sky of summer and the stark beauty of this land I had only just gained knowledge of, but had already come to love, I opened my hand instead, and let the other place lift away. Even at its roughest, this is where I wanted to be.

The children came running toward me then, and I would have to wait to talk to Daniel until their needs were satisfied. I handed them each a book, including one for Marie that she had been waiting for. I gave Hugh a *Doctor Dolittle*. I knew he'd love it and it would give Ella a chance to stretch her performance skills. I was falling into the hang of this job and liking it very much. I knew that all my efforts to pique the interests of the children would pay off come fall and that I'd see those little desks full.

Hugh ran off toward the porch and Daniel excused himself to check on him and put the fiddle away. Marie had run off with her long-awaited book and I was left alone with Ella.

"I read your story, Ella. It was delightful. I hope you'll share another one."

I was baiting her, and I knew it. I had something for her amid the books I'd brought for them, and I was anxious to give it to her.

"I'd love to, but I'm all out of paper, Miss Mattie."

"You don't say," I pressed my finger to my lips as if I was pondering something.

Her eyes lit up, figuring me out. I smiled and pulled a package of paper, a new box of pencils and a sharpener that was tucked between the other books I carried. She squealed so loudly that Opal whinnied from the front of the house. Ella took the items from me and quite literally jumped up and down.

"I'm glad you like my surprise," I said and touched the top of her blonde head.

"I love it," she said. "Where did you get these?"

"I had them sent from Asheville," I said and winked at her, "which is a place that more than one author has come to stay and visit. I bet when you're a famous author, you'll go there too. You have to stay at the Grove Park Inn and get a room with a view that stretches across the whole of the mountains in front of you. You can even see the buildings of downtown lit up at night."

She smiled at me and blushed. "I can't imagine a city with lights that you can see from a distance. That sounds like a make-believe place." She pulled the paper and pencils to her chest. "I don't think I'll ever be a real writer, but it's nice to play at."

"Do you want to be a real writer?"

"Of course," she said, her voice confirming it.

"Then you will be," I said and nodded at her as if that was that.

"It must be quite a bit of work to be a writer," she said, her little brow furrowed.

"Oh, it is indeed," I answered. "But what thing isn't if it's something worth doing? Answer me this; what if I said you couldn't write any more stories. That you'd have to use that paper and pencil set for some other thing. No more stories allowed." I said nonchalantly as if it was of no great consequence.

She took in a little gasp of air. "I don't think I could do that," she said and clutched the package to her chest. "I have to write the stories. They keep coming to me, and I can't just not write them."

I smiled at her broadly. "As I suspected. See, you are already a writer. Now we work to let the rest of the world know it." I nodded at her with purpose.

Her eyes began to well with tears. "You tricked me," she said, smiling then, so wide her face could barely contain the expression.

Her happiness turned a light on inside me at that moment and I felt the current of her emotion like an electrical circuit created from her to me. I nearly buzzed from the charge.

"Can I go and start another story right now?" she asked.

I looked around and lowered my voice. "Yes, but before you go may I ask a question." She nodded and I whispered. "Your father and I are going to practice reading today. Can he read at all?"

She hugged the paper to her chest again and looked over her shoulder. "He can read a little, but he's shy about it. People think he's dumb, but he's not." She stepped closer to me as if keeping a secret from the very trees around us. "People think he's bad, but Da is a good man. He ain't like they say."

I didn't need to ask what "they" said. I knew. What broke me was that she did, too.

"I know, sweetie," I said and reached out to touch her hand with mine.

"Thank you for talking to him like you do, all regular and the like," she said. "People are mean to him mostly and I can tell that it makes him sad."

"Mean?" My heart thudded in my chest.

"Before we left, before Mama died, people started saying mean things to Da. Treating him mean. I didn't like it. Then once we came out here, whenever we went into town, people were downright ugly to him."

"I'm sorry to hear that," I said, my heart fluttering. "Is that why you don't go into town anymore?"

She nodded. "He thinks we don't know that, but we do. He doesn't want us to see the way people treat him. We can go up the creek a ways," she said, her voice lifting. "But we have to stop at Turtle Hiding. But we can go off into the woods at the back of the house near about as far as we want. Ain't nobody back that way."

"Do you remember the last time you went to town with Daniel?" I asked, fearful of what might have happened.

She looked over her shoulder again. "There were two ladies at the grocery. One screamed and ran away like she'd seen a monster. The other lady got all giggly and started clinging onto Da. She wanted him to kiss her on the cheek. I don't even know who she was." Ella's voice was raised in remembered distress.

I supposed a bad reputation could be a deterrent to some and an intrigue to others.

"Then," she said, "the giggly lady's husband came in and snatched her away from Da and spit on his shoe. Right there in the store. I think he would have hit Da, but Mr. Gibbons told the man to leave."

I put my hand to my heart.

"Since then, we stay here when he goes out," she said and sighed as if she was happy to have it over with. "It's better that way. Except we don't get to see our kin. Maybe one day. Da says maybe."

I sighed too and decided to change the subject to something lighter. "I've never heard your dad play the violin."

Ella tilted her head and looked off into the past. "It's been a long time. I don't think he's played it since Mama died. He used to play at church. We don't go anymore though. So, I guess he ain't had occasion to play. It's nice to hear it. It makes me think of good things."

A question came to my lips, and I tried hard not to ask it, but I failed.

"Do I remind you of your mother?"

She looked at me for a long moment. "Nope," she said as if she'd been trying her hardest to find some similarity. "Mama was real quiet and you're sort of loud. Like when you laugh. And you're really silly. Like dancing in the yard and telling funny things like falling off your horse and being a bad cook."

She looked sad suddenly and my heart lurched. "I'm sorry sweetie, I shouldn't have asked that."

"No, it's OK. I just thought maybe I had upset you. I meant all those things as good things. My mama was good, too. I didn't mean nothing bad about her."

"I know you didn't, honey." I reached out and touched her shoulder. "I know what it's like to miss your mama so bad you don't even have words for it. I shouldn't have talked about her."

"I forgot," she said and looked at me deeply. "You lost your mama, too. I'm glad you asked about her. Nobody does. Not that we see nobody much, but still. Miss Mattie," she said and then spoke in a whisper. "You shouldn't worry about Da only liking you because you remind him of Mama. Y'all ain't nothing the same. Which is good. I think it would hurt if you were too much like her." She looked me solidly in the eye and pressed her lips together.

"I suppose it would," I said, thinking about how my own father had never done more than date a woman a time or two because he seemed to always be looking for someone like Mama, but then when he found her, he couldn't bring himself to love her.

"You make Da laugh," Ella said, with a sadness that seemed to contradict the comment. "I wasn't even sure he knew how to laugh anymore. I mean, he laughs at stuff Hugh does and Marie is pretty funny, but with you, he laughs like he forgot we're hurting. I'm glad of that. My Da is too sad."

"I don't want him to be sad," I said.

"He was afraid you might not come back," she said, glancing over her shoulder again. "I think he's been playing the fiddle to keep his spirits light waiting on you. I'm glad you came."

I wanted to say something, but there was a lump lodged in my throat. Instead, I clutched the small stack of books I was still holding to my chest like a shield. Ella had hers and I had mine.

"Da really likes you," Ella whispered.

"I like your father very much, too," I said. "I'm sorry it took me so long to get back here. I won't let it happen again."

Daniel came back around the house then and seeing him too, Ella put her finger to her lips, and I nodded my head.

"You ladies telling secrets?" Daniel asked with amusement.

"Girl talk," I said and smiled at him. "You ready for that lesson?"

He wrinkled his nose. "I hoped you'd forgot." He sighed but smiled. "Ella, will you mind Marie and Hugh outside and let Miss Mattie and me have a few minutes. I've got some book learning to do."

Ella seemed a little jealous. "I hope we get to go to school when it starts," she said. "I miss learning and getting to be around the other kids." She looked at Daniel with pleading eyes. "It's Miss Mattie who's teaching. You like her, right. She would be good to us."

My heart ached. Of course, I would. Let the person who wouldn't be good to them show their face to me. The ache in my heart had turned to a low burning flame. Daniel touched the top of Ella's head.

"I'll think on it."

I came to his rescue. "Well, right now, your father has a reading lesson to get to." I patted the top book on my stack which was a reader I thought to teach him with.

"If we must," he said and smiled.

"We must." I leaned over to Ella and whispered, although I knew Daniel could hear me, "I'll work on him about school."

Ella seemed pleased enough and ran off with her paper and pencils.

"You really don't have to bother teaching me," Daniel said, but headed us up toward the house. "I've gotten on without the skill mostly all my life. I can make things out well enough if I have to."

"Enough won't do," I said as we entered the house. "No backing out now," I said looking around the room. "I think the kitchen table will do well."

Without waiting for him to follow me, I went into the room and set the little book I'd brought down on the table. I pulled two of the seats rather close together so that I'd be able to point to things and have him do the same without either of us having to look at the words at a skewed angle. I had never taught anyone to read, truth be told. I had practiced in school, but it wasn't really the same. I had yet to have an actual teaching job. I remembered the lessons I had learned at university about how to teach reading and I hoped I'd be good enough to help Daniel. It would be great practice for when I had actual students. I sat down in one of the chairs and nodded for him to join me. He did, but somewhat reluctantly.

"I hope you're not offended that this is a book for a child," I said, opening the primer to a page that I gathered might be a good starting point, based on what I knew of Daniel's ability to read. "I don't know if there are books for adult learners, but there should be." I made a note to myself to have Ava research that. Perhaps I could write back to the Asheville library and the university and ask as well. I'd have to ask without my father knowing, otherwise he'd put it down on my resume as more volunteer work.

"A children's book is the least of things to offend my pride," Daniel said, settling into the chair. "I weather worse, so don't worry over it."

He scooted the chair even closer to me. He smelled of cleanliness—oats and rosemary. I inhaled deeply the fresh scent of the natural soap that I knew many of the folks used. It was a far more lovely smell than the medicinal notes of the Lifebuoy brand I had brought with me. My father used that brand and although I imagined there were better options, maybe even perfumed ones for women, it was what I knew. I tried to recall what my mother might have washed with, but I didn't know. I was too young to have noticed such things. I did remember that she smelled of roses most of the time and I imagine it was from a cream or lotion, the name of which I never knew. By the time I was old enough to care about such things, it was just me and my father, and his Lifebuoy.

"I'm a might nervous," Daniel said and I stopped sniffing him and pulled my attention back to the task at hand.

"What are you nervous about?"

"That I'll look like a fool stumbling over words that a child can read," he answered with his trademark honesty.

"No need to feel foolish," I said, clearing my throat and trying not to notice how full his lips were, and how endearing it was when he did that little smile with one side of his mouth turning up just slightly. "It's a needed skill and you'll be all the better for it. Reading is a wonderful thing. Just imagine all the worlds you'll be able to enter, all the people you'll meet." I found that I was getting excited. "The smell of a rose garden, the taste of exotic food, the sound of the ocean waves crashing on the shore."

He smiled at me much more fully and then bit his lip as if it was something that he shouldn't do. He was trying to keep from laughing, but in an endearing way.

"What?" I asked, feigning indignation. "Are you laughing at me?"

He shook his head, but the smile still lit his face. "No, ma'am," he said, smiling even more.

I sat up straight and pretended to be put out with him. "You are, too, laughing at me. Pray tell why?"

He winked at me, and I knew he knew I wasn't upset. "You're adorable when you go on like that about books."

I felt all fluttery and girlish. I was sure I was blushing a shade of pink dark enough to see from the other room. I continued. "What exactly does that mean, sir?" I asked.

Daniel sat back a little in his chair and pondered me. His smile slipped into something of a more contemplative countenance. He sat forward and smiled again without explaining the interlude. "You talk about books as if they're magical. Ella surely believes them so. The both of you get so excited when you talk about a new story. It's endearing."

I wasn't sure if that was a good thing or bad. Was I adorable like a child? I deflated a little over the idea that I had misinterpreted what he meant, but I tried not to let that disappointment show.

"They are indeed magical," I said.

"Do tell." He leaned in a bit closer to me as if he was listening to something very important and didn't want to miss a word.

I took up the challenge. "Take your average book," I said, looking around the room. I spotted one of the novels I had brought for Ella on the couch through the fireplace opening. I stood up quickly and retrieved it. I went back to the table where I opened the book and laid it in front of Daniel. I stood just behind him so that I was reading over his shoulder. "Close your eyes," I said, and I leaned in closer so that I was very near his ear. "See this."

"See it?" he said and looked back and up at me. "With my eyes closed?"

I touched the side of his cheek, smooth where he had recently shaved, nudging him to turn back toward the book. "See with your ears."

He did as directed. I leaned around to peek and see that his eyes were closed. They were.

I read a passage about a terrified family on a ship ravaged at sea. The vessel torn through with leaks and damaged sails. Cries of terror and the thundering crash of waves. The sound of the ship coming apart at the seams amid desperate pleas and prayer.

I sat down next to him after the passage was through and touched his arm. He opened his eyes and smiled at me again. "I saw it."

"Look at the book," I said, touching the section from which I had read. "All that's there are little black words on a white page. With few exceptions, including children's books and the illustrations here and there in books like these, that's all you see—with your eyes." I closed the book and pulled it to my chest. "But in your mind, you see much more. You feel the mist from the crashing waves, you hear the shouts and commands, you feel the terror of a storm and then the exhilaration of the cry of 'Land.'" I sighed and set the book back on the table. "Wouldn't you say that's magic? I would."

He smiled at me again. "Teach me to do that magic trick then," he said. He put his chin in his hand and looked at me very sincerely. "I would like to see what you see."

"OK," I said, beaming. "Let's begin."

I started with some basic sounds and small words to try to determine where his education on the skill of reading had stopped. I didn't know who had taught him. His mother, although perhaps she herself had not known how. Pastor Collins or Mrs. Collins once he'd come to live there. Perhaps, but he'd been old enough that he should have known already and perhaps they assumed he did.

He knew the basic sounds of the letters and could sort out words here and there. He knew a little more than I had given him credit for. He must have sat and learned a little somewhere along the way. He touched his fingers to the words as he read. His hands were large and his fingers strong and square at the tips. I liked to look at his hands and think about them holding mine. I liked their roughness, especially since I also knew how tender they were. I drew my eyes away and focused again on the lesson.

He sounded out a short sentence and then closed his eyes and breathed out heavily. He pressed his hands over his face and rubbed at his eyes.

"What's the matter?" I asked. "You're doing well. I might have selected a book that was too easy for you."

"I'm doing well for a child on his first day of school perhaps," he said and shook his head. "Were I not already put in my place in so many other areas, I don't think my pride would allow me to go on like this—fumbling over the smallest of words. It's an awful embarrassment. Especially in front of you."

I touched his arm where it rested on the table. He looked at me and winced.

"Don't be embarrassed about anything with me," I said, tightening my fingers against the firmness of his arm. "I would never aim to put you in your place." I shook my head. "Not that I'm implying you have a place in which to be put. Of course not. You're fine where you are."

"Out here in the wilds, far away from the gentler folk?"

I couldn't tell if he was playing again or if he was serious. I started to move my hand from his arm, but he put his hand over mine to stop me.

"I'm making jokes because I'm nervous," he said.

"I don't want you to be," I said. "I want you to trust me, Daniel. You can trust me."

His eyes registered a forlorn look of longing as if he wanted desperately for that to be the truth.

"Like I said, trust isn't my strong suit anymore," he said and moved his hand from mine. "But I'll try." His eyes found mine and lingered on them as if searching me to see if I meant what I said.

"Do you want to continue with the lesson, or have you had enough of me for today?" I asked.

He tilted his head. "No, but no."

I almost missed his meaning, but then smiled at understanding. "I can stay a while longer."

"Perhaps I could check on the children and then I could walk you part of the way home," he said, scooting back from the table as if already headed to do so. "It is getting a little late and I don't want you out there alone."

Daniel stepped outside to speak to the children. I watched them through the open door. He scooped Hugh up into his arms as he spoke, kissing the child on the head before setting him back onto his feet. The children came inside then and made themselves comfortable on the couch.

"Ella, fix the little ones a tomato sandwich if y'all get to feeling hungry before I'm back." Daniel reached out and took hold of my hand. "I'm going to walk Miss Mattie and Opal a ways up the creek."

Ella looked at our joined fingers and elbowed Marie who glanced up quickly as if she was annoyed, but then at seeing what Ella indicated, she did a bit of a double take and gawked quite openly. Ella elbowed her again and Marie smiled.

Little Hugh tried to wiggle off the couch. "I come, too, Da?"

"Not this time, bud," Daniel said. "I'm going to see that Miss Mattie gets past the rough spots on her way home. It will be a little late for you to be out by the time I'm back. Tomorrow, I will take you fishing. How about that?"

"Deal," Hugh said and snuggled back in next to his sisters.

"I'll be back shortly," he said to the children, and we went outside.

Daniel held tight to my hand, and we walked out into the yard to get Opal. Daniel took the reins and walked her through the yard. I presumed that he didn't want me to ride her, but rather to walk along with him. I was happy to do so. The sky was orange and tinged with pink as the day tried to come to a close. I'd stayed longer than I should have, and I was grateful that Daniel was walking me through the rougher parts of my trip back home. I'd found myself returning after dark before, but I didn't care for it.

As we walked, I fumbled for something to talk about.

"I didn't know you could play the violin."

"I haven't in a while," he said. "I used to play at church. Imagine the likes of me playing fiddle for the God-fearing folks right here on a Sunday morning in the sanctuary."

I put my hand on his arm and laid pressure on it enough for him to stop walking. He turned to face me.

"I'll have no more talk of such things, sir," I said and eyed him firmly. "Deal?"

He lowered his eyes and then looked back at me. "Deal." He sighed and then spoke again as if the thing he wanted to say was weighing heavy. "Mattie, I have to apologize for my behavior when you got here earlier today."

I must have looked confused because I was. "I don't understand."

"I acted as though we were more important to each other than we might be. I was being presumptuous talking to you like a worried suitor."

"Were you?" I asked. "Being presumptuous. I don't think so."

"No?"

I shook my head and he bit at his lip to keep from smiling.

Daniel stepped closer to me, and I matched his move. He stepped back a tad and I returned. Forward and away. Closer and back again. It was our second dance. We chuckled at each other and finally Daniel reached out and took hold of my hand.

I stepped in a bit closer, and he put his other hand on the top of where our fingers were joined. I wanted to say something, but I was focusing all my energy on not trembling. We stood there looking at each other for a long minute. I could all but feel the tug of our bodies wanting to move closer together. I was certain he could hear my breath—slow and composed in an attempt to keep myself from pressing up against him.

His hold on my hand tightened and he closed his eyes. I took that opportunity to look as full on his face as I could. His long dark lashes caught the last of the sunlight. His skin was slightly browner than it had been when I first met him—long hours in his garden. His cheekbones were strong and his jawline firm. His face which had been covered in a shaggy beard when I first met him was smooth now. I liked him either way. I knew I shouldn't, but I reached up to touch his cheek. His skin was smooth against my fingers.

At my touch he took in a short breath, but kept his eyes closed. He put his hand on top of mine and pressed it more firmly to his cheek. He opened his eyes then and looked intently at me. He pulled my hand from his face, and I felt my heart drop, until he pulled it instead to his lips and kissed my fingers. I took in a short breath.

"I hope you'll be back soon," Daniel said and kissed my hand again, letting his lips linger on my skin. "I surely would love to find out how Dick and Jane get out of their current predicament."

His spot of humor caught me off guard and pleased me.

"I wouldn't want you to go on wondering how it all comes out in the end," I said and raised an eyebrow at him for joking at such a time.

He lowered my hand down from his lips but didn't let me go. He stepped in a little closer to me and I could feel the warmth and weight of his presence. He closed his eyes and then stepped back. Ever the gentleman it seemed, no matter how much I wanted him not to be.

Daniel patted Opal's neck and headed us up the path a ways.

"Can I ask you a question?" I dared and Daniel nodded. I took a breath and voiced a fear. "Am I just convenient?"

Daniel wrinkled his brow. My stomach lurched at the thought that I had offended him. His voice wasn't more than a whisper when he spoke.

"Make you no mistake that I wouldn't have you at my house, growing close to my children and them close to you if I had not given that matter long consideration." He looked at me sternly as if I was in trouble and my heart raced. "Nothing about my life is convenient and least of all you, who at any week I will likely not see again."

"I'm not going anywhere," I said, trying to convince him and perhaps myself as well.

He closed his eyes. "Still, I want you here. Not because you are just some woman that will pay me notice. I have done without affections for many years and am accustomed to a lonely life. There's been a woman here and there who has volleyed for my attention in town. I'm only sport to them. I know that." He put his hands in his pockets and I wondered what the action meant in this circumstance. Did he not want me to touch him or vice versa? Was he angry that I had asked?

"I'm sorry," I said and reached my hand out, but then withdrew it. "I didn't mean to imply anything. I just," I stopped and exhaled a short breath. "I just like you very much and I didn't want Claire to be right."

He startled. "Claire," he said and then his whole body relaxed, and he took his hands from his pockets. He laughed a little and I was very confused.

"I met her at the grocer's," I said. "She all but hates your very marrow."

"She hates me through that and back out the other side of the bone, I promise you." He reached for my hand then and I very happily let him take it. "She has right to hate me, but I hope that you'll make your own decisions about me. I feel as though you're giving me more benefit of the doubt already than I deserve."

Before I could press the question back down it flew out. "What on earth could you have done, Daniel? I don't understand."

He took in a deep breath. "I don't have the courage to answer you at the moment, but it doesn't mean I won't work it up. Let's get you home," he said. "It's getting dark faster than I thought it would."

"I'll be OK," I said. "Once I get past this thick patch the rest of the ride to the parsonage is open ground."

He stepped back from me and turned loose of Opal's reins. "Where?"

"The parsonage." I repeated.

He stepped back further as if he might jump into the creek and swim back home.

"I thank you for your company, Miss Mobley, but I should turn back home. You should be fine from here."

"Miss Mobley?" I said, my heart registering the severity of the dismissal. "Daniel, I don't understand what's happening." Terror seemed to be rising in my throat.

"I didn't know you were staying at the parsonage," he said as if that explained something.

"It's just a house," I said.

He looked wounded to the soul, and I knew right away that this was another piece of the puzzle that I didn't have.

"I'm not angry," he said, holding his hands out like he was being held at gunpoint. "It's just best that we don't lose sight of things."

"Things?" I folded my arms across my chest then. I was practically shivering with fear.

"I'll leave the books from the library with Mr. Gibbons when the children are finished with them."

I was summarily dismissed at this point as he turned his back to me and didn't say another word. I stood there shaking as he walked back up the path to his house. I watched until I couldn't make out any sight of him at all.

Chapter 15

Mattie

I spent the next few days stunned and trying to figure out what to do. I had hoped that since Daniel knew where to find me, he might. But he didn't. I couldn't understand how we'd gone from the beginnings of a relationship to the end of it in a matter of seconds. And all because I was living at the parsonage.

I tried to put it all together. Perhaps he had lived there as a boy with Pastor Collins and the memories of happier times with Liam and Zachary were too much to bear. I didn't think that was it though. Daniel had seemed downright spooked, like he'd seen the quintessential ghost.

I needed answers, so I invited Ruby over to play Monopoly. Or so I told her. I really wanted to pump her for information, and I didn't intend to let her go until I had it.

"So, we move these little pegs around and buy property with this colorful fake money?" Ruby asked as we set the board out on the kitchen table and set the game up for play.

I nodded, counting out the money. "And when you get three plots of the same color you can build houses and hotels and charge the other players who land on them tons of rent," I said, handing her a stack of cash and taking out the colorful cards naming all the properties and such.

"Fabulous," she said, scooting her chair closer to the table. "Wait, do we have jobs?"

"No," I said, counting out thin money printed on colorful rectangle papers. "Other than charging people rent, you get money when you pass back around at the starting point."

"Money for nothing but getting back to Go?" Ruby asked, taking a handful of phony bills from me, and counting through them. "If only there was a restart in real life like that. I think I've been back at Go a dozen times. It didn't get me anything."

She winked at me and smiled. I so much admired her ability to press on with humor and hope despite the very real and seemingly unending struggle that was out of our control and beyond our ability to change. I felt the same way about this new development with Daniel.

"Mattie," Ruby said and snapped her fingers in my face. "You start. Show me how to play it."

"Sorry." I shook my head.

"You're a million miles away," she said, thumbing through the real estate cards. "What's the matter?" She took in a worried breath. "Are you ill?"

"No," I said, flattered by her concern. "Just heartsick I guess." It was a risk to open up to her, but I needed to talk.

Ruby looked at me then and raised an eyebrow. "Do tell."

"I upset him," I said and rolled the dice.

I moved my marker and contemplated buying something right away or letting it ride. I passed the dice to Ruby who just looked at me, waiting for me to say more. She gave up and rolled. She landed on Vermont Ave.

"Should I buy this?" she said. "Is that too much money?"

"You should see the prices on the other side of the board," I said, and watched her eyes bug open when she saw the numbers in comparison.

"What did you do that upset him?" she asked, not asking who I was talking about, likely knowing.

I looked at her, realizing this was my chance to talk openly about Daniel.

"I don't know," I said, setting the dice down without rolling. "Things were going well. Very well." She raised her eyebrow again. "Not that well," I said and waved my hand at her.

She winked at me, and I felt bolstered and confident. I had a friend that wasn't judging me even though I was "dating" the most notorious person in town. Having a friend was such a new and novel feeling that I was almost drunk on it.

"So, what happened?" she asked.

"I mentioned I was living here, and he almost fell over himself getting away from me. He called me Miss Mobley."

Ruby winced. "Daniel." She patted my arm across the board and smiled softly.

So there had been some doubt as to who I meant, but now that it was apparently confirmed I knew two things. It was OK that I talked about him, and she definitely knew something about this whole mysterious story.

"Go on," she said. "And it's your turn."

I rolled the dice and moved my marker. "Then I sort of told him it was no big deal, that it was just a house."

Ruby put her hands over her mouth and her eyes opened wide.

"It's not just a house, is it?" I asked.

She shook her head and lowered her hands from her face. "Oh, Mattie," she said and looked almost terrified. "We really should have told you this part." She shook her head. "I should have told you."

"Let me guess," I said, knowing Emily was the pastor's daughter and remembering the children's books I'd seen upstairs. Not to mention the two twin beds and the little bassinet. "They used to live here. Daniel and Emily and the kids."

She nodded and I put my hands over my eyes.

"I should have known," I said from behind my hands. Lowering them after a moment. "Of course, it would bother him to have me living in the house where she lived."

"It's not so much that she lived here," Ruby said, emphasizing "lived."

My heart lurched. "Emily died here?" I asked, although it wasn't really a question. I knew she died of course and as a young woman that would have been some accident or illness as opposed to old age and I had just assumed that she went to the hospital. Again, my own elevated financial station had caused me to forget that not everyone had the opportunities I had.

I was positively miserable. "I feel like the town idiot for not putting that together. It's not like there's a hospital here. Of course, she died at home and of course they lived here. I've been to the Collins homestead, there's not an empty house there." I put my hand to my burning cheeks. "I feel ill."

"That might not be the worst of it," Ruby said and grimaced. "There was sort of a scene here when Daniel found out."

"What do you mean found out?"

She set the dice down and took a breath. "It's a delicate situation for sure," Ruby said and slid her chair around closer to mine. She touched my hair like she was soothing a child. "If he didn't know you were living here, that was sure to be a piece of news he needs time to sort through. His last day here was a hard one. I'm sure the thought of you walking the rooms of this house is a hard pill to swallow."

"What happened?" I pleaded. "I just need to know the truth."

Perhaps I should have waited for Daniel to tell me himself, but I wasn't sure he was ever going to speak to me again. I set down the dice I realized I was still holding, the bright colors of the game board blurring in front of me.

"When Daniel got home," Ruby said, "Liam and Zachary were waiting for him."

"What do you mean?"

"Daniel was like a brother to them," Ruby said, her eyes searching around the room as if she was looking for where to start the story. "They all grew up together."

I nodded; I knew that part. "They must have known how upset he'd be." I began to picture them standing on the porch waiting to comfort him.

Ruby grimaced again, and I realized I had things wrong. Of course, I was always wrong. Clearly things were not well between the three and this night must have been the start of it.

"I don't think they cared too much if he was upset," Ruby said. "Least of all Liam. From the stories I hear, Liam didn't even say anything to Daniel. He just met him on the front porch and punched him in the face."

"What?" I leaned back in my chair from the shock. "Why?"

"Daniel didn't even know Emily had died," Ruby said and wrung her hands. "Ava tells it that she and Pastor were there too, and that Liam just started screaming it at Daniel. 'She's dead, she's dead.' It must have been a horrible way to find out."

"I feel sick to my stomach," I said. My heart was racing, and a lump clogged my throat.

Ruby took hold of my hand. "Apparently Daniel thought she was still in the house and went in calling for her and calling for the kids. He must have been so confused. People were gathered around the house."

"Why?" I asked, fearful.

Ruby just shook her head. "It was an ugly time. This whole thing with the economy was still fresh and people were scared. Mad. It wasn't good."

"Poor Daniel," I said.

Ruby took in a breath and went on. "Ava said he tore all through the house looking for Emily and the kids. She said she found him in their bedroom sitting on the floor weeping these terrible sobs. His whole body was trembling like he was going to break clean down the middle and crumble into rubble. Those were her words," Ruby said, shaking her head.

"Where were the kids?" I asked, my voice not much more than a whisper. I didn't know how to ask where Emily herself was.

"With Emily's mother."

"So, he went to get them and then they moved up to the cabin where they are now?" I asked. I picked up the dice like I was going to roll a different outcome.

"Well, that's the watered-down version," Ruby said.

"There's more?" I asked fearfully. Already I couldn't take it all in. I felt so awful at the thought of Daniel weeping for Emily.

"When Daniel said he was going to go find them all, Liam told him it was best he left the kids where they were and that Emily was already in the ground." Ruby took the dice from my hands and set them on the table. She put her hands over mine. "Then Daniel laid into Liam and the two of them fought like animals right out there in the street." She nodded her head in that direction. "I don't really know what happened after that, but I've heard the stories."

I had a certain feeling that she hadn't gotten the whole truth from those tales. "What did people say happened?"

"Daniel hitched Opal to the wagon and rode out to the homestead. Burst into Pastor's house and grabbed the kids up by the collars, snatched the baby out of Mrs. Collins's arms, and rode away. They say the whole thing broke Mrs. Collins and that's why she is the way she is today."

I thought of her silent and still on the porch. She seemed like a memory of a person who had once existed.

"Did they come back to the parsonage for the rest of their things?"

"Apparently Daniel came back to town later that night," Ruby said, picking up her little game marker and moving it around in its space like it was pacing. "He took a few things from the house and then went into the church." Ruby looked ashen.

Oh right, the church. I took a deep breath.

"For heaven's sake," I said, surprising myself that I was getting angry. "What on earth could he have done? He's just a man."

"He tore it all up," Ruby said, shaking her head. "Ripped the pews out with his bare hands and smashed the altar. Mr. Gibbons apparently stopped him. He must have been at the store late and seen the flames."

"Flames?" I asked, my voice raised.

"Fire," Ruby said. "Little tufts of it all up and down the aisle in the center of the church. You can still see the marks. People said it was the devil's footsteps. That the Devil got the best of Daniel, and he was trampling fire up and down the aisle right out of the bottom of Daniel's boots."

I lifted my hands in confusion. I was at a loss for words. I made some noises, but they didn't amount to actual speech.

Ruby twisted her mouth as if she wasn't sure whether or not to continue. "He'd also set the altar on fire apparently. People said he was calling up Hell. Gibbons must have seen the glow."

I hung my head and covered my face. "That's why Daniel thinks he's practically Satan himself."

Ruby put her hand on my shoulder. I lifted my head and turned toward her. She took both my hands in hers. The comfort and support meant everything to me in that moment.

"What happened after things caught fire?" I asked.

"He broke out one of the windows," Ruby said. "I think he might have been trying to let the smoke out. I don't know. Maybe he was going to break them all. I guess it could have gone either way. People have told a million stories."

"People who weren't there," I said and sighed. "What happened then?"

Ruby shrugged. "By morning the fire was out, the church was a wreck, and Daniel and the kids were gone."

"Did anyone look for them?"

"Ava went to the cabin a time or two I think," Ruby said. "It was hard for the kids to see her though, I imagine. Daniel, too. I don't know how they made it that first year. I suppose Pastor took them things they needed. It's a mercy that people let him stay in Certain at all."

"Really?" I asked, my face bent in growing anger. "The way people treat him is a mercy?"

"People have been looking to get rid of the Barrett family for generations," Ruby said and shrugged. "I think people forgot who he was until he let his wife die and tried to burn the church down."

"Is that what you think he did?" I asked her. I knew my stare was intense and I didn't mean it to be, I just wanted Daniel to have someone on his side.

She shook her head. "Not really. Daniel was a good man."

"He still is," I said emphatically.

Ruby nodded. "People have let the stories grow and it's too thick to unwind now. He became the very devil to some people, a cautionary tale to others, and a ghost to the rest."

"He's not a ghost," I said harshly and stood up, shaking the table, and making some of the game pieces flutter and fall to the floor. "And he's certainly not the devil." I looked around the little kitchen like I was lost. "What do I do now?" I asked.

Ruby stood up as well and put her arms around me. The intimacy of it almost made me cry. "Show him you're different," she said, pulling back to look at me. "Show him you see who he really is."

"I thought I had," I said, deflating. "I thought I had shown him he could trust me. I thought I had made it clear how I felt."

"Those things are all about you," she said, giving me a challenging look. "Show him something about himself."

Chapter 16

Mattie

I didn't know if I'd have a chance to show Daniel anything as another letter from my father arrived. Sitting in the kitchen, I opened the letter with one eye closed. I read it mostly the same. Nothing of great importance; just a list of social engagements he had promised me to in an effort to appeal to my sense of duty to come home. And of course, an update on the teaching position. *I sent in your resume like you asked, including your time served in the community of Certain.* I hadn't really asked him to send the resume and he made it sound like I was in prison here. *Bigger things await you, Mattie,* the letter also read. I knew he meant well. He was only trying to support the dreams I had told him I had.

I sighed and folded the letter back up. I needed something to do to keep my mind busy. I went into the church to sort and put away some books. There was a new box of donations to catalog, and we still needed to finish the rotation for the centers we serviced. Work had become second nature. I had the systems down and knew all the ins and outs. I was all set up for school to start and had a solid handful of kids who claimed they'd come. Ava had even put in a request with the other libraries for a blackboard should one become available. School seemed set to start without a hitch. Maybe it was for the best that my father put in for the job in Asheville for me. I supposed there was some other lady here in Certain who could teach if she wanted to. It didn't come with much salary, but there was free housing and if I got the garden going, there would be food enough. Perhaps when Lizzie came back, she might want the job.

"And you're just going to leave Daniel and the kids," I said aloud to myself. "I didn't think so." I sighed. I didn't want to leave, but it suddenly didn't seem like Daniel cared if I stayed. Perhaps I'd see what happened with the job. If I got it, maybe it would be a sign that I should go home.

I didn't feel much like cataloging books, so I walked across the street toward the grocery. I put my hand on the door to go in but turned first to look back at the church. Sure enough, I could see the windows of the church. I imagined that late at night, with a fire blazing behind the colored glass, the windows would have certainly caught the attention of anyone who glanced that way. I recalled Daniel telling me that Mr. Gibbons was one of the few who treated him well. I already admired Mr. Gibbons, but I thought all the more of him now knowing he had been the one to catch Daniel at his worst, but still treated him respectfully.

The bell over the door jangled as I walked in.

"Good afternoon, Miss Mattie," Mr. Gibbons said, standing just inside the door, straightening the barrels and baskets.

"I'm trying to pretend it is," I said as I closed the door behind me.

"Perspective is everything," he said.

The doorbell jangled again, and Adaline came running up to me. Mr. Gibbons excused himself to check on a pick-up order that he needed to see to, he said.

"Miss Mattie," Adaline called with a flattering delight in her voice. "I read all the stories you left for us. I even drew a picture about one of them like you suggested. I would have brought it if I'd known you were going to be here."

I let her hug me around the waist. I needed that. "That's OK, Adaline, I can get it when I come by your house in a couple of days." The thought of being back at the Collins' homestead now that I knew so much more about the story made my heart sink. "Are you here by yourself?"

A deep voice sounded behind me. "She's here with me."

I turned to see Liam and a few of the other Collins family kids coming through the door. Liam's dark hair was slicked back as if he'd just taken a shower. He was handsome, but in a harsh sort of way. It was hard to look at him for more than a moment, without thinking there was some punishment for doing so, like his very appearance was a trial to be faced. I nodded to him, and he stared at me for a long, painful moment before moving past me. He opened the same countertop flap that Mr. Gibbons had opened and went into the back of the store as if he owned the place.

He called over his shoulder as he left, "Adaline, take the children and get what we need. I'll be out back."

Once he was gone and the screen door at the back of the store banged closed, I asked. "What's out back?"

Adaline shrugged her shoulders and looked disinterested. "He waits to make sure things go like they should."

"Things?" I asked.

"I don't know. We're not really allowed to ask." She picked up a basket and walked to the other side of the store.

Suddenly I knew what she meant. This was Daniel's trade day, and he would pull up behind the store where no one could see him. I was about to let myself through the countertop flap and into the back of the store when the doorbell sounded again.

"Uncle Daniel," one of the little girls shouted and my knees buckled beneath me. I reached out to take hold of the shelf nearest me, rattling the boxes of corn flakes so hard one threatened to fall to the floor.

Calls and squeals erupted from the rest of the children as well and they all ran past me on their way to Daniel, leaving me pushed and pulled along with them like I was caught in a strong current. I righted myself and upon turning, I saw Daniel standing in the doorway. The children were clinging to him and jumping up and down all at once. He looked at me over the tops of their heads. Our eyes lingered for a moment, and then he looked down at the children. His mouth turned up in a smile, but his eyes were forlorn.

Daniel

It was foolish to come in the front door of the store, but I had seen the children going in as I pulled into town, and I wanted to see them. Maybe I wanted them to see me, too. To see that I wasn't whatever monster they'd heard stories about.

"Uncle Daniel," Adaline said, looking all around her as if there was something she was missing, "are Ella and Marie here? Where's baby Hugh?"

"They're not with me, sweetie," I said to her. "I'm just here to," but I caught sight of Mattie and my voice got trapped in my throat for a second. "To get a few things. I should make it quick."

"When are you all coming back around," one of the other kids asked.

"We miss you, Uncle Daniel," another said in a sad voice. "We haven't seen you in forever."

I was relieved that they still wanted to, that they hadn't been told to fear me. I felt a pang of shame as well. Pastor Collins and his family had always treated me well. They had never allowed talk of an unkind nature about me. It seemed that despite it all, they still didn't. At least around the children.

Adaline tugged on my arm, and I turned my attention to her more fully. "What is it, sweetie?"

"Will you tell Ella and Marie and baby Hugh that we said hello?" Adaline said. "Please. It's important."

One of the older boys piped up. "Hugh probably ain't a baby anymore. I bet he can talk and everything now."

"I'll tell them y'all said hello."

I tried not to glance over at Mattie, but I did anyway. Several times in fact, and she caught me at least once. Once all the kids left the store to head for the library it seemed, I thought to try and say something to Mattie, but Mr. Gibbons came out from the back of the store.

"I'm glad to see you walk in like a proper customer again," Mr. Gibbons said. "I apologize for not being at the register. I was waiting out back with your brother."

"I better make it quick then. The usual if you have it available," I said and glanced at Mattie again. She was staring directly at me, and she did not look pleased to see me.

"I readied your order," Mr. Gibbons said. "Anything for me?"

"It's in the wagon," I said. "I don't have the yield I expected, but it's still a good amount. If you need to take out the oatmeal and the toothpaste, we can do without for a while. I got a peppermint mash what does the same. We don't need luxuries." I looked at Mattie again and she had folded her arms over her chest. I hadn't meant no slight to her, but she seemed to take it that way.

Mr. Gibbons was shaking his head. "I'm sure what you've brought is enough. And if it ain't, so be it."

"You got anything else for me?" I asked.

Mr. Gibbons patted his shirt pocket and removed a slip of paper. I glanced at it quickly. A couple of names and a few words. I'd get Ella to help me like I usually did.

"Thank you," I said. "I've got my goods out front."

Mr. Gibbons ducked behind the partition that separated the store from the storeroom and office. I could feel Mattie staring at me, but I didn't dare look at her. Mr. Gibbons was quickly back with a box filled with things that did not grow in a garden in exchange for things that did.

"Go quickly, son," he said and handed the box to me. "I'm not sure why you're risking yourself like this, but I hope it's worth it." He glanced at Mattie and then back at me.

I lowered my eyes and left out the front door without so much as a word to her. I put the box of goods on the seat and went around to fetch my produce and the things I'd made this time around: a lock box, a rocking chair, and a small hope chest. I was pulling things out when I heard Mattie's voice behind me.

"I know good and well that you saw me standing there. And I know you came through town hoping to see me. Are you really planning to leave now and not say a word? That's not like you."

"You know me well enough to know what I would and wouldn't do?" I challenged.

"I think I do," she said.

"I've got to get going, Mattie," I said more dismissively than I meant. "This was foolish of me. There's no use in it. Go on back to Asheville."

"And what makes you think I'm leaving," she said, her hands on her hips and her eyes fixed tightly on mine. "And especially because you tell me to. I can stay here if I want to."

I wanted her to. She moved so that if I looked directly at her, I'd see the parsonage over her shoulder. I couldn't look at it. It had been stupid to come in the front. The back was safer. No one saw me and I didn't see anything for any longer than necessary. This was too hard.

"I told you," I said and turned to fetch one of the boxes. "It's best that we not carry on as if there's some future in the whole thing. I don't know what I was thinking, coming through town. I can't be here like this. I can't be with you."

I had wanted to see her. I thought that perhaps after I'd come in to see Mr. Gibbons and I'd heard whatever it was that Liam had to say for the moment, that I might work up the courage to go to the parsonage to see Mattie. Pipe dreams. I'd treated her terribly and here I was doing it again.

"Daniel," she said, and her voice was soft and wounded. "What's happening? I thought there was something between us?"

I didn't get a chance to answer though. Liam appeared suddenly and shoved her to the side. He grabbed me by the shoulder and punched me solidly in the face before I'd had a chance to process anything. I heard my teeth clack together against the blow.

"Stop," Mattie shouted out and reached for Liam's arm as if there was something she was going to do.

"Mattie," I called out to her.

Liam's eyes flashed with anger, and I knew he wasn't one to be tangled with. I lunged toward him, but Ava came running across the street yelling at us both and calling for the kids trailing behind her to stay back. Her dark hair lifted and swirled in the hot breeze as she approached. My eyes went instinctively to Mattie who stood with her mouth slightly agape and a look on her face that could have been terror or pity. I wasn't sure. Liam swung toward me again, but I could tell that he wasn't aiming for me. His fist landed against the crate of vegetables to my left. I was taken aback by the ferocity of it all. Like flashes of lightning loosed from a storm. I lifted my hands as if I was being held up or arrested.

"I'll go," I said, feeling a thin line of blood trailing from my lip. I held a hand out to Ava. "Take the kids back. I'll leave. I'm sorry."

Ava shook her head, but she didn't speak. I closed my eyes to be rid of her face.

It was Mattie's voice that I heard next. "You don't have to leave, Daniel," she said, and when I opened my eyes, she was looking at Liam in challenge. "This is your home, too."

Liam nudged her aside before stepping closer to me. I wanted to speak out, but I was too cowardly to stand up to him. He rounded his attention to me.

"You was supposed to come around the back," Liam said, lurching at me as if he might strike again. I didn't make to fight back, just held my ground, and only that. Liam spat on the ground by my feet. "He knows his place."

I couldn't do anything but look at the ground. I wiped at the blood on my chin.

"That's ridiculous," Mattie said, clearly outraged. "What do you do, wait out there each week or however often it is to make sure that Daniel doesn't interact with the good people of Certain?"

I hazarded to lift my eyes back up. Mattie glanced at me, but then looked away quickly.

Liam scoffed at her. "You think you know it all. Got us all figured out. Got Daniel figured out. Got me figured out." Liam pressed his hair back into place and eyed me solidly. "What's gotten into you anyway? Coming in the front door. What were you hoping to accomplish?"

I didn't dare look at Mattie again. If Liam hadn't put it all together by how she acted, I wasn't going to finish the puzzle. I shouldn't have made her part of this. She would be better off back in Asheville.

"I'll take these in and go," I said, shooting a painful glance at Ava before gathering one of the crates in my arms and going back inside the store.

Mattie

Daniel took a crate from the wagon and walked it inside the store. Liam, Ava, and I formed a sort of triangle of angst. Across the street, I could see that Adaline had tears in her eyes. Ava stared angrily at Liam who spit on the ground again. I looked back and forth between the lot of them without a clue as to how to fix this long festering wound. I was making things worse.

A bravery came over me and I stepped closer to Liam. I spoke to him in a hard whisper.

"You're the one who makes this difficult. Not Daniel. Let it go."

"Do you have a brother?" he asked me, and I shook my head. "Then what do you know of family and how far you'd go for them?"

I opened my mouth to say something smart, but two things happened at once. I realized he hadn't asked me if I had a sister. He had said brother. This wasn't about Emily after all. Not all of it anyway. Not now. The other thing was that Mr. Gibbons came storming out.

"You can brawl out back all you want to, Mr. Collins, but you'll not be striking my customers in front of my shop. Get on out of here." Mr. Gibbons swung a broom he carried as if he was chasing off a raccoon or some other varmint. Liam made like he was going to spit again. "Do it, son," Mr. Gibbons challenged.

"Liam!" Ava's voice sounded sharply as she crossed the street. "Please, stop."

I looked over toward the church, but the children were gone inside or elsewhere. Ava reached out to Liam and took hold of his hand. He yanked free of her and stomped off.

"I'm so sorry, Mr. Gibbons," Ava said, a dreadful sadness on her face.

He waved her comment off. "Just let Mr. Barrett finish his business without your brother coming back over here and we'll call it done today. We'll get back on schedule next week. I can manage if anything happens."

There was a sternness on his face that I had not seen before, but now greatly appreciated. He went back inside without another word. Daniel came out then and walked without speaking to the wagon to retrieve another crate.

Ava took in a breath and spoke his name. "Daniel."

He stopped, but he didn't look at her. "I'll talk to you later, Ava," he said, looking at the ground. "Let me be."

She nodded even though he didn't see it and walked back across the street without another word. Daniel took the last two crates balanced on top of each other and walked back into the store.

I waited for him to come back out.

When he saw me still standing there he sighed and ran his hand through his hair. "Why are you still here?" he asked and wiped the beads of sweat from his forehead.

I looked up into the burning sky, squinting at the sun. It was easier to look at than the disinterest that radiated off Daniel's face. I closed my eyes, still seeing the white sunspots behind my lids. When I opened my eyes, I caught sight of a tomato that had fallen from one of the crates. I picked it up and threw it at Daniel with all my might. He dodged it, of course, and it hit the wagon behind him.

"What on earth are you doing," he said. "That's terribly childish."

He was trying to make me angry. I knew it. I felt my eyebrow raise at the thought of it. He was being a coward, trying to shun me away for my own good. I didn't want that. I wanted him to fight.

"Why are you pretending that we aren't anything to each other?" I said rather loudly. "Because last I was at your house, it seemed to me that we were getting a little cozy." I noticed that two ladies passing by on the street stopped to listen quite blatantly.

"Cozy?" he said and looked at the women harshly. "I should say not. I have not so much as touched you."

"That's a lie," I said. I knew what he meant, and that part was true, but it was clear that we desired each other's affections, and I was hurt that he was trying to dismiss me publicly.

He clenched his jaw and lurched forward grabbing me by the arm. He yelled at the gawkers to mind their own business and they scurried away. He walked us quickly around the side of the building where I jerked loose from his grip.

"What was that?" I yelled at him.

He leaned forward a bit and put his hands on his knees. His breath was quick and shallow. "What are you trying to do, accusing me of things right out there in the street," he asked when he finally stood up, "have me hunted down and beaten? Because Liam will do it, if you didn't gather that before."

"And I supposed you'd let him," I countered with the real issue I took.

Daniel ran both hands over his hair and breathed out slowly. He stood up straight and looked at me for a long moment.

"I'd have my reasons if I did," he said.

"Daniel," I said and reached for his hand, but he stepped away. "I know the stories. I know Emily died at the parsonage and I know how you took the kids and left. I know about the church and all of it."

Daniel sighed. "Liam's right. You just know the series of events, Mattie. That's the least of it. I deserve to be driven away. I did the things they all accuse me of. All the things you know and some that you obviously don't. I'm too much of a coward to tell you the things I did. If you knew all of it, you'd leave now."

"Everybody makes mistakes, Daniel."

He looked at me and started to say something, but then looked again at the ground.

"I did come around front today because I hoped to see you," he said, changing the subject. "I know you gathered that. I was acting that way because I didn't know what to say to you once you were there. I know you gathered that too."

I nodded.

"I want you, Mattie," he said and stepped in close. "But it's a mistake," he said. "I was wrong. I was better off playing the monk and accepting the life I have. Which isn't a bad one, mind you. I should have known that I'd fall for someone I couldn't have. It's OK. You go on and do what you need to do. I won't be angry with you for going back to your regular life."

"I'm not going anywhere, Daniel."

"This novelty will wear off, Mattie," he said, gesturing at himself. "You think you know all there is to know, but you don't. Liam does and he punched me square in the jaw for it even after all this time. You should take your cue from Liam."

"And punch you?"

"Why not," he said and shrugged.

I don't know what came over me, but I raised my hand and aimed to slap him across the face. He caught my wrist before I made contact. He held tight, bringing my hand down to my side, but not letting it go.

"You should go back to Asheville," he said, calmly.

"Let me go then," I said and tried to yank free of his grasp. He tightened his hold.

"I can't," he said desperately and stepped closer to me again. He closed his eyes and after a long minute he let go of my wrist. His chest heaved with shallow breaths. His eyes remained closed. "Go. If you're going, go. Please."

He clenched his jaw, but I could tell that it wasn't in anger. It was to keep from trembling. I looked at the scruff of his beard where it was returning. Trying to be different but going back time and again to the man he'd become. He saw that man as a monster for reasons I supposed I didn't understand yet. I saw his beauty no matter what. His black lashes were long and thick. His jaw was square and rugged. The side of his mouth where the punch had landed was starting to swell and turn purple, but still he was beautiful. It was a beauty that came from the inside out whether he wanted to believe in that or not.

I raised up on my toes and pressed my lips softly to the spot Liam had injured. I placed my hand over Daniel's heart, the spot that held the most injury of all. His eyes fluttered open, and he grabbed hold of me with both hands on my hips. He pushed against me until my back was pressed to the brick wall of the Certain Grocery. I sucked in a tiny breath, and he kissed me hard on the mouth. Rough and desperate at first and then he sank into it as did I, and his lips found a softer measure and his kiss slowed and deepened. His hands stayed on my hips while mine searched for a place to land firmly—his arm, his face, his hair. His beard stubble was rough on my face, but it felt like the finest pleasure against my skin.

He pulled away before I wanted him to, and he stepped back from me. "I apologize," he said. "I don't know how to do this."

"I beg to differ," I said, flushed through and through. "I've not had much experience, but I wager that was pretty good."

He smiled, a blush across his cheeks, but he shook his head and stepped closer to me. He put his hands first on my shoulders and then on the sides of my face. "Mattie," he said and touched my hair. "I don't know how to know you, when you don't know me."

"I do know you," I said. "As much as you know me. That's sort of what the start of it is."

He nodded. "I don't know how to start when I'm already at the end."

Suddenly I felt that prickle of anger rising again. I knew what he was doing. Pushing me away. "Don't you dare," I said. "Don't you dare take the easy way out again."

He pushed me slightly, more to make a greater distance between us than in anger. This wasn't going to end with another kiss, I knew it, but I needed him to understand.

"Don't you dare run away," I said. "Hiding out with the kids and exiling them from their family all these years. Letting Liam punch you in the face in the parking lot of the grocery store and not fighting back. Looking at the ground when people talk to you like you're a dog." I was nearly shouting at him. "Fight, Daniel. Don't let people spit at your feet and tell you you're no good. Don't play into some family history of dancing with the devil. Fight. If not for yourself, then for Hugh. Don't turn him into that lost little boy you were."

He looked at me and I couldn't tell what thoughts were behind the eyes that glared green and hard. He shouted out like that day I'd come up on him chopping wood. He punched the wall beside me.

He cursed and put his hands over his face. He reared back like he was going to hit the wall again and I could see the way he'd busted up his knuckles already; he would be lucky if he hadn't broken his hand.

"Don't," I yelled. "Daniel, stop."

He pulled his hand back like maybe he wasn't going to do it, but then he couldn't seem to control himself, and he hit the wall again anyway. He whispered something, but I couldn't hear him. He turned and walked back around to the front of the building. I heard him get into the seat of his wagon, call to his horse, and pull away. I closed my eyes, not wanting to see him go.

I stood shaking and trying to get myself back together for a long few minutes before walking back to the parsonage on wobbly legs. I had thought I might make myself a cup of tea, but when I went inside, I bypassed the kitchen and went directly up the stairs to the room in which I had noticed the books. They were Daniel's children's books of course.

I knelt in front of the small bookcase and pulled a book from the low shelves. I looked at the inside cover. There was an inscription penned in lovely writing—*To Ella and Marie from your Mother and Father.* I opened another one to see the name Ella scrawled in a child's writing. A lump formed in my throat as I ran my fingers over the script. My heart broke for Daniel and for his children—and for Emily who was gone. I ran my fingers over the spines on the other books and pulled one last one to me. I opened the front cover and a photograph fell out onto the floor. I picked it up and on turning it, I gasped. The photo showed a family standing in front of the church. Two little girls in Sunday dresses smiled out at the camera. They were younger, but it was clearly Ella and Marie. And a woman, very pregnant, looked down at them. My eyes blinked at the face I had seen before. Ava's face. I studied it hard and then realized why Daniel wouldn't—couldn't— look at her and why she hadn't taken to bringing books to the kids when their original carrier left. She and Emily were twins. The very image of each other. My whole body broke out in chills, and I could feel my skin raise up in little bumps—all the way into my hair.

I looked at Daniel in the picture. His arm was slung over Emily's shoulder, and he was looking down at Ella and Marie with such a look of adoration that my heart ached. I touched the little family reverently and tucked the picture back into the book. I stuck the book back onto the shelf and sat back on my heels.

I was still for a long while, and then I crawled up onto one of the little beds and burrowed underneath the covers. It was still broad daylight, but I closed my eyes and let a sleep born of exhaustion take hold of me.

Chapter 17

Mattie

The next day at the library, I couldn't stop looking at Ava. My eyes continuously flitted away from the scrapbook I was making and over to the circulation desk where she worked. Every time she passed her hand over her hair or shifted in her seat to cross or uncross her legs, I wondered about Emily. Were their mannerisms the same, or just their face? Would Emily have worn her hair shorter to her shoulders the way Ava did now or would it be longer like it was in that photograph.

"You didn't know they were twins, did you?" Ruby's voice found not just my ears, but my very heart.

She had brought her chair with her to the table where I worked and sat down beside me.

"No, I did not," I said and ran my fingers lightly over the drawing I was positioning in the scrapbook. "I suppose it doesn't matter. It's just a shock."

I looked at Ruby and she nodded her head. "What are you making?"

I picked up the scrapbook gingerly, but proudly. "It's nearly done,"

I said and handed it to Ruby. "It's a collection of stories and pictures. I was going to show it to Ava and see if we could put it in circulation, but now, after yesterday," I paused and didn't finish the sentence. "It seemed like a good idea at the time."

"What happened yesterday?" she asked. "Did you and Daniel talk?"

"I guess you could say that," I said. "I think we argued, but we kissed, but then he punched the wall and left." I was telling it all wrong, but that was the gist of it.

Ruby lowered her voice, but her whisper was still loud enough that I waved my hands around to shush her when she spoke. "You kissed?" she asked, her eyes wide open.

"It's neither here nor there, really," I said. "I don't want to talk about it."

Which was a lie.

Ruby eyed me for a moment and then flipped through the pages of the scrapbook, pausing here and there either to look more closely at a picture or to read a few lines of story. "It's delightful," she said and pointed to the creek pictured in one of the drawings. "Is that the Hell for Certain?"

I beamed. "It is," I said. "This is Certain's very first illustrated short story collection. Pictures by Adaline Norris and stories by Ella Barrett."

Ruby made a little gasping sound. She looked at me and paused. "You do know who those children are, yes?"

I laughed. "I do," I said, "but thank you for being ready to offer a fast clarification."

Ruby opened back to the first story and read a couple of pages. She skipped ahead, reading a paragraph here and there. There were six stories in all and about twice as many pictures.

"This is about Daniel and his kids," she said and closed the book reverently. "If they were raccoons that is. Are they happy stories in the end?"

"Eventually," I said, recalling the progression of the overall story arc. "They don't start out that way, but there is hope by the end."

I opened the scrapbook and turned to the last story which Ella had just given me not long ago. I read a passage that was clearly about

Daniel, and his family, and even about me.

The daddy raccoon asked his daughter what she wanted most of all from the forest, for he had been planning to go on a gathering trip. It wasn't his usual trip and she wondered if perhaps he himself was going in search of something special.

"Da," the little girl raccoon said and tucked her tail underneath her because she was afraid to ask for what she really wanted.

"What is it, my darling," her father asked her. "I will do my best to get you anything your heart desires."

He said things like that to her often and although she knew he wasn't able to get her anything much at all, she knew that he wanted to more than anything, and so that made the offer of it even more special than whatever the thing itself might have been.

But this time, she did have something that she wanted. She couldn't bring herself to ask, and so her father tried to guess, naming all the things that he knew she loved.

"Is it berries from the thicket," he asked. "The ripe red juicy ones?"

She shook her raccoon head and closed her eyes.

"Is it a great wiggly fish from the cold waters of the creek?"

She squeezed her eyes tighter and shook her head again.

"Is it a song on your old Da's fiddle," he asked, guessing the thing that she usually wanted the most.

She shook her head again and opened her eyes. She would take a chance and ask for the things that she desired the most. Now, dear reader, you might think that you could guess as you know well by now the sad little story of the little raccoon's life and all the things that she and her father had lost. You'd be right, she wanted those things, but those things weren't possible. This new thing that she wanted was.

"I want you not to be lonely," she said. "I want me and my brother and sister to not be lonely. I want you to gather up our cousins from across the creek and I want you to shake hands with our uncles and I want them to shake hands with you. I want you to play your fiddle around the fire and for us all to dance and sing like we used to do, and," she paused, about to ask for something she didn't know if she should, but since it was all spilling out faster than she could keep control of, she let the words fall out of her mouth, "I want you to go through the forest and into the city and back to our old house where a new raccoon lives and I want you to invite her to come live with us. We don't have much room, but we love her very much and we know you do as well."

After the girl was finished, she realized she had once again closed her eyes, so afraid was she to ask for all these things. When she opened them, she could see that her father was crying. She'd like to say she had never seen him cry and as far as he knew, she hadn't, but he cried from time to time, just not in front of her and not like this where the tears glistened off his shiny black and brown fur like little diamonds that were beautiful but weren't worth anything to people who didn't know him.

"If only I could," he said. "But no one wants to visit us, my darling. I wish there was something I could do to change that."

"But Da," she said. "If they knew how nice you were, they'd come back."

She said this, because the other creatures in the forest thought that her father was a bad raccoon as sometimes raccoons can be. Even the other raccoons along the creek thought that and the other creatures that weren't really all that different from raccoons themselves thought that too. She and her brother and sister knew the truth. And so did the new raccoon that lived in their old den.

"What if I ask and she says no," her father asked and wiped his tears away with his paw. "It's scary to try again. I think I'm just used to the life we live now. It's not the best, but it's happy enough. I have you three little cubs and that's all I need."

But it wasn't all he needed, and she knew that. He needed love and forgiveness and a chance to be happy again. So, she decided that she'd go on the gathering trip and gather things up for herself, her sibling raccoons, and for her darling father who loved her so dearly that he could hardly stand it. She knew this of course, because he told his children that every night before they went to sleep in their cozy straw beds, in the corner of their tiny but perfect little cabin.

"Stop," Ava said, the word catching in her throat and her breath coming out in jagged little puffs.

I looked up sharply to see her standing there with tears streaming down her face. I looked quickly to Ruby whose hands were both planted against her own heart and who wore a tortured look.

"Ava," I said and nearly jumped from my seat. "I'm sorry. I thought the book would be a fun idea at first. Something cute that perhaps the cousins could make, and I could share it with you. I thought it would be some sort of bridge back to better communication, but that was before I knew the depth of it all. How naive of me."

"Not naive at all," she said and reached out toward me. I took it that she wanted the book, so I held it out to her. She took the book and upon seeing the picture that I had used for the cover, she put one hand over her mouth and tears rolled again from her eyes. "This is Adaline's."

Ava stepped backward and sat down instinctively on the end of one of the pews. She turned toward the front of the church and let her gaze fall on the place that the altar once was. Ruby touched my shoulder and nodded for me to go and sit with Ava. I touched Ruby's hand in friendship and nodded back.

I went to stand at the end of the pew. "May I?"

Ava scooted over and I sat down. Ava sighed then and opened the book. "It's different when you hear it from a child," she said and then looked back at me. "Or maybe it isn't really. Maybe it just causes you to listen differently."

"The story ends on a hopeful note," I added.

"I'm glad," she said and reverently turned one page and then the next.

"I was going to ask you if I could put it in circulation," I said, "but that was before I could so clearly see what it was about and before I knew all the things I know now."

"Daniel was a good man," she said.

"He still is."

She nodded and hugged the book to her chest. "Show it to the girls and to Daniel. If they agree, we'll put it in circulation." She handed it back to me. "Have you talked to him since yesterday? I suppose not, as you're here."

"No," I said. "Things went from strange to worse, and I'm not sure that he wants to see me."

"I'm sure he does," she said and stood up. "You should go before too much time passes. He'll be churning things over in his mind, and he's not kind to himself in his thoughts."

She was right about that.

She put her chin in her hands and looked at me sideways. "Did Daniel ever tell you how he and Zach and Liam used to get on?"

"He said they were close," I answered, recalling the story he'd told about Pastor Collins taking him to live with them after his parents died. "Like brothers."

"Like brothers," Ava repeated in confirmation. She smiled as she recalled it. "Daniel was eleven when he came to live with us. Dad called them the three musketeers. They had a fort in the woods that Emily and I used to try and infiltrate, but they always caught us and sent us running and squealing back home." She laughed to herself and shook her head. "I have tons of stories, don't let me get started."

"I'd love to hear them," I said.

"One day," she nodded at me. "Thing is, Daniel was like their little brother. Zach was thirteen and Liam already fifteen by the time Daniel came. We knew him. Well, we knew of him. Everyone did."

"The stories about his family?"

She nodded. "Dad said that Daniel didn't have anywhere else to go and we were to take him in like one of our own. He said that he'd best not hear one breath of talk about the Barretts being bad seeds or anything of the sort. He told us that a man can be whatever he aims to be, and we were to help Daniel aim to see that he was a child of God, not the son of Satan like people were wont to think of that family. We were his new family and that was that."

"I can't imagine Liam ever liking Daniel," I said, scoffing at the thought.

"Oh, they were the closest of all," Ava said.

"What?"

"So much so that Zachary was fairly jealous," Ava said. "More than once he and Liam came to fists over it. It took them a while, but they all worked it out. I swear, if you didn't know that Daniel wasn't blood, you wouldn't have known he wasn't. Those three were thick as thieves and in and out of trouble like them too," she said and smiled again at memories I knew nothing of. "They loved Daniel like he was indeed their little brother. They loved him so much they didn't balk when he and Emily started to have eyes for each other several years later. Liam actually encouraged her when she wasn't sure if she wanted to claim Daniel as her beau."

"Liam?" I questioned. "Are you sure?"

Perhaps that explained his anger. Maybe he felt like her death had been his fault.

"I was there," she said. "I should know." She winked at me.

"I just can't imagine it," I said. I had seen the look in Daniel's eyes when he talked about Liam and Zachary. He missed them; I could see that. "I guess I knew how he felt about them, but I didn't realize they had felt the same."

"Oh indeed," she said. "Just you let anyone say anything about him and either of them get wind of it," she shook her head. "More than once Daddy had to get one of them out of jail over a beating they'd given someone for looking at Daniel wrong."

Perhaps she thought she was making me feel more kindly toward Liam, but the more she talked about the way things had been the angrier I got. How could Liam treat Daniel the way he did now, considering all that.

"I'm sorry, I'm just not in the mood to be told how wonderful Liam is right now," I said and stood up. Ava stood up as well, but I stepped away before she could stop me.

"I'm sorry, Mattie," she called, even as I walked away from her. "I just wanted you to know that things weren't always like this. There was a time when they were better."

I turned to say something, but I couldn't think what. I shook my head and left quickly through the side door. I headed around toward the parsonage and out of the corner of my eye, I saw Liam exit the front of the grocery. Before I gave myself a chance to think better of it, I hightailed it across the street and near about burned up the very ground underfoot making tracks toward him. I didn't even announce myself, I just started talking.

"You better have an explanation for the way you treated Daniel the other day," I said, my voice raised as I had started my rant before I even got across the street good.

Liam turned around slowly, like he either didn't think I was talking to him or didn't care.

"Pardon?" he said and ran a hand through perfect hair.

I walked right up to him, stopping on the other side of the common threshold of personal space. I thought he might back up, but he didn't.

"Ava told me all about how close the three of you were, how much you were like family, how it was three Collins sons and not just the two once Daniel came to live with you."

"Did she?"

I scoffed. I knew what he was doing. "I can see you coming halfway down the mountain, Liam," I said, thinking I was calling him out. "Answering me short and sweet with that tone in your voice like you know something I don't know."

I suspected that part might be true, but his way about it annoyed me, nonetheless.

"There's your problem right there," he said without seeming to be annoyed by me at all. He pointed his finger at me when he said it, but matter-of-factly. "You come over here from the big city with your big mouth, talking about things you don't know nothing about." His voice was mostly calm, but there was a hint of a rising storm as he spoke. "You think you've got it all pieced out, and maybe you know a good portion of it, but you ain't in it. You ain't from it."

I knew what he was getting at. The history. The length of it. The weight of it. But I wasn't in total agreement.

"I might not be from it," I said. "But make no mistake, I am in it."

He cocked his head and smirked. "You ain't nothing but talk. It takes a lot longer of knowing these hills and these people to have a right to judge anything we do. You think you know why I show up here to keep Daniel in line?"

"I know exactly why you do," I said, my hands finding my hips. "You hate him. Despite your history and your brotherhood," I said making quotes in the air, "you can't forgive him for a turn of fate that wasn't his fault. No matter what you think he did or didn't do. He didn't kill Emily."

"Is that right?" he asked.

He was baiting me, I knew, but I was biting no matter. "Yes, and now you're taking your justice by making his life miserable."

He shook his head and chortled. "Like I figured," he said, and spit on the ground just shy of my shoes. "You're about as wrong as snow falling in the summertime. That ain't it at all."

I put my hands back on my hips. "Well, do enlighten me."

Liam's eyes flashed a cold blue flame of anger and he stepped, at first, closer to me like he might grab me by the shirt collar, but then he stepped away.

"Sure, I'm sick to my gut over Emily every day since she died, but I don't hate Daniel. I love Daniel," he said, looking me hard in the eyes. "Daniel is my brother sure as blood and I dare you to question me about that again." He paused like he was waiting for me to. I didn't say a word and he nodded. "I come here to protect him. I come to make sure he does his business here in town and gets on back home before those less tolerant of the man who let the pastor's daughter die while he was off running moonshine get to him first. I come here to keep him safe."

"Safe?" I shifted my weight. This explanation was not what I had expected, but I wasn't ready to see Liam in a more gracious light just yet. "That's why you punched him in the mouth?"

"It surely is," Liam said. "And that's on you."

"Me," I said, indignantly.

"People don't take kindly to the man who turned the devil loose and almost burned down the church while he was at it," Liam said. "That's why people don't go anymore. They think the devil's taken up residence there."

"There's nothing in there but books," I said, incredulous.

Liam shook his head. "I don't know what got into Daniel—thinking he could come right up to the front door," Liam said and gave me a hateful look. "Trying to fool you or impress you, heck, I don't know what he was doing, but that kind of recklessness gets tongues wagging and next thing you know people start to plotting."

"Plotting what?"

"Use your booksy imagination, Miss Library, and I bet you still won't come up with something ugly enough. People get scared and they look for someone to take things out on."

"So, you hurt Daniel to keep him safe?" I was the one baiting the hook then.

"We take care of our own, here," Liam said. "The way we might do it ain't none of your business, so I'd advise you keep your big mouth shut."

"Well, with my big mouth I'm going to suggest you come up with a better way to take care of your brother," I said, spitting that word out at him just like he'd spit his disdain for me on the ground. "Because he thinks you hate him. He says as much and his heart breaks over it every time he sees you, sees Ava, sees anyone in this wretched place." Which it wasn't—I loved this place more than I knew how to manage, and I didn't mean that part, but that's what it felt like in that moment. "So, you take your theories of what the townsfolk might do to him and weigh that against a lifetime of loneliness and sorrow. Which do you think hurts worse? Maybe it would be a kindness to put him out of his misery. And that's on you," I said and pointed my finger back at Liam as he had done to me.

I spun on my heels and stalked back over to the parsonage without so much as a look back. My whole body trembled with anger, confusion and mostly fear. I could barely stand up by the time I wobbled up the steps and reached for the doorknob. I stumbled up the stairs and fell straight away onto the bed where I let myself cry until there was nothing left of me but heaving sobs.

Chapter 18

Daniel

I didn't want to admit that I had taken to sitting out on the front porch of an afternoon so that I could watch for Mattie, but admit it or not, that was the truth of it. I knew right where I could find her, but I hadn't worked up the courage to go. Perhaps it was best that we just stopped now. It was better for everyone that way.

So, why, when I thought I heard Opal's whinny in the wind, did I sit up straight and train my eyes on the clearing? I shook my head at myself for imagining things and I closed my eyes against the bright understanding that I wanted more than anything to see that stubborn horse and its stubborn rider come up from the creek bed.

Then there they were. I hurried off the porch fast enough to give my hand away if she was looking for such signs. It wasn't a day she'd usually come, so I counted this a good thing. Although she was one to speak her mind and she could just as soon be here to finish telling me off.

I tried to gauge what I might have in store, but her face was blank.

She pulled Opal to a stop and dismounted.

"I'm glad you came," I said, deciding to speak first. "I tried to go see you again, but I was too much of a coward."

She exhaled heavily and I wasn't sure I'd said the right thing or just the opposite.

"I wasn't the nicest version of myself," she said, and gave an apologetic smile.

Relief poured over me. "I've never had someone kiss me and then yell at me all in the same breath," I said, and she smiled.

"You've got me off kilter," she said.

"Likewise."

Her smile was easy, even if there was still an apprehension in her eyes. She had something yet that she wanted to say. I could tell.

"I have some things for you," she said, opening the saddlebag and removing the small stack of books. "They're from your old house. I thought the children would want them."

She held out the books to me, and I took them carefully. I recognized them, of course.

"I found something else as well," she said and touched the top book on the stack in my hands. "Open it."

I opened the front flap of the top book to find a photograph of my family. I looked back at Mattie to find that she was very obviously nervous. She needn't be.

"Thank you," I said, and placed the photograph in my shirt pocket. I nodded at the books. "The children will like these very much. I didn't think to take them that night."

She touched my arm and my eyes again found hers. I could see the relief on her face, and I knew she had been as worried as I was about our next meeting, or if there would be one.

"Would you like to come inside?" I asked, shifting the load of books to one arm and when she nodded yes, I put my other hand behind her to guide her in. I wanted to touch her, to hold her hand or place my palm on her back, but I didn't dare too much.

Inside, the house was dark due to the overcast nature of the day and the air inside was unexpectedly cool. The children were all sitting on my bed and Ella was reading them a story. They all jumped up at seeing Mattie and ran to circle their little arms around her waist and legs.

"Miss Mattie, Miss Mattie," Marie chimed.

"We didn't know you were a-comin'," little Hugh said. He had grown so much more talkative since Mattie had come around the first time. "Did you bringed us a book?"

"Actually, she did," I said and offered the books out to them. "Girls, do you remember these? Your mother used to read them to you."

The girls practically squealed at the sight of them, clearly recognizing them from years gone by.

"Can we keep them, Miss. Mattie?" Ella asked, hugging the ones she'd grabbed close to her chest.

"Of course," Mattie said and then looked at me. "They're yours after all."

"Thank you, Miss Mattie," Ella said and hugged her again.

I left the photograph in my pocket. Showing them would be best suited for a different time. Looking at Hugh, I realized that he'd never seen what his mother looked like. He had seen Ava a time or two very early on when we got here, but he was too little to understand, and there was no point in confusing him.

"Ella," I said, having to touch her arm to actually get her attention away from the books, "why don't you take the children onto the porch and read for a while. It's light yet. I'd like to talk to Miss Mattie."

Ella looked at me and smiled as if she was pleased by this. She nodded and tugged the children outside the house. I stepped to the door and closed it softly. I nodded toward the couch, and we sat. The small sofa didn't allow much space between the two of us, and I could all but feel the racing of her heart. I figured she could feel my nervousness, too. After a moment I took the picture from my pocket and looked at it again.

"Thank you for giving this to me," I said. "I wondered what became of it. It's the only photograph I have of the girls when they were younger. I have none of Hugh. I thought perhaps my in-laws had it." I shook my head. "I shouldn't call them that. They aren't anymore, I suppose, and I don't want you to think that I am still attached to them in that way."

"But you are," she said, shifting her position on the couch to be able to look straight at me "They're still your family, and that's OK. More than OK."

I looked back at the picture. "Did you know that she and Ava were twins?"

"Not until I saw that photograph," she said and winced a bit. "Is that why you wouldn't look at her the other day in town? Is it too hard to see the reminder of Emily?"

"No," I said, wishing it were that easy. "It's hard not to look at Ava and think about what I did to her."

Mattie sat back and I knew I was delivering news she didn't know. This was what I meant when I told her she didn't know the worst of it.

"I'm sure she didn't tell you, did she?" I asked. Mattie shook her head and I nodded. "I figured as much. She's too kind to me."

"Ava cares for you and the kids very much," she said.

Although that should have been a lovely statement, it was painful to hear.

"I don't deserve her grace," I said and took in a deep breath. I stood up and moved away from Mattie. At first, I kept my back to her, but if I was going to tell this, I needed to see her reaction. It would tell me everything. "I knew Emily was sick, but I didn't know how to fix it and I was too ashamed to ask for help. I had begged God for Hugh. I wanted a son. Not that I didn't love my daughters, don't understand me wrong." I winced. I wasn't telling it in a way that made sense, but I hadn't planned for this conversation. "I got what I asked for, a boy, but something inside Emily never healed after the birth. She didn't get well like she had with the girls."

I looked at Mattie, she was listening intently. She either didn't know this part already or was at least offering me the chance to tell my side of it.

"It's my fault," I said. "Liam was right. I had picked up work running moonshine. I wasn't making it or selling it. Just delivering. It was a little bit of money at least, but I was gone for days and days at a time. Emily died while I was away."

"You couldn't have known that would happen," Mattie said, and I wanted to feel relief at her understanding, but I didn't deserve that either.

"I was trying to help," I said of my misguided efforts. "I didn't manage nothing but to neglect my own family and be gone when my wife passed alone in the house with the kids. Thank God it was Ava who found her."

I closed my eyes and when I opened them again Mattie had stood up from the couch and had come closer to me. She looked at me as if asking permission to comfort me. I wanted it. I didn't know how to accept it. I closed my eyes again and felt her hand circle around mine. I covered my face with my other hand to try and stifle the emotion that I knew showed all over it.

"God forgive me," I said, and I heard my voice break across the words. "When I was on the road, I could put it all out of my head." I uncovered my face and scraped my hand through my hair. I felt Mattie's grip on me tighten.

"Daniel," she whispered. "You don't have to tell me all this. It doesn't matter."

But I did. I needed her to know how bad I'd done. I didn't want her to fall for some idea of me that wasn't true.

"I even thought about leaving," I said, looking her hard in the eyes. "That shames me more than anything. I thought about the freedom of going somewhere no one knew me. Getting a job, starting over." I was sick to my stomach to tell it. "I wouldn't have, though. It was just a sad dream of things being easy. Those desperate things that cross your mind when you don't mean for them to."

"I know that Daniel," she said and reached up to let her fingers touch my cheek. I flinched and looked away. "Daniel, look at me," she whispered.

"I can't."

I hung my head and she stood on her toes and kissed the top of it. My whole body trembled.

"I told you my mother passed when I was a child, right?" Mattie asked and I looked at her, confused.

"Yes."

"Come sit," she said and pulled us back to the couch. "I didn't tell you that it was because of something so simple and unnecessary that it doesn't even seem like a reason someone would die." She took a breath and took both my hands in hers. "I wanted a cake from the bakery across the street from my father's office. She told me no because it was nearly time for dinner and that we'd make a cake together later. I loved baking with my mother, but I wanted cake right then. I was insistent, and she felt guilty. I knew that, and I used it against her." Mattie squeezed my hands, and I knew that it was she who needed the comfort. I squeezed back.

Mattie took in a breath and blew it out. "She'd had to cancel a picnic we were planning in order to help my father at work, and it was already late when she finished her work. I knew how to push her buttons and get what I wanted. It worked. So, she said she'd go across the street and get one small cake. I remember it so vividly. She held up one finger and tilted her head just a little. She whispered for me not to tell my father and winked at me. Then she went to get my cake and she died."

I closed my eyes and breathed in deeply. My heart ached for her. "What happened?" I asked her.

"She was hit by an automobile," Mattie said. "The owner had just gotten it and was not accustomed to driving at all. I don't know the whole circumstance as my father would never speak to me about it. I don't know if she died later at the hospital or if she died right there. I know the driver went off the road and she was struck on the sidewalk and because he didn't know how to brake, she was run up against the side of the bakery where I had sent her to buy a cake."

Her eyes had drifted from me and to the far off in memory.

"I am so sorry, Mattie," I said softly. What a devastation. "That was an accident, you know that, right?"

She nodded. "Sure, but one that I caused. Or at least I feel like I did."

I nodded my understanding. I breathed in and out slowly, closing my eyes. I needed to finish my confession. It was only fair after she had shared hers.

"After I brought the kids here that night, I rode back into town," I said, opening my eyes. "I meant to get a few of the things I knew we'd left in my haste to go. When I got to the house it was empty and I couldn't make myself go back in. So, I went over to the church thinking I'd pray or cry or something, I don't even know, Mattie. I had lost myself entirely."

"It's OK, Daniel," she said as if to stop me from telling this part.

I imagine she'd heard some of it, but she didn't know it all. "Ava and Pastor Collins were there," he said and shook his head. "I wonder sometimes how things would be if they hadn't been there. Not like I think anything I did was their fault, but if it hadn't happened. Or if I'd had the sense to just turn around and leave." I shrugged. I'd already thought on that more times than I could count. "Maybe it would have been worse. Who's to say?"

I felt my heart beating fast and fluttery like a bird. Mattie's gaze was steady, and her hands were tight on mine. I felt as if I could say anything to her and she wouldn't leave me. It was a heady feeling and it spurred me on.

"My eyes landed on Ava's face, and I forgot everything Pastor Collins ever told me. I forgot the person he said I could be and became the man I thought I was. I rushed at Ava and grabbed her by the throat." I stopped to see if she'd leave. Mattie's eyes widened a bit, but she didn't flinch. "I don't know what came over me, Mattie," I said, the worst of it about to come out. "I had her down on the ground. I begged God to take her and give me back Emily." My voice hitched. "I screamed it, loud, and I could have killed her right there if I thought it would have worked."

I stopped and pulled my hands from Mattie's. I felt ill. I pulled in a ragged breath and had to work hard not to vomit up my guilt and loathing.

"She didn't even try to get away," I continued and shivered against the thought of it.

I didn't know my eyes had welled with tears until the water dropped over my lids and ran down my cheeks. Mattie's hand moved quickly to brush them away. The intimacy of the gesture moved me. I could tell that she wasn't clearing them from my face because she didn't want to see me cry, but rather that she was trying to remove the sadness from my soul. I opened my mouth to speak again, and my voice quivered. "Then Liam and Zach were there pulling me off her. I guess they'd been in the house and heard me yelling. I think Liam held Zachary back from killing me straight out."

"Liam?" she asked, but then nodded. "Daniel, I'm so sorry. I can't imagine how hard this is to hold inside like you do."

I almost couldn't bear the acceptance. There was more yet and I wondered what the tipping point would be where she'd change her mind.

"Pastor Collins collapsed," I said. "He dropped to his knees and Ava got up and rushed toward him yelling for Liam and Zach. They all crowded around Pastor, and I gathered that he was having a heart attack. Because of me and what I was doing, what I did to Emily and to Ava. I lost myself. I just started tearing things up. There he was lying on the ground, this man who had saved me and I was tearing up the whole church, Mattie. Busting up the altar and kicking in the pews. I was an animal. I was the devil."

"Daniel," she said quietly, slipping down on the floor in front of me and wrapping her arms around me. "You're not the devil. You're not."

I relaxed into her embrace and spoke the rest of it into her hair.

"They took him out of the church," I said, seeing it all as clear as yesterday in my mind. "I thought he'd died. I saw a little candle sitting on the floor. My mother always lit candles when she prayed. I thought maybe I could call on God one last time and try to make things right. I lit that candle before I had thought about where I was going to put it. It was just a nub of a thing and not much flame, but it was burning my hand before long, and I dropped it."

I could hear Mattie shushing me like you would a child. She didn't need to hear the rest, but I needed to tell it. I wasn't sure that I'd ever told anyone this part.

"I figured the candle had gone out when it hit the floor," I said. "So, I walked up to the window with the picture of Mary and baby

Jesus. I tried to pray, but I didn't know how to start, so I just sat down on the floor and cried. Before long I could hear a crackling, like fire. I turned to see that a stack of hymnals I had torn up was on fire. I guess the candle had caught them. I tried to step it out, but it was suddenly too big and all I was doing was spreading it around. The door was open, and the wind came in, just hard enough to fuel the flames. I didn't know what to do, so I just gave in to it."

I straightened up and pulled back so that I could see her face. It was full of kindness and the sort of pity that is really understanding without the ability to change anything for the person.

"I pulled out another match and lit it," I said, shaking my head at the strangeness of the act. "I lit the Bible that Pastor preached from and then tossed it onto the pile of wood that had been the altar." I could barely get the words out. It was such a horrible thing to have done.

I scoffed at myself and shrugged. "I had given up. Then Mr. Gibbons came running in asking if I was OK, checking me over like I was hurt. I yelled for him to get out and just let me burn up, but he wouldn't go. I reached into the fire and grabbed a board. I threw it at him, but he ducked, and it smashed out the window instead." I exhaled hard. The telling of the thing was exhausting. "I laughed, Mattie. Can you believe that? I busted out that picture of Mary and little baby Jesus and the angels all around. Heaven itself. I busted down Heaven and I laughed. The devil inside me laughed."

"Daniel, stop," she said and put her fingers to my lips. "It's OK. It's over."

"God himself hates me," I said against her fingers. "What chance have I left?"

She turned me loose then and I was relieved in a way to have finally convinced her I was not worth her time. Saddened, but relieved. I thought she was leaving when she stood up, but instead she put her hands on her hips like she did when she was readying to give someone what for.

"God does not hate you," she said forcibly. "Nor does Emily. Nor will the children. Nor does Liam for that matter. Nor do I think you are not worth having." She leaned forward and pressed her lips to my forehead, leaving them there for a long moment.

"How can you hear what I did and not hate me," I asked. "What sort of person can do those things?"

"That's not who you are," she said. "It's something you did. That's all."

I closed my eyes and squeezed them shut tight. I felt her sit back beside me on the couch. I looked at her hopefully.

"Perhaps God has some small measure of love for me, after all," I said.

"More than small, Daniel," she replied in a pleading voice. Willing me to believe her. "And I do as well. You know that right? That I love you."

I looked down, but she nudged my chin until my eyes met hers again.

"I'm not going anywhere," she said. I'm not going back to Asheville. I'm not going to leave you. You can trust me, Daniel," she said. "Is that all of it? Everything you've been keeping inside?"

I nodded. That was it. All of it, told finally.

"OK then," she said as if that was that.

"OK then?" I repeated.

She leaned close to me and kissed my cheek, then she pressed her lips softly to mine. I could taste the salt of my own tears on her lips. I pulled her solidly to me and kissed her deeply. My arms wound around her, and her lips left mine only long enough here and there to whisper things against my skin. I might have forgotten myself had the front door not opened and Ella came in with Hugh crying in her arms.

Mattie and I pulled away from each other like one of us was electric and we didn't know which one it was. Ella glanced at us and I could see in her eyes what she longed for. She smiled slightly and crossed the room to lay Hugh down on the bed.

I stood up quickly. "Is he alright?"

"He fell on the steps," Ella said and kissed Hugh's head. "He's OK. He's just ready for bed, I think."

Marie came in then carrying all their books. "It ain't even dark out," she was saying, not paying me or Mattie any mind. "Ain't you going to finish the story, Ella. We're supposed to stay outside so that Da and Miss Mattie can hold hands and stuff, right?" She gestured to us standing by the couch now and put her hands over her eyes in an overly dramatic effort not to see anything.

"I'm glad she didn't come in first," I said to Mattie and took her hand in mine. I cleared my throat. "Marie, you can uncover your eyes and Ella, please tuck Hugh in and I'll see Mattie out."

"I could stay a while still," Mattie said.

"I should let you go," I said but didn't let go of her hand or make a move toward the door.

"It doesn't seem that you're able," she said, squeezing my hand and smiling at me.

"You're right," I said. "I imagine that would be a difficult task indeed."

We stepped out onto the porch, and she tightened her hold on my hand. "I'm not going anywhere. I'm staying right here in Certain."

"I hope that's true come morning when you've had a chance to think about things," I said. I moved to kiss her again in case I was right, and this was my last chance, but Hugh let out another wail. "I should check on him."

She let go of my hand and touched my cheek. "I mean it, Daniel."

"Be careful," I said and kissed her quickly on the lips. "I'll be beside myself if you're hurt on the way home."

"I'll come back tomorrow," she said. "If for no other reason than just to prove to you that I mean what I say." She winked at me.

I nodded, fearful and excited all at the same time. Hugh had stopped crying and I could hear Ella whispering to him, so I stayed on the porch and watched Mattie go.

Chapter 19

Mattie

As soon as I was home, I wrote a letter to my father.

> *Dear Pop,*
> *Thank you so much for your loving attempt to help me*
> *obtain the teaching position in Asheville. However, I have*
> *decided to stay and teach in Certain.*

No, that wasn't the whole of it.
I have also decided that this is where I plan to make my home.
The decision not to come back home was something that I really should have told him in person, but I needed to send that message out as soon as I could.

> *I will come back to Asheville soon to talk with you in*
> *person about my decisions. I hope that you understand and*
> *know how much I love you.*
> *Mattie.*

Of course, I knew he would. I knew he'd miss me being there, but my father had always only wanted me to be happy. And I was happy now.

The next morning, I raced Opal down the paths and rocky trails that led to Daniel's house. I usually took my regular book route when I went to see him, even if I wasn't delivering. I didn't make all the turns up and around to the houses, but rather stayed along the creek and close to the familiar paths. It wasn't the shortest way there, though. I had traveled those paths enough to get an idea of how one thing branched off into another, so today I opted for a route I'd surmised, but never taken.

It was chilly enough that I had worn the pants Ruby gave me instead of one of my skirts. I hoped it meant summer was on its way out for good. A hard rain had beat down the night before and the ground was slick with fallen leaves and mud. Opal was none too happy to tread over rocky paths covered in camouflage. She lost her footing a time or two and she was blaming it all on me. Thrashing her head around and puffing breath both visible and forceful through her flared nostrils.

"It's OK, girl," I said, pulling up on her reins, hoping to get her to slow down rather than speed through, which was what she seemed to want to do. "Slow down. We'll go slow."

But we were already in too much of a bind with water too high up her legs for her comfort to think clearly. Me or her. Before I knew what was happening, I felt her trip again and then I felt myself going backwards as she reared up in front of me. I tried to hang on, but that only caused her to whip her head from side to side against the unexpected force. I knew the moment that I lost my grip and would fall. I felt it as much as I processed it—that sliding back beyond the point of correction—that understanding that I would hit the ground. All of it jerked backward for just a moment as my foot caught up in the stirrups and I was whipped in a different direction and then flung onto the ground where I landed harshly amid the same leaf-covered rocks that Opal had fought against.

As Opal thundered away from me, I saw my boot drop to the ground. Somehow, my foot had come loose from it, setting me free. Otherwise, I imagine I'd be dangling alongside her as she went. I yelled out to her, but she didn't so much as twitch her ears back in my direction.

I sat up, already feeling the bruises that would come from the jagged rocks I'd landed on.

"Here I thought you and I were getting along," I said to Opal even though she was gone.

I scooted over enough to get a better footing before standing up, only to find that when I tried, I couldn't. The ankle I'd wrenched on my way off the horse would no more bear weight than a feather trying to balance a rock. I dropped to my knees. I eased back over onto my backside and breathed out angrily.

I stretched my legs out in front of me and pulled the hurt ankle up to me. Pushing up my pant leg, I could see the swelling starting already. I touched it but winced at the tingling and pulsing the small pressure caused. I didn't think it broken, but it hurt enough to make me a little lightheaded. I pondered my options but was done quickly as I didn't really have any. I figured I was closer to Daniel's house than my own. I could hobble, perhaps. Crawl. Well, one less desirable way or the next, I was going to have to move, but first I lay back on the ground, head in the muck even, and stared up through trees at the sky. The light dappled down and caught the colors of the leaves so that every shade of green lit up from behind like nature's stained glass. The veins of the leaves were highlighted like the pictures on the church windows. I closed my eyes and let the cool of the breeze blow over me. I opened them again and the patterns of the leaves seemed to have moved. A real kaleidoscope. I was basking in the beauty of it all until one of the leaves blew down and hit me in the eye. Typical.

I removed the leaf from my face and just lay there, still, in the damp of the creek bed. I closed my eyes and tried to calm my breathing so that I might lessen the aching throb of my ankle. My head ached and I figured I had hit it on a rock when I tumbled down. That would explain the wooziness. Perhaps I drifted off to sleep just a little, I don't know, but I opened my eyes to see Opal coming back through the brush ahead and heard Daniel's voice calling out to me.

"Mattie," he shouted in a panic. "Mattie."

Just my name over and over, and I realized he thought maybe I was dead. Maybe I was.

I intended to form some words as a response, but I just groaned instead. I suppose that was enough of a relief because I could hear Daniel thanking God and telling Opal to stay put, both with a tone of terror. I also meant to turn my head and open my eyes, but I'm not sure I did those things. I could hear water splash and I figured that was Daniel's dismount into the edge of the creek. Twigs and things that had been blown by the storm the night before crunched and I could feel a large presence run toward me and slide in beside me. It was rather like the preceding moments of a bear attack I surmised.

"Grizzly bear," I mumbled, chuckling to myself.

I opened my eyes then and Daniel's terrified face loomed before me. He sighed heavily as our gaze met and his hands touched my face and then my hair.

"Can you sit up," he asked, already pulling on my hand, and sliding his arm around my waist.

"You and Opal are like Dick and Spot," I said, pulling myself up against him. "Come to rescue Jane."

"You're always talking about books," he said and pulled me to a seated position. He made sure I was steady and then sat back on his heels so that he knelt beside me. "Is that one of the stories in our lesson book?"

"It could be," I said, finding my mind was clouded and I felt woozy still.

"Well, since I know how this one will end, we can skip it and call it good."

"You're always trying to get out of a lesson," I said and winked at him.

"That's true," he said and looked at me sideways. "Is that why you were coming? To make me study from the book."

"No," I said and realized how badly my head was throbbing. I put my hand to it and winced.

"What are you doing out here?" he asked. "This is a terribly rough patch of land to cross when you already know a better way."

"I thought this would be quicker," I said and shrugged. "I just needed to get to you. How did you find me?"

He scooted around to sit beside me. "Opal came up to the house and you weren't on her. The saddle was barely hanging on, so I knew something had happened. I tried to ride her out the regular route, but she reared up at me and so I just let her go where she wanted to go."

"She came to me?" I asked, flattered.

"No, we went into town first and got some apples from Gibbons and then came here."

"You did?"

He chuckled. "It's too easy to best you," he said. "Of course not. She came straight here."

I looked toward Opal who was eating the last stalks of grass around the tree nearest her. Maybe she didn't hate me after all.

"I guess she didn't mean to throw me off and into the rocks," I said. "I'm surprised she knew where I was going and went there anyway."

"She knows her way around," he said. "And she knows you. I'm sure she knew you were hurt. She wasn't running off from you, she was running to get help." He stood up and reached his hand down to me.

"I can't stand up," I said, pointing at my ankle and wrinkling my nose. I didn't like to be helpless.

He nodded and bent down to me, picking me up in his arms. He took care not to swing my hurt ankle as he carried me toward Opal.

"Hold onto me," Daniel said, and I did. He reached out to Opal's reins and pulled her a little closer. "OK, put the good leg over and I'll mind the other one."

I let him hold me up and guide me over. I didn't feel helpless after all. I felt supported and there was a big difference. I hadn't realized how much I needed that feeling. I liked to think of myself as independent and self-reliant. I was, but it didn't hurt to have a companion.

"OK, hang on. I'm going to swing up next to you. I'll go slow so I don't hurt you."

Daniel gripped the reins as well and hoisted himself up. He nestled in behind me and put one arm around my waist. He got Opal moving but headed her off in the direction of his house first.

"Are we going to your place?"

"No," he said. "Just getting us back on more stable ground."

I leaned back into him, and his grip tightened on me. We came to a low rising of the bank, and he led Opal up it. It came out into a clearing, and we wound around unfamiliar territory for a while. Unfamiliar to me, he and Opal seemed to know their way. Before long we were back to a spot I knew.

"There's my shoe," I said excitedly.

Daniel stopped and slid off Opal to retrieve it. I thought Daniel might take his leave once I was sure where I was going and had my shoe back. But he tucked the shoe under his arm and hoisted himself back up.

"Don't you want to get back home?" I asked. "I can make it from here."

"That's not an option," he said and kissed the back of my head. "I'll see you all the way home lest Opal comes riding back up to the house without you again."

"But home is the parsonage," I said, knowing he didn't want to go there.

"I know," he said.

I thought he might say more, but he didn't. We rode in silence the rest of the way. I knew this route well, but I had never ridden it when I was not the one leading. With the freedom to look in any direction, I let my eyes linger on patches of ground and standings of trees that before I had only glanced at as Opal and I rode by. Sure, riding a horse was different than driving an automobile as there was time to look and see the world around me from the saddle, even to close my eyes and enjoy the rolling sound of the water and feel the rush of the air, but with Daniel's arms around me holding Opal's reins and guiding the horse, I had time to rest on it all. To really see and feel it. I lifted my eyes to the sky and watched the rolling clouds move and shift above us. Thin and feathery in some places but layered thicker and more solid in others. The white of the clouds struck stark against the hazy blue of the sky. The mountains in Asheville seemed that color blue at times. I lingered over the thought of my hometown, trying to see if I'd feel a pang of longing for it. I thought the city lovely and wonderful, but I didn't want to go back to stay. Not that it wasn't a beautiful place filled with interesting people. It was. Or that it wasn't a place that still sought joy during this dark depression the country was in. It did. The art and music, theater, and literature, it was all alive even in the worst of times.

But this was my home now. The church library with its old and tattered books was far more glorious to me now than any other library I had seen. The bare shelves at Gibbons' provided more luxuries than any market I knew before because the items were more precious for their sparseness. I couldn't think of leaving my patrons without the books and pamphlets that they clung to. Even though no manner of recipe they held inside made them edible and no explanation of medical illness cured anything, I knew how important the knowledge was because it gave people resources. It gave them the ability to create new dishes from the food they had, and it taught them how to care for themselves. It made their independent way of life more possible. It gave them hope.

And school started in a matter of weeks. I was finally going to be a teacher and I couldn't wait. I was going to care for the kids with knowledge and meals, breakfast and lunch and snack before they went home. I had it all worked out. Maybe it wouldn't always be something of luxury, but it would be something.

Then, of course, there was Daniel. I could feel the press of his body against my back where he held onto me so I wouldn't fall. Every so often as we jostled across the path, his cheek would come down close to mine when he pulled the reins or leaned in to give Opal a command. I hadn't let myself think about leaving him and the kids. It just wasn't something I could do.

All my ponderings and long looks at the scenery ended as we arrived at the parsonage before I was ready. I didn't expect that Daniel would come in with me, and I wasn't ready for him to go.

He spoke to Opal and pulled her up near the front porch.

"Hang on," he instructed me and slid off the backside of Opal like falling from a tree branch.

"Graceful," I chided him, but I knew he had elected the clumsy dismount so as not to jostle me.

He came around and held his arms out to me. "Slide off easy. I'll catch you before that ankle touches the ground. Don't worry."

I wasn't. I wasn't worried about anything with him. I reached out to him and slid into his arms. I thought he might set me down, but he carried me toward the house. Neither of us had spoken about the evening before. I wondered if he was worried over what I had been coming to say.

"You're going to hurt your back," I said.

"I'm trying to be gentlemanly and romantic here," he said. "You're not that heavy." Then he made a noise like I was.

"I'm not that light, either," I said, putting my arms more firmly around his neck to try and take some of the pressure off.

"I'll do my best," he said. "I might have to leave you on the front porch if I'm able to make it up the stairs."

I wiggled around a little, trying to get him to let me go. "You don't have to come up," I said.

"I'm joking," he said. "I'll at least get you to the living room. I can't promise the upstairs, at least not without banging that foot."

He spoke about the house as if it wasn't the source of grief and pain that I knew it must be. He managed the few steps that led to the porch and then shifted me around and down beside him so that he could open the door and we could go through it.

"Careful not to bang your foot on the door frame. It's swelling up pretty badly."

I had rolled the pant leg up so that I could monitor the swelling. I groaned at the sight of my ankle. Good thing I had not decided to become a nurse. He held onto me as I hopped in through the doorway.

"I'm so sorry, Daniel," I said. "I know you don't want to be here."

"It's a school," he said, his gaze flitting and darting around the room as if he was trying to see it without having seen it. "I thought it would still look the same." His voice was without much inflection, but I knew him well enough to know that he was guarding his emotions.

"You don't have to stay. I'm alright."

"Sit down," he said and pointed to the only chair big enough for an adult. "Let me look at that ankle." He knelt in front of me and lifted my leg up in his hands. "I wonder if Gibbons has a bandage wrap or something for the pain. It must hurt."

"It's sort of gone numb."

He looked at me with concern. "That doesn't sound good."

"I'll be fine," I said. "I'm sure it's just sprained. I won't die from it." I winced at my misstep. "I'm sorry. That was rude to say. I wasn't thinking."

He chuckled a bit. "Stop worrying over it. It's fine." He looked at me intently until I nodded at him. He nodded back. "Can I make you some tea or fetch you some water?"

"That would be nice," I said.

"You really need to keep this leg raised up," he said. "Let's get up the stairs. There are still beds up there, right?"

I nodded. He helped me hobble up the stairs and saw me into the bedroom that I now knew used to be his. He held my arm and helped me sit down on the bed.

"Daniel," I said, watching him look around the room. "You really don't need to stay. I'm alright."

He shook his head. "No, it's good that I came. I needed to stop thinking about this place like it was haunted. It's just a house that I used to live in." Again, his voice was empty.

I opened my mouth to protest, but he held out his hand. He turned and went back down the stairs. I thought he was leaving, but I could hear that he opened the cupboard that housed the coffee mugs. I heard him fill the tea kettle and light the stove. He knew where things were and how they worked. This was his house after all. I could hear that he pulled a chair out at the table and sat down.

I felt suddenly exhausted and closed my eyes for a moment. I was startled awake at the sound of the kettle whistling.

Daniel?" I called out, but he didn't answer. I put my feet on the floor and tried to stand, but my ankle sparked in agony, and I sat back down on the bed.

I heard the chair pushing back from the table and sighed. The whistling stopped, but I didn't hear anything else.

"Daniel, are you down there?" I called again. I stood on one foot and hobbled to the doorway, holding onto the furniture as I went. I stood in the hallway, staring down the stairwell and listened. Daniel came into view at the bottom of the stairs. He didn't have a cup of tea in his hand, but rather a stack of papers.

"What's this?" he asked, holding them out. His eyes were angry which surprised me.

I knew what they were. All the letters from my father and one from the school committee in Asheville asking me to write an essay which I hadn't done.

"They're letters from my father," I said, stalling. I didn't know how much he'd been able to read, but I hoped not enough to gather that the letters were about a job back in Asheville.

"These are about a job in Asheville," he said. "Aren't they?"

My heart sank. I knew he was misunderstanding.

"You could read them?" I asked, hoping he was just worried and hadn't really been able to garner any information.

"You know I can't," he said, his voice angrier than I'd ever heard. "But I can make out the word job and I know what Asheville looks like from signs and maps. It might not be as easy as Dick and Jane, but I can piece it together."

"I'm sorry," I said, shaking my head. "That was rude of me to ask. I just meant that I think you're misunderstanding. It's not a job that I'm going to take," I said. "Besides, I probably didn't even get the job."

"But you went after it?"

"No," I said and tried to take a step down the stairs. It smarted, but I tried anyway. "My father sent my resume, but I didn't actually want the job."

"Why did he send it then?" Daniel's expression was guarded but hopeful.

There was a right answer to this, but I was sure I wasn't going to give it. I wanted to be honest. I wanted him to know he could trust me.

"He asked if he could, and I said yes." I hobbled down another couple of stairs.

Daniel turned away and went back into the kitchen. I heard him move the tea kettle. The sound of water pouring into a cup was followed by his return at the bottom of the stairs. He had the papers in one hand and a cup of tea in the other. Perhaps he was willing to talk this thing through. It was a simple misunderstanding after all.

"Here's your tea," he said and sat it and the letters on the bottom step. He turned toward the front door.

"Daniel," I called out and he stopped, but didn't turn around. "You're just misunderstanding what it all means. If you could read the rest of it, you'd understand. If you could see the letters I sent back as well. I was just stalling for time. I only told him to send the resume because I thought it would make him happy to think I was coming home."

He turned then and looked at me sternly. "So, you were just playing him along so as not to hurt his feelings when you decided not to go home?"

I was about to answer this one incorrectly as well. "Yes," I said and hobbled the rest of the way down. I nearly tripped trying to get past the tea and letters. "But I didn't mean it in a bad way. I was just too afraid to tell him the truth."

"So, you lied?"

"Daniel, stop," I said. I wanted to go closer to him, but there was nothing to grab onto that was close enough and I didn't want to put weight on my foot. "You're reading this all wrong."

"You're right Miss Book Woman," he said and folded his arms across his chest. "The big words got me. I can't read them. Ella's been helping me read all those little stories about Dick and Jane, but the big words in Mattie's daddy's letters got the better of me."

"Daniel, I wasn't trying to insult you." I had injured his pride. "I just meant that it isn't what you think."

"I think there was a chance you might get a teaching job in Asheville, so you agreed to have your father send your information to the school and you're still waiting to hear whether or not you got the job. Did you get it?"

"They haven't decided," I said, and then when he shook his head at me, I snapped back. "Which I don't care about one way or the next. I'm not going to take it."

"We'll see," he said, his arms still folded across his chest.

"Daniel," I said, confused. "I don't understand why this is upsetting you. I was never going to take a job back in Asheville."

"Then why did you keep it from me?" he asked.

I was struck silent. Why indeed.

"It never came up," I said, feeling horrible at such a sorry excuse.

"Of all the things you've talked to me about, you didn't mention that you got a letter from your father, who you must miss," Daniel said, and I knew he was about to dismantle any inadequate reason I might have. "Two letters. Or that you wrote back to him. You brought paper and pencils to Ella that came from Asheville, but no mention of a job that your father suggested or the reassurance that you didn't want it?"

I opened my mouth, but I didn't know what to say. What was I supposed to do, suggest that he trust me again? I had gone on and on about how he could. Why had I not told him about the letter and the job? I lowered my eyes. I knew why. I wanted to see if I'd get it. I wanted to keep the doors open in case things didn't work out here. In case Daniel didn't want me. But he had, and I was messing everything up.

He squeezed his eyes shut. "You ain't going to stay here, so you might as well go on and go."

"I am staying here," I said, emphatically. "Daniel, I love you."

"No," he shouted out. "Don't say that. Don't do that."

"Why?" I didn't know what was happening. Everything that I thought would make him understand seemed to have the opposite effect.

"We can't bear it, Mattie," he said, incredulous like I should have known. "I can, maybe, but the kids can't. Don't you see that? Don't you dare make them think you love them."

"But I do," I said. I was terrified at this point. And a little angry.

He shook his head at me. "Go back to Asheville before you hurt my children. I can't abide that. I won't. If you really do love us, leave now while we still have a shot at surviving this."

I didn't know what to say that wouldn't make it worse, but I tried. "I don't want Asheville. I want you. I want the kids and I want this life right here. I want to be with you."

He looked at me sternly. "Well, I can't take you in. I can't feed the mouths I have, and I don't have room for you. If you're thinking that we're going to get married and live happily ever after like in one of the books you bring the kids, then you haven't taken much of a look around you. This whole place is as good as ghost. Maybe I'm the one stringing you along. You ever think that?" He turned and opened the door to leave. He looked back. "You should have listened to them. They were right. You done let the devil in and it's your own fault."

I shook my head. Could that be true? Did he find enough information in the letters to think that I might go on home, and he wouldn't have to worry over me? That he might be able to have a little fun and then I'd be on my way. I thought about the warning that I'd gotten from the lady in the grocery. Was he the devil after all? The devilish playboy in a nice-looking suit.

He turned, then, and went out the door. He slammed it hard behind him.

"Daniel," I shouted at the closed door.

There was no way he meant that. I didn't know what he was trying to do, but I didn't believe a word of it. I hobbled over to the door as best I could. Still, I stepped on the sore foot a time or two and yelled out. I made it to the door and flung it open. Both Opal and Daniel were gone.

I stumbled back in. I spent a very long time going up the stairs where I then fell to the bed and cried into the night.

The next morning, my ankle was black and blue, but not nearly as swollen. I looked out the window to the pen and saw that Opal was eating from her trough. Daniel had been back, and my heart leapt at it, but then sank at the understanding that he might only have put her away properly yesterday and then walked home.

I had to step very gingerly, mostly putting the weight on the other leg, but I made it down the stairs and headed for the front door. I guess I thought Daniel might be out there or something stupid and romantic. I opened the door, but the porch was empty. I sighed and turned to head back in when I noticed that there was a bandage with clips lying on the porch swing.

Daniel was not the devil, but nonetheless, he was gone. I picked the bandage up and underneath it was a letter from my father. It was open. My heart sank.

> *Dear Mattie,*
> *Happy news! The board would like to offer you the teaching position. As you know, school starts in a matter of days. I have already arranged a car for you. Pack your bags, dear one. Your time in the wilds is done. Look for the car this Saturday. I will see you soon.*
> *Your loving father*

I felt sick. Today. The car would be here today. And Daniel had obviously read the letter. It had probably been at the grocery where I received my mail. Mr. Gibbons, no doubt had given it to Daniel to give to me when he dropped off the bandage. I didn't fault him for reading it. However much he was able to read, I knew he could read "Happy News" and that it was the death knell ringing all the way from Asheville. He probably hoped there was some news in it that would shed a different light on what he thought to be the truth. No. There hadn't been.

I looked over toward Gibbons'. It was a trade day for Daniel. I knew his schedule well. I sat on the porch swing and watched the road. I'd be able to see his wagon come up the path that led to the back of the store. I didn't think he'd come in through the front hoping to accidentally see me this time. He was angry for real, and he'd avoid me as best he could, especially now that he was sure I was leaving.

I sat on the porch swing and wrapped my ankle, then I headed over to the Certain Grocery. My aim was to go through the front, announce my purpose to Mr. Gibbons and then proceed to the back of the store where I was prepared to deal with Liam as I waited for Daniel. My plan after that was a bit murkier.

The bell dinged as I walked in the store and Mr. Gibbons appeared from behind the counter as if he'd been hiding there waiting to surprise me.

"I'm here to see Daniel," I said with purpose. "He's upset with me and I need to set things straight."

He nodded knowingly. "That would explain his countenance yesterday when he came to trade."

"Yesterday?" I said, confused. "But today is Daniel's day."

Mr. Gibbons nodded again and came out from behind the counter. "It is, but he came in yesterday. Late. Almost missed me. Said he'd had to make a trip or two back and forth. Something about Opal and that you'd hurt your leg." He looked down at my ankle. "Are you OK?"

"Why did he do that?" I asked, but I knew. He knew that I knew when he'd be here, and he wanted to make sure that I didn't surprise him like I was planning to now.

Mr. Gibbons put his hand on my shoulder, knowing that, too, it seemed. He offered a weak smile and let himself back in behind the counter. He nodded past me out the window.

"Seems like you're not the only one who didn't know he came yesterday."

I turned to look out the front glass. A wagon had pulled up and Zachary was stepping down from the seat. I could tell that someone else was with him and I took it to be Liam. I rolled my eyes and turned back to Mr. Gibbons.

"This is going from bad to worse," I said and shrugged. "Well, I guess it's just another couple of people who will be glad to see me go."

"Are you leaving?" Mr. Gibbons asked, surprised. "I sure hope not."

I couldn't answer, so I took in a breath and pulled open the door. I thought I was about to get into another row with Liam, but once I'd marched past Zachary in a huff and rounded the back of the wagon, I saw that it wasn't Liam at all.

Pastor Collins stood at the back wheel running his hand over one of the spokes. "Not broken," he called out in a loud voice, aiming to find Zachary's ear I supposed. He was about to shout something else when he saw me there and startled. "I'm sorry, Mattie. I didn't mean to yell at you. Was trying to get Zachary's attention before he went in."

I looked back toward the store and saw Zachary heading inside.

"He's not here," I shouted toward him, but he went in anyway.

"Daniel?" Pastor Collins asked.

I nodded. "He's avoiding me."

Pastor Collins nodded back but didn't say anything.

"I hurt his feelings," I said and then I put my hands on my hips. "No, that's not true. He misunderstood something and flew off the handle and then assumed some things that aren't true and wouldn't listen to me when I tried to explain myself, and then he told me he didn't love me and that I should go back to Asheville."

Pastor Collins smiled and nodded his head. "That sounds like my boy," he said and laughed a little.

"It wasn't supposed to be a funny story," I said.

"It's not," he said and sighed. "Nothing about my Daniel's story is funny. It's a good thing you didn't take the lad seriously and actually leave."

"Only because the car didn't get here yet," I said, although that wasn't true. I dreaded the car showing up.

"Do you know much about the devil, Mattie?"

I shook my head.

"Satan's number one job is to make you feel like you aren't worthy," Pastor Collins said. "That you don't deserve to be loved, or forgiven, that you're beyond mercy. If he can convince you of those things, he's got you."

I nodded. He'd certainly convinced Daniel of as much and more.

"That's what happened to Daniel's father," Pastor said. "John Barrett could have been a good man, but the devil got in his head and worse, in his heart. He's pretty well got Daniel convinced at this point, too. You've been the only person who's made him think he might be worth a second chance."

"But I messed it all up," I said. "He doesn't trust me now. I'm not sure what to do about that."

"Your first decision is," Pastor Collins said and pointed toward the parsonage over my shoulder, "to get in the car and go back to Asheville, or stay here where you know you belong?"

I turned to see the black Studebaker sitting out front of the parsonage. My heart dropped so quickly in my chest that I thought I might get woozy and fall over.

"Decide wisely," Pastor Collins said. "Daniel needs you to make a smart and lasting decision. He's afraid of needing people. He's afraid to have people love him. But you knew that."

I nodded. I did know that. "Sounds like you're pretty sure what I should do."

He smiled at me. "I think you are too. You just have to be brave. You have to fight for what you want. What do you want, Mattie?"

I glanced over at the church across the street. "Why didn't you ever go back?"

Pastor Collins followed my gaze. He exhaled hard enough that his shoulders dropped, and his chest sank. He looked at me and then lowered his eyes to the ground. "I felt like I failed. Failed Daniel. My family. My congregation." He raised his eyes to meet mine. "I suppose I haven't been being brave."

Zachary came banging out of the store then and stomped over to where we stood. "You could have told me he wasn't coming. Gibbons let me stand out there for ten minutes waiting on him, too."

"I did tell you," I said. "You weren't listening."

A car horn blared, and we all looked to see the driver leaning in the window to press the horn. He stood up and gestured at me.

"Leaving?" Zachary asked. He turned then and went back to the front of the wagon where he hoisted himself into the seat and grabbed the reins. "I figured you would," he said without looking back.

Pastor Collins leaned closer to me. "He's jealous and always has been. He wanted to be Daniel's favorite. You being here just pushes him further down the list."

"That's not true," I said. "And I'm not the one keeping them from Daniel. They're doing that all on their own."

"Mattie," Pastor Collins said my name softly. "Don't give up on my boys. Any of them."

"I'll be brave if you will," I answered back and nodded toward the church. "It's a nice library, but I think it would make a better church."

Pastor Collins pressed his lips together in a small smile. I looked back over at the car and driver that waited for me. I squared my shoulders and walked across the street.

Chapter 20

Daniel

If I wasn't going to stay in Certain any longer it was best to get going. The kids and I had scouted out a new piece of land up in the hills and maybe it was all for the best that we left. I needed to get Mattie out of my mind and that wasn't going to happen here. Zachary had come up to the house a couple of weeks ago, which was a flabbergasting first, and told me a fancy car had shown up from Asheville, so I figured Mattie was back home, teaching school like she wanted to do. He'd assured me it was for the best. It was wonderful to talk to him, and it almost made me think twice about leaving, but just almost. Besides, I had talked about wanting a better life for my kids, yet I'd stayed right there in Certain where that wasn't possible. And we needed to go before it got cold. Fall was settling in and no good would come from waiting. I brushed my hands together like I was clearing the dirt off them. It was time to get going.

Late September was wet and cold already. We'd seen an early frost and the mud along the creek beds was a murky mix of wet, frozen, and wet again. Much of the leaves had fallen and it was a slick hazard along the rough places. Leaving wouldn't be easy, but it was for the best. If we left soon, I could build a one room house that would see us through the winter. Then come spring, I'd add on. We could start over.

The kids weren't that happy about it, but I was trying to make it out like a great adventure. Like a story in a book. We'd been exploring the land these last couple of weeks and were just now back home to gather our things for our next and best adventure yet. I think I had Marie and Hugh convinced, but Ella was in a different story altogether. She was still hoping for a happy ending in our old book. That story was over.

We'd made it back here last night with just enough energy left to fall in our beds. This morning the kids had gotten up early despite our late travels, but I was too tired to move. I think I might have been stalling just a tad as well. It would be a long day of packing and then when we left, that would be that. I couldn't imagine this old cabin finally being left to rot. But that's what I was doing here, rotting.

When I finally roused up and stepped out onto the porch, I expected to see the kids playing in the yard, but everything was quiet. I listened for the sounds of the children, but the air was still and silent. The sound of nothing was terribly loud. I went back into the house and out through the back door. My eyes fell on the stained-glass pieces I had taken from the church years ago. I supposed I'd leave them here too. Funny, I didn't feel as relieved at leaving as I thought I would.

I stood in the quiet of the backyard and for a moment, I thought I heard Opal's whinny in the distance. All at once, it was as if the sound came back on. The wind rustled the leaves overhead and a squeal of laughter came from the front of the house. I heard the whinny again and I knew I was right. I hurried around the side of the house and there the children were, frozen as if they had spied a ghost. I stepped further around the house and there she was. Our ghost. Mattie.

The kids began to squeal again, realizing that she was real. They ran to her and threw themselves into her arms. I wanted to run to her too, but I stood still and folded my arms across my chest.

"We thought you were gone," Ella said, her voice muffled from where her face pressed against Mattie's skirt.

"Da said you left," Marie chimed in and then pinched her on the hand.

"Ouch," Mattie said and laughed. "What was that for?"

"I just wanted to see if you was real," Marie said.

Mattie was indeed real and standing in my yard.

"Of course, she's real," Ella said, looking around and settling her eyes on me. "We couldn't hug her if she wasn't."

Hugh clung to Mattie's leg. She patted his head and then bent down to scoop him up into her arms.

"I've missed you all," Mattie said softly. "I'm sorry it's been so long. It won't happen again."

I looked at the ground and thought about what to say.

"We're leaving though," Ella said before I could figure out what to make of all this.

At her words, Hugh buried his face in Mattie's neck and tightened his whole body around her.

"I have books for you," Mattie said, shifting Hugh to her hip and turning to her pack. "And I wanted to invite you to school. I had hoped you'd come, but since it's been a couple of weeks and I haven't seen you, I thought I'd come check."

"We can't go to school all the way over in Asheville," Marie said.

Mattie chuckled. "Well of course not. School is here in Certain. At my house."

I spoke finally. My words came out cold, but I didn't mean them to. "I thought you were gone back to Asheville."

"Nope," she said, brushing her hands over her hair. "I'm still here."

"I see that."

Marie was beside me then. "She's still here, Da." She said in confirmation.

"Ella, take your siblings into the house. Close the door behind you."

I sounded angry and accusatory, which surprised me.

"I'm not an intruder," Mattie said and smiled.

I wasn't angry though. I was scared. Scared of the news that she was still here. Scared that she seemed so casual, and I was so nervous.

Scared that she'd leave after all.

"Why are you here?" I asked.

"I just came to invite the kids to school. I'm the new teacher. From in town." She was trying to make a joke, but I didn't know how to process what was happening or what wasn't. She winked at me. "We've met before, remember?"

"I don't understand what's happening," I said.

"I'm introducing myself," she said and stuck out her hand.

I shook my head and stepped back. "You should go."

"This is my home," she said. "I'm not going anywhere."

"Good for you, but it's not mine anymore," I said. "Done found us another spot. It's all for the best. It was foolish of me to think I'd be able to have a normal life and foolish of you to let yourself become enamored with me. The novelty is over. Go back to Asheville."

She put her hands on her hips. "You do not make my decisions for me, Daniel Barrett. I can stay in Certain if I so well please. You are not the only reason I didn't get into that car when it came for me. Didn't you hear me. I'm a teacher."

"So, you got the job in Asheville?'

"I did," she said and cocked her head. "Yet here I am. And this is not a foolish infatuation. I know I seemed silly to you when I first got here, talking about movies, and teaching your children to dance, but I'm not some ninny."

The word and the memories of that day made me smile just a tiny bit, despite myself.

"I am a strong woman," she said, giving me what for, "who has a history of heartache all her own, which I have shared with you. I take my job seriously. I am a teacher here in Certain. I have several students who depend on me, and I will not go flitting back to Asheville when I have responsibilities here."

"That's all," I said. "You came here to invite the kids to school? You're seeing to your responsibilities."

She looked injured, which I had not meant to do. I didn't want to be acting that way, but fear held me tight.

"No," she said. "That is not all. I have come to love this town, your children, and you as well, you beast."

"Beast?" I said, aiming for insulted, but not quite getting there.

"And a stubborn one at that," she said. "You were so sure that I was leaving, which scared you to no end, that you bit first and tried to send me packing. Well, it didn't work, Mr. Barrett. I'm still here."

"I can see that you're still here," I said, and stepped in closer to her. "Is there something that you'd like me to do about it?"

I found myself hopeful and fearful at the same time. I wasn't so stupid as to not know she was giving me a chance to take her back. Moreover, that she was giving herself a chance to take me back. But I just didn't know if I'd be able to risk it.

She squinted her eyes at me. "I have a question for you, and I expect an answer. And I expect you to believe me when I tell you something and to not run away from me again. Also, I will make sure that I don't, even on accident, keep things from you. And I expect that if we have a fight in the future, you will not run off and not speak to me for weeks so that I have to wait anxiously for you to show up and then give up and go find you instead."

"The future?" I asked, too nervous to hope we might have one.

"Yes," she said, "it's that time frame that people refer to when they mean not now, but a ways off."

"I know what it means," I said. She had an infuriating and endearing way of explaining things in what I knew was jest but had serious intent as well.

She handed me a little book from her pack. It looked handmade. "It's poetry."

"I don't like poems," I interrupted.

"I didn't get it because I thought you'd like it," she said. "I marked one in particular. If you can't read it, ask Ella to help you. I expect an answer one way or the other."

"An answer to what?" I asked.

"Read the poem and I expect an answer tomorrow," she said and shrugged like she was apologizing for the short deadline. "I'm having a gathering at the school tomorrow for the kids, just a fun afternoon of games and if you're in, I expect to see you."

"If I'm in?"

"That's right."

"What are you doing?" I asked. "Other than telling me off and making me read poetry."

"I'm fighting because you're tired and can't right now, and that's OK," she said, and nudged Opal to turn toward the creek. "That's what people do. They hold each other up." She gave Opal a tap with her foot to start her moving.

I looked at the little book of poems. I opened to the spot Mattie had marked with a slip of paper. Poetry made me nervous. I was bad with words already and already Mattie had been angry with me for misreading a situation. Why on earth would she give me poetry to try and help sort anything out.

"Ella," I called loudly, already walking up toward the house. "Never mind the packing. We have to read some poems."

Ella appeared in the doorway. A smile lit her entire face.

Chapter 21

Mattie

"When We Two Parted," I said to Ava as we sat on the porch swing of the parsonage the following day, looking off toward the turn of the Hell for Certain that led eventually to Daniel's house. Thunder clapped hard in the sky and we both looked up at the same time.

"Pardon?" she asked, not taking her eyes off the opening in the trees that he'd most likely come through if he was coming.

I was thankful she'd come to help with the kids today, and more thankful she'd come to sit with me in case things didn't go my way. I looked at her and felt calm. I imagined it was hard to go around with Emily's face. I'm sure Ava just wanted to be seen as Ava. I supposed I might be the only person in town who saw her that way.

"The poem that I marked for Daniel," I said, clarifying. "I don't think I told you which one it was." I had told her everything else about the encounter.

"Lord Byron was a little too much of a scoundrel for my tastes," Ava said, "but the poem does speak to your situation perfectly."

I didn't mean to be all weepy and sentimental, what with the "silence and tears" but then again, I imagined that Byron wasn't either. I supposed that it was actually quite nice that he had such a depth of feeling for someone given his reputation.

Reputations were a hard sentence. I wondered if history had gotten Byron all wrong. Thunder clapped again and I jumped.

"Is it normal to have storms like this in the fall?" I asked. "I suppose we should cancel the gathering. I doubt anyone will come anyway."

Ava looked toward the gray sky. "It's not normal, but what's normal these days? It's all one massive storm if you think about it." She reached over and took my hand. "Do you have a back-up plan?"

I shook my head. "If he doesn't show, I guess that's it. I still want to move forward with the plan to rehouse the library in the parsonage so that the church can reopen. I want to stay and hold school at the church on weekdays like before. I'll find a place to live and if there's not money enough to pay a teacher, well, I'll cross that bridge later."

Ava looked at me and chuckled. "I meant what's your back-up plan for the kid's party today." She squeezed my hand in hers and leaned into me compassionately.

I laughed at myself a bit as well. "Next week. I told them if we weren't able to do it now, we'd try again then."

Rain dropped sudden and hard from the sky. Water beat down on the tin roof over the porch. Ava and I looked at each other.

"Next week it seems to be," she said. "And you know that if you want to stay, we'll find you a place."

I smiled at her and sat back in the swing as the rain fell harder. "Daniel won't come. Not in this weather."

Ava turned my hand loose and shifted around to face me better. "I wouldn't be so sure. He can be pretty stubborn. If he's set to come, he'll come."

"If," I repeated.

She nodded and we sat for a while listening to the rain pelt the roof above us and the ground around. A racket of men yelling sounded in the near distance and Ava and I stood up in anticipation. Through the rain, we could see a cart coming into view from the main road up the mountain.

"That's my father's cart," Ava said.

Liam was at the helm and Zachary sat beside him. They rode straight to the parsonage and pulled up sharply enough that Ava and I feared they were going to hit the porch. Ava ran inside and came out quickly with a towel. Zachary bounded up the steps, wiping water from his face.

"What are you both doing here," Ava said, handing the towel to Zachary.

He took it and wiped his face. "You said Daniel might come into town today."

Liam was still out in the rain securing the horse and cart. He wiped the pounding water out of his face as he worked, but he still took care to do things properly. When he got to the porch, he took the towel from Zachary. "Dad told us to come," Liam said.

Ava said, "Let's wait inside. No sense standing out here in the weather."

"How will we see if he comes," I asked.

"His brothers will watch for him," Ava said, and put her arm around me to lead me inside. She glanced back at Liam and Zachary and nodded.

Inside, I busied myself with making tea. My hands shook and the cups clanked loudly against the saucers as I carried them into the living room. I gave one to Ava and then carried the other cups out onto the porch.

Zachary declined, but Liam took a cup and thanked me. We held each other's gaze for a long few seconds, truce acknowledged. He nodded as he drank another sip and then continued. "It's a mess up those twists and turns. Creek's rising like nobody's business. Flooding like it hasn't in ages."

"Someone done made the devil mad," Zachary said.

"Why did you come?" I asked, not in judgment, but in hope.

Zachary looked from me to Liam and then back up the road. He was a man of few words and that was no different today.

Liam spoke, "We don't want to lose our brother. He's making to leave Certain, and we want to keep that from happening. If there's a chance he's coming to town to see you we're going to be here."

"I appreciate that, Liam," I said.

He nodded. "He's going to have a devil of a time getting through that creek. It's as high as I've ever seen it. Hell for Certain indeed."

My heart thudded hard. I recalled Pastor Collins's words. The devil will do whatever it takes to win.

"Daniel's horse," Zachary said suddenly, pointing past us toward the creek. "I see the kids, but not him. Something's wrong."

Zachary rushed down the porch steps. Liam and I both dropped our cups of tea, the shattering of the fine China I'd brought was like a tinkling chime. We were fast behind Zachary, who was already in the road running toward the horse. Marie was holding the reins, which I thought odd until I could make out through the fog of pouring water that Ella was behind her holding onto Hugh who lay limp in her arms. I froze.

Ava, who had joined us, gasped, and rushed ahead of me. Liam slipped in the mud and went down on his knee only to pop right back up and lunge toward them again. The men reached the horse and Zachary took Hugh from Ella. Liam pulled Marie down as Ava and I got to them as well. I lifted my arms out to Ella who slid into them. Liam passed Marie to Ava and took lead of the horse.

"Where's Daniel," Liam called over the rain.

Ella was crying too hard to speak. I tucked her to me and ran for the porch. We took the children inside, but there was nowhere to lay Hugh down.

"Let me see to him," Ava said and reached out for Hugh's small and fragile looking body.

"There are beds upstairs, still," I said, and Ava nodded.

"Come upstairs, girls," she said, freeing one hand from her hold on Hugh and ushering them to follow her.

Liam grabbed hold of Ella's arm. "Where's your father?"

"I don't know," she said, crying again. "Hugh fell and he tried to get him. I don't know."

Zachary stepped out on the porch and shouted, "Daniel. Daniel."

No response came back. Zachary came back inside, and he and Liam looked frantically at each other.

I couldn't stand it all anymore and ran up the stairs to check on the kids. They had gone into the children's room where Hugh lay on one of the small beds. Ava had her hand on Hugh's chest and her ear to Hugh's nose.

"He's breathing. He's OK. Hugh?" Ava said and tried to rouse him. She looked to the girls. "Tell me what's happened." Her voice was kind but firm.

Ella pulled up straight and tried to speak around the jagged sobs. "The rain," she said. "It came up quick and the thunder spooked Cody. He reared up and the buggy hitched funny or something, I don't know," she said and shook her head.

"Then what," Ava urged. "Where's your father?"

Ella looked at me and her eyes were filled with fear. "The cart turned, and we fell out. The water is usually low enough that the cart goes through it fine, but it was too high today, and the water was rolling too fast. Hugh went falling into the creek. Da jumped out to get him, and Cody started forward. The cart jerked and it knocked Da down, I think. I think he hit his head or something because he wouldn't get up. Marie and I got to Hugh, but he wasn't moving either. He spit up some water and I thought he was OK, but then he sort of closed his eyes and we didn't know what to do." Ella burst back into tears and Marie sobbed even harder. "We didn't know what to do, so we came here."

Hugh stirred and blinked. Ava let out a sigh.

Hugh's little voice cracked, but he spoke. "Splashy tail."

Ava looked at me in question.

"Splashy tail," Hugh said again.

I jumped. "I know where Daniel is."

Chapter 22

Mattie

I raced out the door and around the back of the house to get Opal from her stall. I could have taken Cody, but Cody didn't really know me. I needed Opal. She'd know exactly where we were going. I knew she wasn't a fan of the water and really wouldn't like it today, but I trusted that she'd pick up on the importance of this trip and find the courage to power through.

I grabbed the bridle from the hook outside the stall and put it on her. She seemed to sense my urgency and whinnied in question. I opened the stall door and let her out. I didn't have time to fuss with the saddle and instead, just tried to swing myself up and over. I missed twice and then she seemed to know what I was doing, if not why, and knelt low enough that I managed to get on.

I patted her neck. "Good, girl. We're going to find Daniel," I said and held the reins tight as she started forward. She hesitated as if to tell me that things weren't right. I knew that and nudged her with a little tap. I needed her to trust me. She shook her head a bit to make her point, but she stepped forward and let me lead her out.

We were at a bit of a trot as we rounded back in front of the house. Liam had his horse unhitched from the wagon they'd ridden in, and Zachary was just then mounting Cody.

"Ava says you're going to find Daniel," Liam called out over the wind and rain. "We're coming, too."

"I know exactly where he is," I called to them over my shoulder as Opal and I picked up speed.

I didn't wait for them. I slapped the reins and called for Opal to ride faster. The ground was messy, and the rain was not letting up. Opal didn't like the conditions one bit and her whole body let me know that. Still, she went. I could hear Liam and Zachary calling to each other behind me. I knew a couple of shortcuts through the passage to get to Splashy Tail. It wasn't far from their house; Daniel and I had made the walk several times. Just beyond Devil's Branch and into a section wily enough for the creek to run fast if it wanted to, and rocky enough to make one hard fall a man's last.

My heart raced and I had to fight the urge to stop and retch from nerves. Mud and water flung up and out to the sides of us as we went. When she could, Opal would open up into a gallop and then when the land closed in around us she fell back to a slower gait. All the while, I called out for Daniel if for nothing else than to let him know I was coming.

Finally, we got close enough that I knew he'd hear me if he could. "Daniel," I yelled.

I heard Liam's and Zachary's voices doing the same somewhere behind me. I saw the overturned cart up ahead and pulled on the reins to slow Opal down. I didn't see Daniel at first, but then a swatch of red cloth under the cart caught my eye. I recognized his shirt and jumped from Opal recklessly enough to find myself landed flat of my behind in the mud. I scrambled to get to my feet. Slipping and sliding down the incline I fell in close to him, screaming his name all the while. His head rested on a rock. His eyes were closed, and the rising water covered one eye and pooled up closer to his nose. His dark hair floated out around his head like a black halo. He was still as stone. I could see how the children thought he was gone. Hugh had probably been pushed down the creek past the cart and by the time they all got to Hugh, Daniel was too far behind in the water and rain, and half hidden under the cart to see.

"Daniel," I yelled again as fruitlessly as any of my calls had been.

I had to get partially into the creek myself to squirm up next to him. I didn't know if I should move him or not, but I knew I couldn't leave his face in the water. I scooped my arm under his torso as best as the sucking ground and the dead weight of him would allow. With the other hand, I turned his face out of the water. His head lolled over harshly, and I had to stop it from wrenching his neck.

Liam and Zachary were there then. Liam pulled at the cart that was over the top of Daniel and Zachary splashed out into the creek beside me.

"I got him," Zachary said, pushing his arms underneath Daniel as well.

I didn't want to let go, but I knew if his body washed loose when the cart was moved that Zachary would have a better chance of catching him.

I slid my arm out from under Daniel and let Zachary take my place. I watched Zachary's face as he looked on Daniel's closed eyes and at the gash now visible on the side of his head where he'd hit the rock. Blood seeped into the water and around Zachary's hand where he held Daniel's head. Zachary closed his eyes for a moment and when he opened them, I could see the pain there.

"Mattie," Zachary called to me. "Tear my sleeve and put pressure on that wound." He held his arm out.

I tugged, but the garment was well sewn and didn't budge.

"Harder," Zachary yelled, positioning his body to hold Daniel in place and putting the hand that had been underneath him against the wound itself.

I looked back at the blood in the water and ripped the seam of Zachary's sleeve. I pulled the material down and off his arm, him aiding me with his movements. He took the cloth from me and put it against Daniel's head. Everything was wet with blood and water.

"Hold this," he said and put his arms under Daniel again.

I leaned in and put my hand on the cloth against the side of Daniel's head. Liam was yelling and grunting as he pulled the cart up and away from Daniel. We thought we were about to be able to free him, but once the cart was moved, we saw that a large rock had been dislodged from somewhere and had rolled over onto his legs.

Liam looked up to the bank where another similar rock had rolled from its mooring a bit as well. "All this water over the last months must have loosed these things," He called, already sliding in next to the rock that trapped Daniel. "This one might have tumbled down as they passed."

Zachary was nodding his head and breathing fast and shallow. "We shouldn't have left him up here." Zachary looked at me with pained eyes. "We should have taken him home."

"We don't have time for that, now, Zach," Liam said. "We got to get him out from under this thing and get him to a doctor."

Zachary was shaking his head. "He's already gone. I know it."

I gasped and then a firmness hit my spirit. "That is not an option," I said. "The two of you are going to get him out of this creek and fix this. We're going to fix this."

The water was rising a bit, but Daniel was still close enough to the bank that the water was too shallow to cover him so far. Still Zachary pulled him up so that his head was off the ground. I had to move in close to Zachary as well to keep pressure on the wound.

"Hold his head," Zachary was saying.

I couldn't take my eyes off Daniel's slack face.

"I can't budge this thing," Liam shouted over the ever-increasing noise of the falling rain.

Thunder clapped again, louder than it had been before. I didn't mean to, but I screamed out. Daniel flinched and his eyes fluttered.

"Daniel," I shouted, the small indication of life jolting me. "He's alive."

Liam grunted as he pulled at the rock. "Of course, he's alive. He's too stubborn to be dead." Liam grunted again and cursed when his efforts failed. "Zach, help me. I can't get this."

"I got him," I said and pushed at Zachary to go. He splashed up out of the water and squatted down by the rock. His feet slipped and he righted himself. The two brothers called to each other about moving the rock. Their voices blended.

"Stand here, the ground is more firm."

"I can't get a grip from this position."

"On three."

"I don't have it."

"Get it."

Daniel's eyes fluttered again, staying open for a second before closing once more. Thunder banged overhead and the sound of it caused Daniel to startle.

"He's coming to," I shouted.

The overcast afternoon sky brightened suddenly with lightning in the distance.

"We have to get him out of this," Zachary called.

"We can't budge this rock," Liam shouted.

"So, what, we just leave him here?" Zachary cried. He sounded more frightened than angry. "That's your plan?"

"Of course not," Liam shouted back. "Why would that be my plan?"

"Because you said he was better off alone," Zachary called. "Does that look better off to you?"

I looked up at the brothers who had stopped trying to move the rock and were standing there on the bank arguing.

"Knock it off," I screamed at them. "You move that rock, and you move it right now. You will not let your brother lay here in this freezing water with a bleeding head wound and broken legs most likely while you argue over which of you loves him more or has treated him more poorly." I spit against the water that was running in my face because I didn't have a free hand to wipe it off. "Don't just stand there looking at me. Move that rock."

Zachary and Liam nodded at each other, and Liam counted down from three. I looked back to Daniel then to see that his eyes were open and looking directly at me. The corner of his mouth twitched up and I bent down quickly to kiss his lips.

"You came for me," he whispered.

"Of course, I did." I said and because I knew he would ask if he could, I said quickly, "and the kids are OK. They're at the parsonage with Ava."

The brothers made a loud noise of effort and combined strength in motion and Daniel slid suddenly toward me once the weight of the boulder was released. Daniel yelled out in pain and his eyes squeezed shut.

Chapter 23

Daniel

The release of pressure and the sudden movement hurt like the devil, but it was worth it to be free.

"Help me," Mattie called, and I felt bad that I'd scared her, but glad she was there with me.

Liam and Zachary splashed toward me, tugging me out of the water. To see them there, fighting for me, was like being in a dream. I wanted it to be real, but there was also a chance that I had hit my head hard enough to hallucinate, or that perhaps I was dying. Maybe they were all taking me off to Heaven. Or Hell.

"Hold his legs."

"Keep his head up."

"Careful, everyone be careful."

It all sounded real enough.

Zachary and Liam carried me up and out of the creek. I could feel Mattie behind me, her hands touching me. They all called to each other to be careful in the mud and to watch this or that rock or root. I hadn't realized I was in such a precarious state, but the urgency of their voices seemed to indicate so.

I felt myself laid down on the loamy soil of the bank. My eyes fluttered open and closed and in the moments I could see anything, I saw their concerned faces and their lips moving over the words they spoke to assess the damage.

Broken leg.

Head wound.

Knot forming.

Zachary's face, when it came into view, looked terribly concerned and I sensed his hands hovering over my head.

"That's good," Mattie said, nodding at us both reassuringly. "The knot forming outward is good. The wound is trying to clot, but he'll need attention to it. Maybe stitches, maybe not. It's looking better. The bleeding has stopped."

I felt myself coming back to a bit.

Liam rubbed at his face. "What about the leg? How do we get him home on this?"

"Tear up your shirt," Mattie said to Liam and to Zachary she said, "Get some branches at least as thick as your forearm. Make a splint and use the torn cloth to tie it tight."

Zach and Liam nodded and set to work. I was lucky she was here, pressing forward as she always did.

"Laurel's gonna tan my hide for ripping this shirt," Liam said as he took off the outer garment, his undershirt immediately getting soaked from the rain that I was now aware of.

I shivered as a thunderclap sounded overhead. The more I came to, the more dire the situation seemed to get.

Zachary laughed and pointed at his own ripped shirt. "We'll go down together."

"It's worth it, brother," Liam said, leaning over me and patting my shoulder. "Bring those limbs," Liam yelled to Zachary and scooted down by my legs.

Brother. He was talking to me. I felt myself smile.

Mattie held my head up in her lap. "Daniel, are you OK?"

I nodded; I supposed the smile seemed strange at such a time.

"Done," Liam called and looked over to Mattie. "What now?"

"Is the cart usable?" she asked.

Liam shook his head. Mattie nodded acceptance and looked at the horses.

"We'll get up on one of the horses. One of you will have to walk alongside and stabilize his leg. I'll sit behind him and hold his head and make sure he's stable. He's awake now, but if he drifts out again and falls, he'll be in worse shape. He probably has a concussion, and we don't need another head wound. This probably isn't the best course of action, but it's the best we've got."

That was my Mattie.

"How do you know all this?" Zachary asked.

"I read it in a book," she said and looked down at me. "Ready?"

"Yes," I said, my voice barely a whisper.

I tried to hold in my cries of anguish as they moved me. I was in hellacious pain, but I didn't want them to know that. Liam rode Cody and led their horse behind him. Zachary walked, holding my broken leg up as steady as possible, alongside Opal with me and Mattie riding. We must have been a sight. Every jostle was agony, but I kept it to myself as best I could.

I leaned back against Mattie, and she wrapped one arm around my waist to steady me. It was a nice feeling. She sighed and kissed the top of my head. That was nice too. I had rescued her once, and now she was saving me.

We moved quickly, but cautiously back along the creek. The unrelenting rain of the swirling storm held any thoughts of happy celebration at bay though. I could feel myself shivering and I knew that wasn't good.

Finally, we entered town, and I felt Mattie breathe a tentative sigh of relief. "Let's take him to the church," She called out to Liam and Zachary.

I stirred then, despite the pain. "No. I can't go in there."

But no one paid me any mind. Liam and Zachary led the horses around to the front doors of the church.

"We can open both doors, and it will be easier to get him inside," Zachary said.

Liam jumped from his horse and pulled the doors open. He took hold of Opal's reins and led her right inside the doors.

"Get me out of here," I said, suddenly very awake and thrashing like a man possessed. "It's not right for me to be here."

Mattie held on tight. "Daniel, stop," she said firmly.

I relaxed back against her, breathing heavily.

"No more nonsense, Daniel," Liam said, walking alongside us. "Not from you, or us, or anyone else." I tried to speak, but Liam reached up and put a hand to my arm. "Let's get you off that horse and onto a pew."

"Mattie," Zachary said, "hold him steady until Liam and I have him, and then can you swing down and clear that first pew?"

"Ava is going to kill you both," she said.

"You're the one who suggested coming in here," Liam said.

"Yes," Mattie said, "but I'm going to blame it on the two of you."

Liam smiled a crooked smile at her. That was his acceptance smile. She had won him over.

My brothers worked together to get me off Opal with the least jostling of my leg possible. Mattie hurried down and pushed a line of books off the pew. They laid me down so my hurt leg was resting along the back of the seat. It wasn't a great fit as I was half falling off, but it kept my leg supported. Mattie sat down by my head and slid herself beneath me so that my head was resting in her lap. Liam and Zach came into view pushing the old couch from my house which was now in the church for some reason down beside my waist and legs to make as much room to hold me as possible. It worked well. Mattie had the top half of me, and the couch and pew supported the rest.

Liam asked, "You OK, Danny?"

I nodded, happy, despite the pain. Mattie leaned down and kissed my forehead.

"Am I going to make it, doc?" I said to her.

"Yes, you stubborn mule. You probably will."

"Probably," I said, amused. "I guess those are decent odds."

Ava burst in through the side door and stopped short. She looked around in shock, her eyes landing on the books on the floor, me on the pew, and a horse in the middle of the room.

"Get that animal out of this church," she said, her hands going straight to her hips.

Zachary turned to Liam. "Get out, animal."

I smiled. I had missed the way they joked. The way we all joked with each other.

Ava rushed over to us and knelt beside me. I turned away from her and winced as if stung. She touched the side of my face.

"Daniel, look at me."

I looked up at Mattie and she nodded. I turned to Ava. "I don't expect you to forgive me, Ava."

She sighed and shook her head. "You were forgiven ages ago. Daniel, I just want to be part of your life again. I want to be part of the children's lives. Please."

"I didn't mean to keep you away," I said, my voice hitching a bit. "I'm sorry, Ava. I just…" But she held a hand up to stop me.

"We both know that old story," she said. "It's time to let it loose."

"What about everything I did here in the church?" I asked, barely able to get the words out. I looked at the still broken window and the place where the altar should be. "I destroyed it."

"It wouldn't be the first temple that ever had to be rebuilt," she said and smiled at me graciously.

"I'll help," I said. "I'm good at building things. I'll fix it."

She touched my face and her eyes welled with tears. One dropped quickly over the edge and ran quickly down her cheek. "We'll fix it together."

I exhaled a hard little puff of air and a tear rolled from my own eye. She brushed it away and ran her hand over my hair. "Daddy will be happy."

I nodded at the thought of Pastor Collins here again in the church and of being here with him.

Ava patted my arm, stood up, and turned to Zachary. "I'm serious, get that horse out of here and bring your brother a blanket. Somebody pick those books up off the floor."

Liam was already coming toward us with what I could tell were the blankets off the twin beds in the parsonage. "I told the kids to hang on and we'd bring them over in a minute."

"I'll go sit with them," Ava said.

I wanted to say something, but a knot was forming in my throat. I nodded and reached out for her hand. She kissed me on the forehead and hurried back to the parsonage.

I watched Liam and Zachary bustling about. Liam covered me with one blanket while Zach set about dragging an ornery Opal back outside. They argued over who would go to Gibbons' store to use the phone to call the doctor and who would clean up the books. They both went to the store.

Mattie and I were alone.

"So," she said, cautiously, "why exactly were you and the kids coming to town in the middle of a downpour?"

"Because you told me to," I said.

"And suddenly you're the obedient type?"

"I read that poem," I said. "Well, Ella helped, but I did right good by myself. I was coming to answer you, like you said."

"I could have waited a day," she said. "Or until it stopped raining."

"It couldn't," I said. "I tried to get booksy for you and memorize a poem in return. Me and the kids sat around and read the rest of the ones in that little book. I found one I like. The kids thought it was too romantic for their father to be quoting. Well, Marie did. Ella tried to help me memorize it, but I couldn't remember the whole thing," I said, "but I got enough that you'd know my answer."

"What is your answer?" she asked, obviously nervous even though she should have been able to guess it.

I took in a breath and said, "And the sunlight clasps the earth, and the moonbeams kiss the sea."

She smiled and I knew I was right. She'd recognize it right away and know.

I continued, "What is all this sweet work worth? If thou kiss not me?"

"'Love's Philosophy,'" she said. "I'll take that as a yes."

She leaned down and kissed me softly on the lips. I wanted to kiss her deeper, longer, but I could see Liam and Zachary had come back in and were headed toward us.

"Poetry, Danny?" Liam said but smiled.

"Must be the lump on his head. Next, he's gonna sing us a tune," Zachary pulled up a chair and sat beside us. "Doc's on his way. We'll probably have to get you into the office somehow to get that leg set."

I reached out and took hold of Mattie's hand. She looked worried for me.

"I'll be alright," I said, comforting her now. Reassurance was reciprocal, like things should be. I didn't know what would happen after this, but it didn't matter. This part alone was worth it.

Chapter 24

Mattie

Ava opened the side door again and sunlight found its way in. The storm had burned off without us noticing its departure. I looked at the stained-glass windows. The pictures grew vivid as I watched the sunlight find its way through them as well. The room filled with color, and I eased Daniel into a sitting position with some pillows Liam had brought as well. The kids were clinging to Ava, and I went to them. Liam pulled a chair up beside Zachary and I watched the brothers, all three, talk.

I could almost see them as young boys, brothers welcoming a lost child into their fold. Zachary looked the most pained. He bit at his knuckles as Liam spoke about starting over. Tears ran down Zachary's cheeks and I knew there was much I didn't know about the hearts of these men, the depth of feeling they had for each other. Liam clapped Zachary on the back and Zachary wiped at his eyes.

I scooped Hugh up in my arms and took hold of Marie's hand. I nodded Ella forward and we went to Daniel. Sunlight shone in again through the windows and a burst of red, blue, orange, and green filled the room. I had always thought that kaleidoscopes were something like magic, but this was better. This was something real.

The kids were cautious, but I could tell they wanted to fling themselves onto their father.

"Just mind the leg," he said, opening his arms to them. "I'm alright. Everything is going to be fine."

They hugged to him for a while and then Ava came and ushered them back. "We'll be in the parsonage."

'Wait," I said. "Before you go, I want to show Ella something and I need to talk to Daniel about something pressing."

"More pressing than this?" he asked and gestured to himself and his busted leg.

"In many ways, yes," I said with all seriousness.

"Well in that case, do tell."

I went to my worktable on the other side of the room and brought back the scrapbook of stories and pictures the girls had written and drawn. I handed it to Daniel.

"I need your permission to put it in circulation if Ella agrees. Adaline has already said yes."

Daniel looked at the book and then back at me. He waved Ella over and held it where she could see it. A smile began shyly and then spread all over her face.

She took the book from Daniel and read from the cover. "Stories by Ella Barrett. Illustrated by Adaline Norris," she said, and her eyes welled with tears. "It's just like a real book of stories."

"It is a real book of stories," I said. I looked at Daniel.

He winked at me. "I suppose you've read these stories and they pass muster," he said, pretending to have his doubts.

"Oh, they are quite good, sir," I said formally. "You should read them and see. I think you'll find yourself in the stories a time or two or more. All the best books let us see ourselves in their words."

"I would like that," he said. "I suppose that means that you'll have to come by for more reading lessons. I want to make sure that I don't miss anything because I don't know the words." He winked at me.

"I suppose I could," I said as if it would be a chore.

Marie and Hugh started jumping up and down, not buying our act at all, which of course is all it was.

"And we can come to school?" Ella asked, excitedly, but with a touch of apprehension at the coming answer.

Daniel looked at her lovingly. "Of course. Since Miss Mattie is still teaching and I suppose she's staying?" He asked, with a touch of apprehension at the coming answer.

"Yes," I said with firmness and clarity. "She is."

"Then yes you have my permission to circulate Ella's book," he said and looked to Ella. "If she approves."

"Oh yes," Ella said, her smile so wide I thought she might never be able to recover from it.

"And the children can go to school," he said, then held his hand out to me, "and you will please come back to visit us and let us come here as well and," he looked at his children and then lowered his voice, "some of the mushy stuff in the poetry book."

"Da," they all screamed at once.

I knew I was blushing deeply, but I didn't care. I nodded, mostly because words would have brought up tears.

Ava cleared her throat. "Now, I do think it's time for us to go to the parsonage. Perhaps get you kids a bite to eat."

Ella looked at Daniel. "Will Da be able to come home tonight?"

"Not tonight, but soon," I said. "Maybe you all will want to stay with me tonight? Yes?"

Their little faces lit up and I kissed them each on the head. Zachary and Liam excused themselves to wait on the doctor out front and Daniel and I were alone in the church again. I pulled one of the chairs closer to him. He scooted himself up better against the pillows so that he was sitting up straight. I touched his face and leaned in closer. I kissed him deeply and felt him relax into me as well.

"I don't think you're supposed to kiss me like that in church," he said when I reluctantly pulled back from him.

"This is a library, too," I said. "At least for a little longer. Kissing is allowed in the library."

"Is it, now?"

I made a face of concentrated thought. "I don't know technically," I said. "But this was the romance section mind you." I looked at the books still lying on the floor.

"Romance novels" he said and winked at me. "Scandalous. So, when do we start those reading lessons again?"

I smacked his hand where he reached out, trying to pull me back to him. I didn't for one second really want him to stop. He didn't give up on it and pulled me to him anyway, kissing me sweetly, but with a hint of passion that he'd yet held in. Once we'd parted, I sighed out heavily, content in the knowledge of the way our poem would end—or rather—begin.

The little book of poetry I'd marked for him had been another one of the library scrapbooks. It was a mix of poems and pictures and other pages that had fallen apart from other books. It felt like a metaphor for life. All our lives are a mixture of moments and memories—pieces that have fallen apart and come together, been stitched, and glued and melded to make the story of who we are. Our stories are worth telling. Each and every one. Where would we be without them? Without each other? We were all part of the shifting patterns of life. We changed each other in big ways and in small ones. Every piece mattered. I was exactly where I wanted to be. Of that, I was certain.

Mercy, forgiveness, and love were their own colors in the kaleidoscope. The best colors of all.

Acknowledgments

It never gets old to have a book published, and I am so grateful to so many people for seeing this one along its journey from thought to finish. There's an idea that writers write alone and even though for large portions of the work, that's true, thankfully, there are many people in a writer's community and life who contribute to her success in ways that they know, and even some they don't.

There's no way to put anyone in order of importance as writing and publishing is a circular endeavor, so bear with me as I ramble on about the many people who have made this dream of publishing come true again.

Thank you to Fireship Press/ Cortero, Mary Monahan, and Jacquie Cook for loving this book enough to make me and it a part of your publishing family. What an honor it is to be published by a house that adores and specializes in historical fiction. Thank you also Jacquie for putting up with me through all the drafts and answering all my questions. Good editors make a writer's work what she always meant it to be.

Thank you to my wonderful agent, Julie Gwinn at the Seymour Agency. Julie, you work so tirelessly to find the perfect house for your authors and their stories. You have succeeded again! I am so grateful for the time and care you put into nurturing me as a writer and helping my work find a home. I am blessed to also call you a friend and that means the world to me.

Thank you to Lisa Mangum for presenting the idea of a story involving the Pack Horse Librarians to me several years ago. I didn't know about them at the time and probably never would have thought to write a book about these amazing women in this beautiful part of the country if you hadn't given me the idea. Thank you for all your support and especially for your friendship which I consider a special gift.

Thank you to my street team for working so hard to help me promote my books, but more importantly than that, being there when I fall off the face of the earth for months at a time and then resurface with my tale of work or woe that has kept me from being in touch. You are there every time with words of support and love. I only wish I could do more for you in return. You are all so important to me.

Thank you to my friends and writing colleagues, who are very often one and the same–how lucky am I, for sharing this journey with me, for encouraging me, for believing that what I write has merit even when I'm not so sure. Thank you for endorsing my books and talking about them online and to your reading communities. Thank you for spending your time with me and calling me your friend. You are all there for me in times of happiness and grief–times that have nothing to do with writing and everything to do with being a person in this world who couldn't get by without her friends. Thank you so very much, all of you.

Thank you always to my Wildacres Writers Workshop family. You have been the end all-be all for me over these decades that we have been a part of each other's lives. There are literally hundreds of you over the years and I love you all. A special thank you this time around to Bill Spencer for such a close read of this novel, helping me to correct some downright silly accidental mistakes all the way to some major oops that I'm glad didn't make it into print. Thank you, Carolyn Elkins, for allowing me his time and for accompanying him as you both drove the hard copy edits out to my house when I needed some feedback in a hurry! What a joy it was to see your faces (well, your eyes at least. I know the smiles well enough to be able to see them even covered.) I love you both dearly.

So, I know I said there was no particular order here, but I have to admit I'm saving my best for last. Thank you to my family who are a constant support and who cheer me on always. Who love me when I'm not that lovable, and who lift me up in big and small ways of which you might not even be aware. I'm aware, and I am blessed. Life would not be anything without you all.

And the best of the best, Jesus Christ my Lord and Savior, without whom I'd never get through the day. We are not the mistakes we've made. We are always welcome in His Church, His arms, and we are forever in His heart. What could be better than that?

All my love,
Amy

About the Author

Amy Willoughby-Burle grew up in the small coastal town of Kure Beach, NC and now lives in Asheville, NC with her husband and four children. She teaches creative writing and works as a freelance editor when not working on her own fiction. She is also the director of Wildacres Writers Workshop.

She is the author of the novels *The Lemonade Year* and *The Year of Thorns and Honey*. Her award-winning short fiction has been published in numerous journals and in her collection, *Out Across the Nowhere*. Her fiction focuses on the importance of family and friends and centers on the themes of forgiveness, second chances, and finding beauty in the world around us. She likes to write about the wonder and mystery of everyday life.

Visit her online at www.amywilloughbyburle.com

Other Titles by Fireship Press

Finding Paradise
Jane Ver Mulm

Ellen Schmidt finds herself out of step with the world around her. Considered a spinster in her community, her closest friends are the slaves that her family owns. After her father arranges her marriage, she must face a cruel set of circumstances and the beginning of the Civil War, setting her on a path that seems to be out of her control. Strong and independent, Ellen continues in her own unique way to forge a future that can include a paradise of her own.

"If you enjoy reading about the Civil War era, this book [*Finding Paradise*] should be placed on top of your reading list."

—Trudi LoPreto, *Readers' Favorite*

Molly's Song
Lee Hutch

Amidst the turmoil of Civil War era New York, a young, immigrant woman seeks to escape a life of prostitution so that she may rescue a child from a terrible fate.

It wasn't supposed to be like this. Cast adrift in an unfamiliar city, a young Irish immigrant named Molly finds herself forced into prostitution and has a child stolen out of her arms. With the city descending into the chaos of the Draft Riots, Molly must save herself before she can save the child.

From the green fields of Galway to the crowded streets of New York and the ornate parlors of New Orleans, Molly never stops fighting to free herself and the child she hardly knows from a terrible fate.

"A stunning roller coaster ride of unimaginable tragedies and inspirational triumphs." —Gregory Lee Renz, author of *Beneath the Flames*

For the Finest in Nautical and Historical Fiction and Non-Fiction
www.FireshipPress.com

Interesting • Informative • Authoritative

All Fireship Press books are available through leading bookstores and wholesalers worldwide.

CPSIA information can be obtained
at www.ICGtesting.com
Printed in the USA
BVHW051016250922
647944BV00005B/173

9 781736 620380